SWEET HOME LOUISIANA

BOYS OF THE BAYOU BOOK 2

ERIN NICHOLAS

ISBN: 978-1-7338901-1-3

Editor: Lindsey Faber

Cover design: Angela Waters

Cover photography: Lindee Robinson

Models: Brian Boynton and Krista Ferguson

1

O wen felt his mouth curve into a grin as he heard the familiar *clap, clap, clap* behind him.

That was one of his favorite sounds—high heels on the wooden dock of the Boys of the Bayou swamp boat tour company.

He took his time turning and once he did, he started at the shoes.

They were black and showed off bright red toenails. The straps wrapped sexily around trim ankles and led the eye right up to smooth, toned calves. The heels matched the black polka dots on the white skirt that thankfully didn't start until mid-thigh, and showed off more tanned skin.

He straightened from his kneeling position in one of the boats as his eyes kept moving up past the skirt to the bright red belt that accentuated a narrow waist and then to the silky black tank that molded to a pair of perfect breasts.

He was fully anticipating her lips being bright red to go with that belt and her toenail polish. God, he loved red lipstick. And high heels. In any color.

But before he could get to those lips, she used them, to say, "Oh, dammit, it's you."

Owen's gaze bypassed her mouth to fly to her eyes. Because he'd know that voice anywhere.

Madison Allain was home.

A day early.

Not that an extra day would have helped him prepare. He'd been thinking about her visit for a week and was still as wound tight about it as he'd been when Sawyer, his business partner and cousin, had told him that she was coming home. For a *month*.

Owen stood just watching her, fighting back all of the first words that he was tempted to say.

Like, "Damn, you're even more gorgeous than the last time I saw you."

Or, "I haven't put anyone in the hospital lately."

Or, "I've missed you so fucking much."

Just for instance.

She blew out a breath and now he did focus on her lips.

Yep, red. Terrific. That wasn't going to make ignoring them any easier.

"I was hoping you were Sawyer," she said, propping a hand on her hip.

Owen tossed the wrench he held into the toolbox at his feet. "Nope. Sorry." So she wasn't happy to see him. Big shocker. He hadn't always been the perfect Southern gentleman around Maddie, that was for sure.

He wiped his hands on his jeans. Okay, he was supposed to be *nice* to her. That meant treating her like she was one of the tourists who frequented this dock. Polite. Friendly, but not I've-known-you-my-whole-life-and-kissed-you-a-whole-bunch friendly. Just mildly hey-how's-it-goin' friendly. So that she didn't sell off her portion of the business that not only fed him and his other two partners, but that was their pride and joy. And the only thing he was really good at.

Nice. Polite. A little friendly—but not too much. He could do that. Though it probably meant not saying things like, "I still remember how your nipples taste."

Annoyed that within thirty seconds of seeing her again he was already thinking about her nipples, he kicked the toolbox, trying to slide it into the nook under the bow of the boat. Of course, he kicked it too hard and it tipped, spilling tools over the floor of the boat with loud clangs of metal against metal.

He shoved a hand through his hair. That was typical. Everything was an overreaction when it came to how he acted around Maddie. Even the little stuff. Certainly the big stuff. Always had been.

"Sawyer's over at Ellie's." Owen pulled himself up out of the boat and onto the dock.

That took him about two feet closer to her and he instantly became aware that he wasn't wearing a shirt. Very aware as Maddie's eyes tracked over his shoulders, chest and abs.

The heat that arrowed through him was unwelcome. Though not unexpected. There had always been this crazy chemistry between them. Key word: crazy.

"You're early," he said shortly.

Her eyes bounced back up to his. "Um...yeah. I was able to get away sooner than I'd expected."

"You could have warned us. Quick text or something."

She frowned. "I didn't realize you all needed *warning*."

You all. Not y'all. Seemed that Maddie had lost her drawl living in California for the past twelve years.

Hell yeah, he needed a warning she was on her way. The same way he needed warnings about hurricanes and anything else that was going to blow into his life and potentially turn everything inside out. He needed a chance to batten things down. Like his emotions.

"Would have been nice, that's all I'm saying." He realized he was being kind of a dick. He took a deep breath. She was here because her brother, Tommy, had owned thirty-five percent of Boys of the Bayou. He'd left that to Maddie when he'd died eight months ago. And now she wanted to sell. He and Sawyer and Josh, the remaining three partners, now had thirty days to convince her not to do that.

They didn't want some stranger coming into the business they'd inherited from their grandfather and that had been a part of their lives for as long as they could remember. But they also couldn't afford to buy her out. Maddie being the fourth partner, the silent partner that lived two thousand miles away and simply got her share of the money via check once a month, was perfect. They just had to convince her to keep the status quo.

And him being an ass to her within her first ten minutes in town was probably not the way to do that.

She was already wary of him. Understandably. The last time she'd spent more than a few hours in Autre, Owen had put her brother in the hospital. Sure, *he'd* been in the bed next to Tommy, and really, Tommy had started it, but that didn't change the fact that Owen's actions had freaked her out.

Tommy had just found out that Owen and Maddie were planning to elope. Tommy had said Owen could marry Maddie over his dead body and that had sent Owen over the edge.

And him and Tommy through a plate-glass window.

That wasn't the only time he'd been an idiot over her, but yeah, seeing him and Tommy in matching hospital beds had worried her.

Probably rightly so.

Madison Allain had taught him the true meaning of being *crazy* about someone.

He needed to get a grip. And he needed to keep that grip for the next thirty days. According to the Boys of the Bayou partnership agreement, she had to give them thirty days' notice before changing any part of the agreement. That included selling. Sawyer was determined to use that thirty days to convince her she wanted to keep her share.

One month wasn't very long. Just four weeks.

Owen could keep his shit together for that long.

Maybe.

"I'll take you over to Sawyer," he said, giving her a smile. He bent to grab his shirt from the dock where he'd stripped it off earlier.

It was June in Louisiana. Anyone working outside did so in as little clothing as possible. But as he pulled the soft green Boys of the Bayou tee over his head, he couldn't help but grin a little. He didn't mind making this first impression on Maddie.

Yeah, he scared her, but he made her crazy, too. Maybe even crazier. The things that had happened in Autre from the time his lips first touched hers, to the time she got in the car and drove out of town for the last time were pretty legendary.

So he should be scared of her, too. When this woman touched him, he became a bit of a dumbass. Okay, a great big dumbass. But *she* set shit on fire for him. Literally.

He'd taught her to use a nail gun rebuilding the shed she'd torched. He'd also warned her ex-boyfriend—and the reason for the blaze—to steer clear of the backyard while she had that nail gun in hand. Wade Hillson had fucked up big-time at that Valentine's Day party. It had led to Owen and Maddie's first kiss, so Owen hadn't been *totally* pissed, but he'd still threatened to throw Wade off the Manchac Swamp Bridge. A bigger threat, however, was definitely Maddie putting a nail gun to Wade's junk.

That history and chemistry between him and Maddie was going to make Owen's life hell for the next thirty days, but he didn't mind thinking that she might feel a little of the torture, too.

"Is there any chance I could just wait *here* until Sawyer comes back?" Maddie asked as he stepped forward.

"You don't want to go to Ellie's?" Ellie's was Owen's grandma's bar. It was where Cora, Maddie's grandma—and Ellie's best friend since they were kids—worked, too. Cora ran the kitchen and Ellie tended the bar and kept the patrons—mostly old fishermen and tourists—in line. It was also where everyone in their big, boisterous family gathered. For just about any and every occasion. Or just to shoot the shit and catch up. They were over there planning Maddie's return right now.

Maddie sighed. "I don't know if I'm ready to see them *all* at once."

Yeah, their families were a lot, especially when all together. And excited about something. They were definitely excited about Maddie being home.

"I don't suppose that bottom drawer of the file cabinet in the office still functions as a minibar?" she asked.

Owen chuckled, surprised that she remembered that. But her grandpa and his had been best friends and had started the company to take people out hunting and fishing on the bayou. It had evolved over the years into the tourist attraction it was now. All of the kids had spent plenty of time down on these docks and in t growing up. The office had always had a drawer full of candy and one full of liquor.

"It does, as a matter of fact," he told her. And taking the edge off of...everything that was to come...wasn't a bad idea.

They were twelve years older. When they'd been together, they'd been kids, newly in love, newly having sex. Then her mom had died and her dad had gone to jail trying to avenge her mom's death.

That had been a lot. *A lot.*

But it had been a long time ago. Maddie was a sophisticated city girl now and he was a laid-back bayou boy. They both knew that you couldn't go around setting shit on fire just because someone pissed you off. You also couldn't dangle people off a bridge or throw people through plate-glass windows.

He and Maddie were past all of that. They knew better now. And they didn't feel that way about each other anymore.

It took a lot of heat, hormones, and more than a little bit of stupidity to act the way they had back then. His hormones were now under control, thank you. He was a lot smarter. Okay, a little smarter at least. And heat? Yeah, he hadn't felt heat like that in years. That had been first love stuff. No matter what his grandfather said.

The Landrys were well-known for falling hard and fast and having big, crazy love stories. But Owen was...skeptical. That was the best way to say it. He was skeptical about the level of in-love crazy that truly ran through the family tree. His mom sure hadn't found true love in spite of having Landry blood flowing through her veins. She'd raised Owen on her own—at least as alone as someone with an involved-in-everything family could be—and not once had there been even a maybe-a-soul-mate in her life. Not even when Owen, from ages seven to nineteen, had tried everything he could to find her one. Now, after all these years, she was finally dating a nice guy who treated her well. But she'd met Paul at Home Depot when buying a new toilet. No one fell madly in love over toilets.

"I think I need a shot or two before I walk into the bar across the street," Maddie said with a small, sardonic smile.

Owen looked at her closely. Past the red lips and the silky blonde hair and the California tan and into her eyes. She was nervous. Well, hell.

Okay, so he felt a *niggle* of protectiveness at that. But she looked vulnerable, and she was here because her brother had died, and Owen was a good guy. He felt bad for her. She'd come to Autre for Tommy's funeral, but she'd shown up at the last minute and had high-tailed it back out of town before he'd spoken even a word to her. She'd talked briefly with Sawyer and she'd hugged Cora. Then she'd gotten in an Uber—that she'd paid to wait for her—and headed back to the West Coast. So if he felt *a little* like hugging her and a *tiny* bit like putting his fist through a wall because he couldn't fix this for her, well, that was just because he was *nice*. He gave a shit about other people. That was all.

There was nothing special about Madison Allain.

He couldn't fix that her brother was dead and that she owned thirty-five percent of a business she didn't want, but he could do *something*. He could get her tipsy.

"Come on." He felt himself start to reach for her hand, but he balled his hand into a fist and stepped back, gesturing toward the office.

She started in that direction, and he noted that she had a big red purse hanging from one hand. She looked every bit the sophisticated city girl and it poked at him. She was gorgeous this way, of course. She looked a lot like tourists they got down here on a regular basis. He always got a kick out of the girls who had clearly never been on a boat and were wearing their expensive dresses and impractical shoes down here. Those were the girls who were most likely to get splashed with swamp water at some point. He put them right up front.

But on Maddie it made him itchy. It wasn't right. She wasn't a city girl.

Except she was. She'd lived in San Francisco for the past twelve years. Through her teens and early twenties. She'd been dressing herself for a long time. Just because she'd *been* a bayou girl, wearing cutoff blue jeans and running barefoot, didn't mean that's who she was now.

Though he remembered a particular pair of cutoff blue jeans when she'd been sixteen that had ended up on the floor of his truck...

He cleared his throat as he pushed the door to the office

open to let her in. He even resisted putting a hand on her lower back. He couldn't, however, escape the scent of her filling his lungs as she brushed past him.

She even smelled sophisticated. Her perfume was probably expensive and couldn't be found within forty miles of Autre.

He remembered when she'd smelled like sunshine and peaches.

She'd tasted like peaches, too.

Maddie paused just inside the door and looked around. She let out a soft sigh.

"You okay?" he asked, crossing to the file cabinet near the windows.

"This place is exactly the same." She went to the chair behind one of the two big wooden desks. It had been her grandfather's chair.

It was nothing fancy. Never had been. But it was as much a part of the office as the windows and exposed wooden beams overhead.

The desks were piled high with stacks of papers, and boxes of everything from fishing lures to engine parts sat all over the floor. The guys didn't really use the office for, well, office work. It was more of a storage area. All of the guys, Tommy included, had always preferred to spend their time on the docks and the bayou itself. They only did what paperwork was absolutely required, and even most of that fell to Sawyer and Josh's little sister, Kennedy. She bitched about them all on a daily basis, but she also didn't trust any of them to do the book work or scheduling.

Owen glanced over to find Maddie sitting in her grandpa's chair, looking around the office with a slightly dazed expression. Yeah, he imagined it was a little like going back in time. The invoices and lures might be new, but the desks and chairs and file cabinets were original. Even some of the dust had probably been there since the first days.

Oh, who was he kidding? He pulled a glass milk bottle from the bottom drawer. Some of those lures and the invoices on the bottoms of the piles had probably been there since their grandfathers had owned the place, and the dust was *definitely* original. Kennedy drew the line at cleaning. Anything.

He held the bottle up. "This okay?"

"Is it at least 90 proof?"

He laughed. "Doesn't make it through that door if it's not." He set the bottle on the nearest desk. The one *his* grandfather had used. The bottle hadn't held milk in years, but it had been refilled several times with the moonshine Mitch made with Kenny Allain's recipe. Owen reached for a coffee cup sitting on the desk, looked inside, saw it was empty and dry—not necessarily clean, but the moonshine would kill any germs—blew into it to dislodge any possible dust, and poured two fingers' worth. He handed it over to her.

"Whiskey?" she asked. She didn't seem worried about the possibility, just curious.

He fought his grin. She might drink martinis or something now, but she'd first gotten drunk on good old "bayou whiskey," as Kenny had called it. She wasn't intimidated by a little you-can-drink-it-or-remove-paint-with-it   liquor. "Kenny's moonshine."

Maddie gave a little smile that seemed slightly wistful before lifting her cup. She took that first swallow without so much as a wince.

Right. Kenny's moonshine. Maddie's grandpa's moonshine.

Owen poured more into an empty, clean-ish plastic cup from the *Stop It Now*, the convenience store at the end of the road that led to Boys of the Bayou.

He was going to need this as much as she did.

They both needed to take the edge off of...everything.

He toasted her and she touched her cup to his. Then they both drank. Their eyes locked.

Owen swallowed the set-your-gut-on-fire liquor. Neither of them said anything for a long moment.

"I'm sorry I didn't get to talk to you at Tommy's funeral," he finally managed. Okay, not really small talk, but he had to say *something* and that was the first thing on his mind.

She nodded and held her cup out. "There wasn't much to say."

Yeah, maybe. But he'd still felt empty after she'd left. Much like the bottle of tequila he'd woken up with the next morning.

He poured another inch of moonshine into her cup.

If he thought too hard about everything she'd been through, it twisted his heart like someone wringing out a sponge. There was something about Madison Allain that had always made him want to fight dragons for her. When he was seventeen, he'd assumed it was the deeply ingrained protective streak that ran strong in the male side of the Landry clan.

But he'd only felt it for Maddie. Which had made him wonder if it was *actually* the voodoo curse Sarah Cutter had put on him when he'd left her on Valentine's Day to go pick Maddie up from a date-gone-bad.

That was actually more believable than some genetic penchant for over-the-top romantic gestures. You didn't grow up on the bayou without respecting voodoo. Even if you didn't believe in it fully, you sure as hell knew not to mess with it.

And now the woman who made him bonkers was sitting a foot away from him. With her legs crossed and a whole lot of smooth, tanned skin showing.

Nah, this wasn't genetics or a curse. This was just good old-fashioned attraction. He wanted to run his hand up her leg and under her skirt. He didn't want to elope with her.

Anymore.

He cleared his throat and shifted on the edge of the desk. "How's California?" he asked, lifting his cup.

She shrugged. "Good. Fine."

"How's the museum?"

"Art gallery," she corrected.

He'd known that. She'd always been a big fan of museums of all kinds, so he just automatically put her there when thinking of her in a big building with lots of beautiful and interesting displays. "Right. How's the art gallery?"

"Good. Fine."

He took another swallow of moonshine. He talked to total strangers all day every day. He could surely make small talk with a woman he'd known since birth. Even if he had been in love with her at one time. And couldn't quite manage to get his attention off her legs. "How was your trip today?"

She nodded. "Good."

"And fine?" he asked dryly.

One corner of her mouth curled. "Yeah. Fine."

He reached for the bottle again. He was going to end up smashed simply because his options here were polite conversation, grabbing her and kissing her, or drinking. The chit-chat was annoying him and kissing her was out of the question. So drinking it was.

"I had a great salad at the airport." She swirled the liquor around in the coffee mug.

"Oh." He honestly didn't care about her salad. He *wanted* to ask if she had a boyfriend. That was stupid. "Glad to hear it."

"And the woman next to me on the plane was very nice. She's visiting her daughter and her new grandbaby."

Uh-huh. He also didn't care about the woman next to her on the plane at all. How long had she and the California douchebag been dating? Was it serious? "How nice."

Maddie nodded. "They didn't have any hazelnut coffee creamer, though, so I had to drink it with plain cream."

"Huh." Yeah, he really hated small talk. At least with the tourists he could tell them something weird about alligators.

Maddie knew all about gators. Which actually made him smile when he thought about it. "I got a new thermos."

She lifted a brow. He lifted one back at her.

"So how long are we going to do this?" she asked.

"Do what?"

"Talk about stupid crap that doesn't matter."

He huffed out a laugh. "Just makin' conversation."

Both of her brows went up now. "And *this* is what comes up when you try to talk to me?"

"When I'm tryin' to be...cordial," he told her.

"You wouldn't be cordial without trying?"

"Well..." Should he just be honest with her? She'd known him all his life, too. "To be honest, I'd probably be inappropriate. At some point. Not very far in."

She looked startled for a moment. Then, if he wasn't mistaken, she seemed relieved. She grinned. "Oh yeah?"

He laughed again. "That surprises you?"

Maddie shook her head. "No, not really."

He appreciated that. He took another swallow of liquor.

"So what kind of inappropriate thing would you have said?"

He swallowed with a little difficulty, his eyes drawn to her heels and her legs before he could stop them.

She noticed and stretched her legs out, crossing her ankles, her shoes on full display.

She knew he loved heels.

Had she worn these just for him? Because she knew better than to wear those things on a boat dock. Or a dirt road. Or an uneven sidewalk and rickety front porch steps. They had a lot of all of those things down here and a distinct lack of smooth stone paths and meticulously manicured green spaces. It was wild and natural down here. Maybe even more so than it had been twelve years ago.

He looked up, meeting her gaze. "I would have said somethin' like, damn girl, if you're here, that means California just got a lot less hot.'"

She gave a soft snort. "Wow."

He grinned.

"I think you're mistaking cheesy for inappropriate."

"Okay, how about, 'thank you?'"

"Thank you?" she repeated. "For what?"

"For bringing those heels and that sassy skirt down here. You're risking sacrificing a lot of sweet skin to the bugs in that and I appreciate it."

That tugged a little smile from her. "Flirtatious maybe, but not really *inappropriate*."

Okay, challenge accepted. He looked down at her feet. "Those heels are gonna feel damned good digging into my ass later."

Her eyes widened and she stared at him for a long moment. Then she nodded. "Yeah, okay, that would have been an inappropriate greeting after twelve years of not seeing each other."

"I *saw* you just a few months ago." At the funeral. Yeah, maybe he was still a little annoyed that he hadn't had a chance to talk to her.

She held his gaze as she chewed her bottom lip. Then she tipped back another swallow of moonshine before saying, "Talking would have made it worse."

"Worse? How could talking make Tommy dying any *worse*?"

She frowned and held out her cup.

He didn't move to fill it. "Tell me."

She gave an irritated sigh and reached out to grab the bottle from him. That gave him a quick glance down her shirt to the matching black bra and the gorgeous tits the black silk held. He let the bottle go. She splashed more in her cup, then set the bottle down with a *thunk* next to his thigh. "What would you have said?" she asked him.

"That I was sorry."

"I knew that. Of course you were sorry. Everyone was sorry." He frowned. "That I was here for you."

"And what would *that* have meant? That we could sit and reminisce about Tommy? My memories are twelve years old and the last ones here with him weren't that pleasant. Or would that mean that you'd hold me while I cried? How would *that* have helped? Either we would have realized there was no way to actually make me feel better and you would have put a fist through a wall and I would have gotten in a huge fight with a TSA agent over the alligator skull I was trying to bring on the plane in my carry-on because I would have been wound up and looking for an outlet." She took a deep breath. "*Or* I would have decided to distract myself from the pain and would have kissed you and we would have slept together and I would have driven out of town the next morning and *then* you would have put your fist through the wall and I would have gotten into a huge fight with a TSA agent over the alligator skull I was trying to bring on the plane in my carry-on. Either way, you would have ended up with a sore hand and I would have ended up in TSA jail for a few hours. What would have been the point?"

Owen stared at her as she finished her rant.

That was all…not completely impossible to imagine. They wound each other up. That was just a fact.

"We're not past those kinds of reactions?" he asked. He'd like to think all of his overreactions had been a product of being a stupid kid who didn't know how to handle the protectiveness and possessiveness Maddie stirred up in him. It probably wasn't true, but he liked to think it.

She slumped back in her chair and crossed her arms. "I was in that room in the airport *forever*. Missed *two* flights back to California."

Owen felt the grin slowly curve his mouth as what she said sunk in. "You *did* get into a fight with a TSA agent over an alligator skull?"

She nodded. "He was an *asshole*. I mean, it wasn't like I was trying to bring a *live* alligator on board."

"We could have shipped it to you." He knew exactly which skull she was talking about. It had belonged to Tommy.

"I wasn't thinking," she said. "I just grabbed it and then when he started giving me a hard time, I lost my mind." She looked up at Owen and took a breath. "But it wasn't about the skull."

He frowned. "What was it about?"

"Autre."

"What do you mean?"

"This place makes me crazy. It's...chaos. It's loud and crazy and *hot*." She plucked the front of her blouse away from her chest. "Good, Lord, it is so *hot* down here."

"It's hot in California."

"No. It's warm. It's sunny. It's pleasant. It's not holy-crap-I'm-melting-hot. And we have wine."

"We have wine."

She snorted. "You don't have *wine*."

He fucking hated wine. "Well, I like the heat. You know that I'm always in favor of anything that encourages the removal of clothes."

She gave him an unimpressed look. "And you're not really the type to...let your alcohol breathe before shooting it back."

He eyed the cup she held. "If that stuff breathes too much, it might get up and walk outta here on its own."

She tipped the rest back.

"So you're pissed about being here because it's hot and there's no wine?" he asked.

"That's part of it."

"What's the rest?"

She sighed. "Everything."

"Real nice, Mad," he said, annoyed. He poured more liquor.

"It's just...agitating and uncomfortable in every way. I just wanted to get the hell home. Back to where it was peaceful and quiet and..." She swallowed.

"And?" His tone was tight. Just like his chest. She didn't like it here. She didn't want to be here. Not for Tommy's funeral and not now.

"Where I'm in control." She blew out a breath. "Here, I never know what's going to happen, or how I'm going to react. Though I *do* know it's not going to be levelheaded and calm and cool."

Owen had never met her grandparents from California, but Tommy had told them that his mom's parents were wealthy. Sophisticated. Cultured. The type of people who would hang out in an art gallery rather than a broken-down shack/bar by the bayou. Levelheaded people. Calm and cool people. People who probably couldn't even handle a little cayenne.

Nobody down *here* was calm and cool. Yeah, they could handle the heat.

So could Maddie, dammit. Of all kinds. Maybe she was used to air-conditioning and ocean breezes keeping her cool. Maybe she hadn't burned anything down in San Francisco. But she was a bayou girl deep down and that meant spice was in her blood.

Suddenly, he had an intense—possibly even crazy—need to make sure she wasn't calm and cool.

That was bad. Dangerous. He knew that. But hell, she was already expecting to be agitated and...*hot*. And Sawyer wanted them to remind her what it was like to be here. Well, here it was hot. In many ways.

"You're not your father, Madison," Owen said, low and firm. That had been what had driven her away. She'd gotten on that airplane to California happily. She'd seen her father lose his mind and land in jail, likely for the rest of his life, and her family fall apart, and after the month she'd spent with Owen just prior to that—sneaking out at night, having sex for the first time, burning people's sheds down—she'd been convinced she was going to end up out-of-control and in trouble. The permanent, life-altering kind of trouble.

She'd gone to California to escape all of that.

She hadn't been back since.

She was shaking her head now. "You don't know that I'm not just like him." She sat up straighter. "I ended up in *jail* after only a couple of hours in this town."

"Airport jail," he said. "Come on."

"I have flown literally a hundred times and never ended up in airport jail, Owen."

Maybe she had a point. "So you've been staying away from Autre because—"

"It makes me crazy," she filled in. "And now I'm stuck here for thirty days because of a partnership agreement our *grandfathers* wrote up, in ink on notebook paper, while drinking"—she held up her cup—"*this*. This agreement should not be legally binding."

Suddenly, for a reason he couldn't name exactly, Owen felt a rush of satisfaction go through him. As if things were working out quite nicely. Even though there was actually not a bit of proof of that. "Mark Maillard says it is. Signed and dated. Even had witnesses."

When Sawyer had told him and Josh about the partnership agreement Leo had given him, Owen had thought for sure it was going to be a huge pain in the ass.

He'd been right. But it was also going to be fun.

"See? Crazy. Everything about this place is crazy."

Owen could see that she was getting a little worked up. She was breathing faster and her cheeks were pink and...she looked gorgeous.

She looked like the Maddie he'd always known. And loved.

"It's been twelve years. Surely you've gained a little self-control," he said. He sincerely hoped not.

She frowned at him. "I don't need self-control in California. I have crazy urges that need to be controlled when I'm here. Hence why I love it *there*."

"So not just the wine then," he said.

Maddie took another sip of her grandfather's recipe. "Not just the wine, no."

He'd bet his last twenty bucks that she didn't even really like wine.

Maddie was a moonshine kind of girl. Bold and down-home with deep roots and a long history in the area. As a kid, she'd thrown herself into everything they all did. Running, climbing, swimming. When she'd gotten older, she'd insisted that her father teach her to ride a motorcycle when he was teaching Tommy. She swore. She drank cheap beer. She'd gotten a fake ID so she could get a tattoo. She could shoot a gun. She could take apart a transmission. She loved to dance and laugh and play pranks and sneak cookies from the kitchen and cigarettes from Leo's truck, all just for the thrill of maybe getting caught. Just as Cora would have happily given her cookies if she'd asked, Leo would have probably given her the hand-rolled cigarettes that he smoked. Hell, he would have just handed over the tobacco and paper and let her roll her own. She knew how. They'd all watched Leo do it enough times.

Maddie had always been right there, having fun, living large, taking risks, pushing boundaries. And he'd known by the time he was twelve that he was going to date her someday. Then she'd started wearing a bra and shaving her legs, and he'd figured he was going to marry her someday. Marrying a girl who could help him rebuild an engine, clean a catfish, and smelled as good as she did seemed like a *very* good idea.

"Have *you* gained some self-control?" she asked.

He'd really like to think so. Truth be told, his control wasn't tested very often. He had a laid-back lifestyle, a laid-back job, a laid-back attitude about pretty much everything.

"I haven't broken a nose or any china for...about twelve years."

He let that sink in. He watched her as it did. She took a little breath but didn't say anything about the fact that he hadn't lost his cool since she'd left town. Then her eyes drifted to the scar that came out of the bottom of his right shirt sleeve and traveled to his elbow.

That scar was because of her. And looking at her, now he knew he would still do anything for her. Even if it meant twenty-nine stitches and risking not being able to throw a football that fall, a police record, almost losing a lifelong friendship, and threatening the future of the business that meant the world to his entire family.

"We should probably go to Ellie's," she finally said.

He nodded. He was feeling lighter than he had when he'd first seen her and had felt that familiar, scary mix of affection and adrenaline. "Okay." He pivoted to put the bottle of booze back in the bottom file cabinet drawer.

She glanced at the cups they'd been using. "Don't we need to wash those?"

He looked down at the cups. He didn't even know how long they'd been in here. "Most people who need a shot of bayou whiskey aren't picky about what they drink it from."

She held out a hand. "I'm going to *not* think about just drinking out of cups that you don't feel strongly about washing."

"Probably for the best." He handed the cups over.

She grabbed her big red purse and tucked them inside, then headed for the door. He followed, keeping his eyes off her legs. But not off her ass. Even in that flared skirt, it was a fine view.

2

Owen and Maddie rounded the building and crossed the narrow dirt road that dead-ended at the Boys of the Bayou main dock. Ellie's sat baking in the June sun across the road. The bar was a mainstay in the tiny town. It had long served hard liquor, beer, and fried seafood to the fishermen, roughnecks from the oil rigs, and any number of other blue-collar guys in the area. It also served as a down-home taste of real Louisiana cuisine for tourists who came for the tours or even the hunting and fishing packages Boys of the Bayou offered. Ellie's Hurricanes were ten times better than those served in the Quarter in New Orleans, and she often gave visitors their first taste of alligator. Usually it was fried, but she sometimes talked people into trying it in her gator and shrimp jambalaya and, every once in a while, someone would try her blackened alligator filets.

Ellie's food and drinks were famous locally and she did very well in online reviews.

Which was good, because the decor of the place was very... backyard-shed-converted-into-a-bar, with some crap-collected-over-the-years hung on the walls. The structure had stood, exactly as it was, inside and out, for over forty years and those years showed.

People didn't come to Ellie's for the ambiance. They came to get full and tipsy. Sometimes more than tipsy. So Ellie and Cora focused on giving people those things and didn't worry so much about the fact that their light fixtures didn't match—they just replaced them as needed and got whatever was cheapest—and that people had to shove a wooden wedge against the bathroom door to "lock" it. But hey, they'd written "wedge this under the door" on it in black sharpie, so it worked. Kind of. Good enough, anyway.

Owen reached around Maddie and grabbed the door handle, but just as he started to pull, she slapped her palm against it.

"Hang on," she said.

He looked at her. They were standing really close now. His chest was millimeters from her shoulder. Her expensive perfume didn't smell like peaches, but that didn't mean he didn't want to lean in and put his nose against her neck and sniff.

"You okay?" he asked her.

"They're *all* in there, huh?"

"Very likely. At least a lot of 'em." He didn't know where else they'd be since they weren't down on the docks or out on the airboats.

They'd done a few tours that morning, but had closed up early so Sawyer and Josh could help move furniture in and out of the room where Maddie would be staying at Cora's. If they hadn't, Leo would have tried to do it and would have thrown his back out. Or pretended to, anyway. He would have been bitching and moaning and hoping that Cora would feel bad and make him cornbread and beans. It was amazing the things Leo would do for Cora's cornbread.

Owen had chosen to stay out of that, volunteering to do some extra repairs and cleanup on the boats instead. He didn't need to be anywhere near Maddie's bed, whether *she* was near it and whether it was temporary and in her grandmother's guest room, or not.

Maddie took a deep breath. "This is going to be a big deal, isn't it?"

"You being home?" he asked.

She shot him a glance. "Me being in *Autre*."

So she wasn't going to refer to Autre as "home?" He frowned. "That's what I said."

"No, you said home."

"This is your home."

She turned to face him more squarely. "I haven't lived here in twelve years."

"So? Home is home. Your roots are here." His heart was thundering now and he felt tension squeezing the back of his neck.

She stepped back, putting more space between them. Which was probably for the best.

"My past is here," she said. "But I only lived here for sixteen years."

"Your family is from here."

"Not my whole family."

Owen shoved his hand through his hair. "You lived here longer than you've lived in California."

She lifted a shoulder as if this topic were no big deal. "For now. But if you consider that I don't remember much of my life here before age three or four, it's almost even."

"It's not almost even," he said, aware he was gritting his teeth.

She frowned, clearly noting his teeth. "Are you really going to make me say this?"

"That you don't feel like you're from here?" he asked.

"That I don't want to be here. That if Tommy hadn't died and left his share to me, I wouldn't be here now."

Owen took a deep breath and worked on being laid-back. He never had to work at that. Apparently Madison could still wind him up. Of course, in the past, he'd had the outlet of hot sex. Whether he was feeling possessive or they were making up after an argument, the sex had been the perfect release. Now they were on opposite sides—she didn't want to be here and wanted to get rid of Boys of the Bayou. He needed her to not only keep Boys of the Bayou, but within twenty minutes of her being in town, he had a gut-deep *need* to make her *want* to be here. Yeah, he wanted her to *like* being here. To miss them. To find things here that were better than California. He didn't just want her to agree to keep the business going. He wanted her to want to be a real part of it.

This business and his family were the center of his life. They were everything that mattered to him. And if Maddie didn't love them and want them, that was going to eat at him.

Damn. This was getting complicated. Already.

And if he didn't have hot sex as the way to blow off steam, he was afraid of how this might all end.

He took a breath. "Yeah, okay, yes, they're very excited to see you. They've been moving furniture in and out of the extra bedroom at Cora's, cooking up a storm, and generally worrying and planning for your visit," he finally said.

Maddie dropped her chin to her chest and blew out a breath. "Okay, then."

He couldn't resist. He reached out and put a hand on her arm. He squeezed. Her head came up quickly and she met his gaze.

"It's going to be okay," he felt compelled to say. Because he was always compelled to comfort her and make her happy.

"A month is a long time."

"Depends on how you look at it."

"I look at it as thirty days surrounded by people who I haven't known in a decade, who are slightly off their rockers, and who are now going to be doing everything they can to convince me not to sell my portion of the company they all love."

So she'd realized this visit was intended to talk her out of selling. He should have known she'd figure that out quickly.

"Okay, that could be a long thirty days," he agreed.

She wet her lips, seeming to hesitate for a moment. Then she said, "I'm going to need a friend. Someone on my side."

That kicked him in the gut. Just as she'd intended. He dropped his hand from her arm. "What do you mean? Everyone here loves you."

She lifted a shoulder at that, as if she wasn't completely convinced. Owen tucked his hands into his front pockets to keep from reaching for her.

"I need someone to help them understand that I need to sell," she said.

He wasn't sure how much Sawyer had told her, but he had to be honest here. "We can't afford to buy you out."

She sighed. "I know. And I'd sell it to you for a dollar if I could."

The partnership agreement said that anyone selling had to get at least fair market value.

"But I have a buyer," she added.

"Yeah. I heard."

She chewed on her bottom lip, studying Owen's face. "He's a great fit. He wants this. He's excited about the company. And he's got money. A lot of it. Enough to invest and really do some big things. Expand. Advertise. Whatever Boys of the Bayou needs."

"And you want me to convince my family that we should let a stranger come in here and be a partner?" he asked. "You have to know that's not going to happen."

"Please," she said, her eyes pleading. "It's a good idea. For everyone. I don't want the company, he does. And you guys could use a partner who's truly involved. And has cash."

"We should go in." He couldn't handle this on his own. Because he was torn between wanting her to keep it, wanting her to feel connected here, and wanting her to be happy and get what she wanted.

This was definitely going to be a long thirty days.

Owen felt his temper spiking and he reached past her to grab the door again. "Let's talk in thirty days. If you don't love it here, and you don't want to have a piece of everything here, and you don't understand that this is about family more than it's about money, then yeah, I'll convince Sawyer to let you sell. I won't want you owning even a sliver."

She again flattened her palm against the door. "I don't want you to be upset."

"Then don't sell the business." *And please go back to California, because I can't even breathe normally when you're here.*

"That's not fair," she said, looking sad.

"Why are you so set on getting rid of it?" he asked crossly. He meant everything he'd said to her. If she didn't feel her roots here, connected to this business and all the people, then he didn't want her to have it. But the idea that she might not feel those things tore him up.

She wet her lips and then seemed to make a decision because she lifted her chin. "I don't like getting those monthly checks from here. It's a monthly reminder of this whole...life. I have no idea why he left it to me and not to you guys, but not only do I *not* feel a connection to the business, I'm happy in California and really just want to be left alone."

See, *this* was going to be hell. He'd thought the torture would be keeping his hands to himself. He hadn't anticipated this. She didn't want to be here. She was unhappy about being forced to come back. That made Owen want to help her get the hell away from here. Maddie being unhappy was unacceptable. Especially if it had anything to do with him. Which it did. Boys of the Bayou was his business. The only thing he was good at. The thing he was most proud of. He loved his life here. He didn't want it to change. Someone else owning thirty-five percent of Boys of the Bayou would definitely mean change.

Thank God he wasn't dealing with this alone. Left alone with this decision, he'd probably look into her eyes for one second too long and totally cave, letting her do whatever she wanted with the company he'd loved and helped build.

"We need to talk to Sawyer." Without letting her respond, he jerked the door open. She was just going to have to get over her trepidation about facing the family. The sooner the better.

Inside it was, well, normal. Which meant it was full of people all talking at once, arguing, laughing, giving each other shit, and eating and drinking. It also meant it was kind of loud.

Maddie hung back, so Owen stepped through the door and called, "Hey, y'all."

Ellie glanced over. "Get in here and hang that up," she said, pointing at the WELCOME HOME banner that was drooping to the floor on one end. "Swear to God these men can't even use Scotch tape right."

She didn't, however, react to seeing Maddie. Surprised, Owen looked over his shoulder to find that Maddie had stepped to the side, out of sight. She better not run. He would definitely chase her down. Throwing her over his shoulder was far too tempting.

"That's because real men use *duct tape*," Mitch, another cousin, told her.

"You can't hang a welcome home banner up with duct tape," Cora told him.

"Why? Guarantee it wouldn't be lyin' on the floor right now," Mitch said.

"Because it doesn't look nice then," Cora said.

"Well, if you're tryin' to make this place look nice, you're gonna need a few more banners to cover stuff up. Big ones," Mitch said.

The other guys, including Owen's grandpa, two uncles, and a few stray guys who were just always around, all laughed.

Ellie slapped Mitch on the back of the head.

Owen sighed and lifted his fingers to his mouth to blow out a sharp whistle.

Blessedly, everyone stopped what they were doing and pivoted to face him.

He turned around, reached around the corner, grabbed the front of Maddie's belt and pulled her through the door. "Look what I found."

Everyone stared. Not saying a word. For three whole seconds. Which was truly a miracle.

Then Cora cried, "Oh. My. *God!*"

And the whole place went wild.

———

MADDIE HAD REHEARSED this moment a million times over the twelve years since she'd been gone. She knew exactly how she wanted to smile, what she wanted to say, how she wanted to dress. This was the last time she was ever going to be here, so she wanted to go out happy. Or happy-ish anyway.

"Hi, everyone," she said with a smile that was Miss America wattage.

"Oh my *God*," her grandmother said again, almost running toward Maddie, her eyes sparkly with tears.

Maddie braced herself. Not only for the impact of Cora's embrace, but also for the wave of emotion it would bring.

Cora pushed Owen out of the way and enfolded Maddie in a hug that, sure enough, made Maddie's throat tighten and her eyes sting. Cora smelled like Cajun-spiced pancakes—a mix of cayenne, garlic, and maple syrup. Maybe not a great combo in actual pancakes, but on her grandmother, it was perfect.

Maddie let Cora hold her, rocking her back and forth, just absorbing it all. Her other grandmother, Patrice Johnson, her mother's mother, was not a hugger. She had always been kind and encouraging to Maddie. Patrice told her that she was proud of her and loved her. But she wasn't as warm and openly affectionate as Cora Allain. Of course, very few people were.

Finally Cora leaned back, her cheeks wet with tears. "I'm so happy you're here."

"Hi, Gran," Maddie said, using the name she and Tommy had always used.

"She might have your blood, but she's got a lot of my pecans in her, too," Ellie Landry said, pushing in next to Cora, moving Owen even farther away.

For a second Maddie felt a little bit of panic at her ally drifting away. But that was stupid. Because Owen Landry represented as big a risk as anyone or anything to ruining Maddie's good feelings and memories of Autre. And this was Ellie. The woman had been a second grandma to Maddie and Tommy.

Ellie could work magic with pecans, that was for sure. Her pie had once led men to literally fight over the last piece, and she made amazing spicy pecans that Maddie could eat by the bushel. "I haven't had a decent piece of pecan pie in forever," Maddie told Ellie, her voice soft because of the tightness still afflicting her throat.

Ellie took Maddie's face between her hands and peered into her eyes with a solemn but affectionate look. "We will fix that, my sweetheart. We will fix a lot of things."

Oh boy, there was that threat of tears again. Maddie blinked quickly and gave Ellie a wobbly smile without answering.

Ellie pulled her into a quick hug and then turned her over to Owen and Sawyer's grandpa, Leo.

"This old man hasn't seen anything so pretty in a long time," Leo told her.

"Thanks, Grandpa!" Kennedy called from somewhere at the back of the crowd.

Everyone laughed.

"You've got a hole in your nose, girl!" Leo called back to Kennedy, referring to her nose piercing, that went along with a lot of others. "That's all I can see when I look at you."

Everyone knew he didn't mean that. Not at all. Kennedy was his self-proclaimed favorite.

"Oh, well, then you've been missing me rolling my eyes, sticking my tongue out, and flipping you off!" Kennedy told him.

Leo chuckled and said to Maddie, "No, I haven't. And if she didn't flip me off once in a while I'd be worried I hadn't raised her right."

Maddie's heart melted further. She'd always loved Leo. "Oh really?"

"No woman should put up with shit from men and I definitely give her my share," he said with a nod.

"Just to keep her in practice for dealing with all the other guys?" Maddie asked, feeling the threat of tears pass and a general warmth settle in her chest. *Thank you, Leo.*

"Exactly." He gave her a wink.

Maddie laughed. She was succumbing to their charm and craziness. She could already feel it. She had to fight it. But... maybe after pecan pie.

This definitely had to be the last time she came back.

She could go weeks without thinking of Autre. And seven out of ten times when she *did* think about the little town or her family or Louisiana in general, it was because of something good—some restaurant in San Francisco trying to make a good jambalaya or serving something they called sweet tea, or a local bar celebrating Mardi Gras, or people building bonfires on the

---

beach, not realizing that no one did jambalaya, sweet tea, Mardi Gras, or bonfire parties like where she'd grown up.

But other times, like every time she sold one of her paintings, she'd think about what prompted her to only paint stormy scenes from the Louisiana coast and dark, haunted images of the bayou.

She'd grown up here. Until age sixteen, she'd loved this place as much as any of these people did. But everything had changed that June night twelve years ago and now her memories and feelings for Autre were a lot more *what-ifs* and *I wishes*.

All of that influenced her art for sure. There was regret and longing that she poured into her painting. But she was okay with that. It was a good outlet, it made her a living, and allowed her to shut all the feelings and memories down other times.

Then she'd started getting monthly checks from the Boys of the Bayou and every single time she looked at that return address, she cried.

That had to stop.

"Welcome home."

The deep voice pulled her out of her thoughts. She looked up—a lot farther up than she'd needed to look for Cora, Ellie, or Leo—into the piercing green eyes of Sawyer Landry.

Her brother's best friend. The guy who had been like a brother to her. The other majority partner in Boys of the Bayou. The reason she was here now.

She should correct him about the "home" thing like she had Owen. But she swallowed and forced a smile. "Hey, Sawyer."

He put a hand on her shoulder and squeezed before dropping it. Yeah, Sawyer wasn't really a touchy-feely guy.

"Good to see you," he said. He was studying her carefully.

He was worried. She could see it. Feel it. Sawyer had always been a bit protective, but it seemed to have been dialed up a few notches. Was he worried she was mad about being here?

And that she might burn something of *his* down? Or just about her in general? She'd just lost her brother. She was being forced to be here. By him. He had reason to worry about her emotional state, she supposed.

She gave him a smile. It was a little forced, but not entirely. It wasn't Sawyer's fault that having someone feel protective of her made her uncomfortable. She didn't want anyone feeling responsible for her.

It wasn't hard to figure out where that came from. Her father, feeling protective of Maddie's mom, had tried to kill a guy and had landed himself in prison. Tommy and Owen, both feeling protective of *her*, had crashed through a window and spent the night in the hospital. Feeling protective of Owen, *she* had set a guy's shed on fire—and it easily could have been his house—and had stolen a car—kind of—and spent a night in jail herself.

That's what happened when you really cared about someone. Cared to your very bones. Cared to the point that you would sacrifice everything. It made you freaking crazy.

She didn't want that. For any of them. She couldn't keep these people from caring about each other, but she could absolutely not be a part of it.

And if Sawyer was concerned about her, Owen definitely would be. Sawyer would try to snap her out of it with a crawfish boil, her favorite locally made root beer, and talk of the good old days. Owen, on the other hand, might end up in jail or the hospital again. Or in the hospital on the way to jail.

She really needed to persuade them that she was fine and didn't want anything to do with Boys of the Bayou or Autre. She just had to prove to them that she was over all of this. Owen had confirmed the theory she'd been mulling over. These people were proud and loyal and protective. If she didn't want the things they did—very especially the business and the family—that would offend them and they would easily let her go.

It wasn't a lie. She didn't want the business. She really didn't. What did she want with a swamp boat tour and fishing company? She had the Pacific Ocean. The massive, gloriously beautiful Pacific Ocean. She didn't need the dirty, kind of creepy bayou. And owning it from afar wasn't a good option, either. She definitely did *not* want to keep getting those checks in the mail.

Plus it was *hot* here. Not hot. But *holy-shit-it's hot*. And the humidity—God, the humidity. Then there were the bugs. There were lots. Big ones. Also, Cora's gumbo was going to give her heartburn. She couldn't handle the spices anymore. She hadn't had a single drop of Tabasco in a decade, and she hadn't eaten any breaded, fried meat in almost seven years.

This was just not her place anymore.

But she was going to have to convince them of that while *they* were trying to convince *her* that she missed all of this and wanted to get back to her roots. She didn't doubt for a second that Owen, Sawyer, and Josh loved the Boys of the Bayou. They got to boat on the bayou, fish, hunt, laugh, tease, and be outdoors in the sun and fresh air. And now they got paid for it. It was the perfect job for them. But she also knew that fifty-percent of their love of the company was that it was a part of the family. In their minds, all it would take was her being here for a month, being a part of this life, to never want to let it go. She didn't know if they thought she'd actually move down here and start over, but it was clear they thought they could tap into her loyalty and love for Autre and the Landrys, and that would keep her from cutting ties.

She really needed to cut those ties. She needed to use these thirty days to show them that she didn't fit here and that they didn't want her here.

But there were more of them.

And they had pecan pie.

This was definitely going to be a battle.

"I think I might have already dropped a couple pounds from the sweating," she told Sawyer. "I guess that's one perk of this trip."

He chuckled softly. "California isn't really the arctic."

"No, but it's not a sauna in an oven on the surface of the sun, either."

He lifted a brow. "That's dramatic."

"So is insisting that I come over two thousand miles and stay for a month-long staff meeting."

His smile grew. "Thanks for coming."

"I didn't really have a choice, did I?"

Of course, that was thanks to Leo and Kenny more than it was Sawyer's doing. The two old men had drawn up a partnership agreement that was, even according to Maddie's lawyer, legal and binding. Even if it was unconventional.

Unconventional. What a word. Everything about this town and her situation here was un-freaking-conventional.

If she wanted to get rid of her share of Boys of the Bayou, she not only had to sell it for fair market value or greater, she had to jump through a few hoops. Crazy, only-Leo-and-Kenny-would-come-up-with-this hoops.

A thin line of sweat trickled down her spine just then reminding her that yeah, no matter how tempting the pecans and laughter and...okay, Owen...were, it was too damned hot to live here now that she'd gotten used to the San Francisco Bay area.

"Madison Evangeline Allain!" Josh, the third of her partners and Sawyer's younger brother, pushed to the front of the little crowd, cutting off any argument she and Sawyer might have gotten into about him coercing her into coming. Josh pulled her into a big hug and said softly in her ear, "Sawyer's a pretty great big brother, if you need one."

And she was suddenly at risk of crying again. She did need one. Hers was gone. And while Tommy had been damned stubborn over the last twelve years about cutting her off and letting her start fresh in California, she knew that he'd done what he thought was best. Being an asshole to her had been his way of taking care of her. But dammit, he'd given her sixteen pretty great years before that.

She sniffed and pulled back, giving Josh a wobbly smile. "Yeah, I guess you turned out pretty good."

"And I'm happy to fill in, too." He gave her an affectionate grin.

"Thanks."

"And the camping trip is going to be fun. I promise."

Right. The camping trip. One of the stipulations in the partnership agreement. Apparently Leo and Kenny had decided that the only reason one of them would be trying to get out of the partnership would be because they'd had a fight and that any conflict between them could be settled the way it had been since they were eight—with a camping trip.

The camping trip that she was *not* going on. She'd sit around a campfire in Cora's backyard or something, but no way was she spending the night in Leo's old cabin.

Sawyer knew that. At least she assumed he knew that. She didn't camp anymore. She didn't get on airboats—which was the only way to get to the cabin. She didn't sleep in bunkbeds—which were the only things to sleep on out there. She didn't go without internet access—which was a complete joke out there. Yeah, there was no way in hell she was going to stay out there in that ramshackle "cabin" with Sawyer, Josh, and Owen overnight to work out their business problems.

But she'd agreed to come to Autre, hoping to placate them by at least showing up in person to discuss all of this. Besides, she was going to meet with Bennett Baxter, the guy who was interested in her share, and it made sense to meet him in person. And be here when he came to check things out. Because God knew what these guys—hell, the whole group of friends and family—would do or say to dissuade him from buying.

"Okay, time for the partners' meeting," Sawyer interrupted, pulling Josh back. He smiled down at Maddie. "Come on. Let's head over to the office. We have a lot to talk about."

"The office?" Kennedy called out. "I just got my fries!"

"The *partner* meeting," Sawyer said.

"Oh, come on!" Leo protested. "We want to hear."

"This is about Boys of the Bayou," Sawyer said.

"We let you hear about all the plans for this place," Ellie said.

"You have *plans* for this place?" Josh asked, looking around.

"We put a new roof on."

"Because there was water pouring in on top of the back tables every time it rained," Josh said with a laugh.

"Still." Ellie shrugged. "You got to hear all about it."

"We couldn't really help it," Sawyer said. "Bill was the roofer and he was in here for lunch when you were talking about it."

"Still."

That was how it went with Ellie. Maddie felt a tug at the corner of her mouth. She remembered Ellie's stubbornness.

"Well, Maddie can't make it to the partner meeting if it's not here," Cora announced. "She hasn't had lunch yet."

"Oh," Maddie started. "I'm not—"

"I've got shrimp and cheesy grits."

Damn. It wasn't pecan pie, but it would take a much stronger woman than Maddie was to turn down Cora's cheesy grits.

She would *not* be worn down by grits. She had to be tougher than that.

Bugs. Heat. Humidity. No spa or gym for forty miles. The heat.

"She'd better eat something." Owen was suddenly beside her again. "She had a few snorts of Kenny's whiskey in the office. Could definitely use some grits to soak that up."

Maddie opened her mouth to say that she was only feeling mildly buzzed—which, in a previous life, would have been something to brag about. Kenny's moonshine was strong stuff. But Sawyer frowned at them before she could reply.

"You two were drinkin' in the office before you came in here?"

Owen suddenly looked like he'd been caught taking candy before dinner. He looked at Maddie. Blew out a breath. Then nodded. "Yeah. But only for—"

"She kiss you?" Leo asked.

Maddie opened her mouth to protest but she was again interrupted. She was maybe a little slow because of the booze. Or maybe because she was out of practice interacting with the people who all talked at once, talked over one another, and said whatever was on their minds.

"No." Owen glared at his grandfather.

"*You* kiss *her*?" Leo asked.

"*No*. Knock it off," Owen told him.

"Anything on fire anywhere?" Ellie asked with a smirk.

"Hilarious," Owen told her dryly. "You're all really hilarious."

Maddie felt her cheeks burning. Yeah, so maybe she'd set a couple of things on fire. But that was twelve years ago. And one had been an accident. Geez. She wasn't going to burn things down just because Owen kissed her.

Probably.

"Nope, nothin's burnin'," Kennedy called, holding up her phone. "Checked Facebook."

Autre was tiny. Someone, probably multiple someones, would definitely have posted any fires or other emergencies to the town's Facebook page. Hopefully, someone would also call

9-1-1. But it wasn't impossible to think that the volunteer fire-fighters would first find out about a blaze from social media. The grapevine here might just be faster than a 9-1-1 dispatcher.

"They must not have messed around then," Ellie decided. "Yet."

Maddie frowned at them all. "*Of course* we haven't kissed. Or anything else." She said it with a tone that clearly conveyed how absurd that idea was. "I've been here for like thirty minutes." Not that she would kiss Owen even if she'd been here longer. They were twelve years, a lot of regrets, and a lot of growing up past kissing each other.

There might have been a moment or two when she'd remembered what it was like to kiss him. Hot. Consuming. Crazy-inducing. All excellent reasons *not* to do it. Even if he was the best kissing she'd ever had. Ever. And he'd only been seventeen and pretty new to it all. God only knew what he'd be like now. She'd probably end up burning the whole town down.

She had to very definitely, absolutely, no-question-about-it *not* kiss him.

It was really unfair that she'd already seen him without his shirt on. Because *damn*, twelve years of growing up and developing and doing manual labor outside in the sun had been very, very kind to Owen Landry and his abs and biceps.

"Yeah, well, it doesn't take thirty minutes to set a fire," Leo said.

"None of you *really* think that she set anything on fire," Owen said. "Stop it."

"I don't mean a fire like that," Leo said. "I mean that fire." He waggled his finger back and forth between Maddie and Owen.

Maddie felt her *cheeks* start to burn a little from blushing. They were all being ridiculous but that's what this group of people did best. "Okay, very funny," she said. "But the shed and…everything else…was a long time ago."

"Sparks like that don't burn out," Leo said. "They just lay banked, waiting for some kindling."

Maddie sighed. They really needed a new topic. "Partner meeting time, right, Sawyer?"

"Really?" Owen asked his grandpa. "Cuz you and Ellie's sparks burned out."

Leo and Ellie were now divorced, even though they were still good friends and—clearly—spent time together.

Maddie groaned. He needed to let it go. They *all* needed to let this go.

Leo shot Ellie a glance and gave her a grin. "Like I said, that kind of fire doesn't burn out."

"You're divorced," Maddie heard herself point out. *She* needed to shut up, too.

"Doesn't mean the spark's gone," Ellie said matter-of-factly. "We're still hot for each other, we just can't live together."

Maddie sighed.

"Trevor know you're still hot for Leo?" Josh asked, referring to Ellie's boyfriend.

Maddie had never met the man and found it all bizarre, but she knew about Trevor, the New Orleans attorney who was twenty years younger than Ellie and, apparently, thought she walked on water. Kennedy, thankfully, had no filter, just like the rest of the Landrys, and she posted everything on Facebook. That worked for Maddie as a communication tool because she could look when she was ready and didn't have to reply. She could stay up to date on the family and Autre in a general sense, but she didn't have to be *involved*.

"Sure he does," Ellie said.

"He trusts you not to act on it?" Josh asked, seeming almost fascinated.

"Of course," Ellie said with a frown.

One thing that was an absolute truth—the Landrys were loyal people. When they made a promise, they kept it.

Which was why this partnership agreement was so important. And binding. Even if it hadn't been legally binding, the guys would have wanted to follow it to the letter. Family roots and doing what you said you were going to do were hallmarks of this group of people.

"Well there was that one time..." Leo trailed off.

Ellie slapped his arm. "Trevor and I were on a break."

Maddie's eyes widened. Sawyer gave a little groan and took her elbow. "Let's change this subject."

She was all for that. Besides not needing any further details about Leo and Ellie rekindling their "fire" once in a while, she really didn't need to be thinking about rekindling fires of any kind down here. Especially given the...smoldering...going on between her and Owen.

3

They made their way toward the back of the bar, people parting like Sawyer was Moses. Mitch and another guy Maddie didn't know were pulling tables together to make one big, rickety conference table.

But Maddie's attention was pulled to Kennedy Landry, who was sitting at the end of the bar, her feet—in black combat boots—propped on the stool next to her. Her black hair was streaked with purple, her eye makeup was a thick, bold mix of the same colors, and her nose and ear piercings glinted in the lights that hung over the bar. It was a sharp contrast to the beauty queen Maddie had known growing up, but Kennedy had started her feminist rebellion against the pageants and what she deemed their "superficial emphasis on defining what makes a woman worthy of attention" when she was thirteen. On stage. At the last beauty pageant she ever entered. She'd left the stage in the semifinals looking like a sweet southern belle and come back out for the finals with jet-black hair, temporary tattoos, a not-so-temporary series of ear piercings, and, yes, combat boots. She'd lost, but she'd made her point, and

Maddie had been the person applauding loudest from the audience.

Kennedy gave Maddie a huge grin and a little salute with one of her chili cheese fries.

Maddie grinned back. She'd always really liked Kennedy. The other woman was a couple years younger than Maddie but their families had spent so much time together, Kennedy felt like a cousin or even a sister. The only two girls in a group with an overload of testosterone, they'd stuck together. They'd drifted apart, too, over the years. Maddie just hadn't had the energy to stay close to anyone in Autre, and Kennedy had only been fourteen when Maddie had left. She'd had a full life, revolving entirely around Autre, and Maddie had figured it was easiest, for them both, to just live their own lives.

"So Maddie was on this horrible date for Valentine's Day," Maddie heard Kennedy say as she drew closer.

She noticed that Kennedy was talking to another woman. One Maddie didn't know. "Hang on, I want to say hi to Kennedy," she said to Sawyer.

He gave her a nod and went over to help the guys arrange the tables and to tell Josh and Owen that it was too early for beer and to help Cora, who had started carrying plates to the tables.

It looked a lot more like a family dinner than a business meeting but that just further emphasized how this business worked. You couldn't untangle the family from the business or vice versa.

Maddie felt her stomach knot a little. She wasn't really family, anymore, but Tommy had been. These guys had been like brothers to him. *Why didn't you just leave the business to them?* she asked her brother silently for the millionth time.

After her grandpa had passed away, his portion of the business had gone to Cora. She'd sold thirty-five percent of her portion to Tommy and fifteen percent to Owen. Leo had sold thirty-five percent of his portion to Sawyer and fifteen to Josh.

Since the guys had owned it, the business had grown and now it was worth far more than they'd paid their grandparents for it. Before they'd taken it over, Leo and Kenny had mostly taken groups out hunting and fishing and camping. The boys had expanded it into a true tourist attraction. They'd also committed to rolling most of their profits back into the business, expanding and improving and advertising. Which meant that, ironically, they couldn't afford to buy Maddie out.

Now she was going to have to break up the family business.

She hated that she was in this position. She, of course, felt guilty. But she also felt panic when she thought about keeping a connection to this place that felt familiar and scary at the same time.

"Owen had the guy up against the wall, cutting off his windpipe, telling him that he was going to throw him off the swamp bridge if he ever touched Maddie again," Kennedy was saying as Maddie slipped onto the stool next to her.

"Hey," she said. "Did I hear my name?"

"Oh, I'm just tellin' Tori you and Owen's story." Kennedy popped a fry into her mouth and chewed.

"Our story?"

"I *love* the stories from around here," the other woman, who Maddie assumed was Tori, said. "I especially love that Owen has one."

Maddie lifted a brow and reached out her hand. "Hi, I'm Madison Allain."

"Oh, I know." The woman took her hand with a huge smile. "I'm Victoria Kramer, but everyone calls me Tori."

"You're new here."

"She's Josh's," Kennedy said, running a fry through some cheese sauce. "Just moved down here from Iowa about three months ago. She's a vet." Kennedy grinned. "Josh bought her a farm. And peacocks."

Maddie looked at Tori, who was now smiling with a touch of pink in her cheeks. She looked a little shy but also very... satisfied. She was an outsider, though. Not from here. New. Maybe Maddie could have a normal friend here for the next month. Someone to remind her of the great big wide world outside of the Autre city limits. "Josh, huh?"

Tori's smile grew. "Yeah." She was dressed in cutoff denim shorts, a basic blue tee, had her hair back in a pony-tail and Converse tennis shoes on her feet. She had a smudge of dirt on one leg, short fingernails, a faint smat-tering of freckles over her nose, and when she reached for one of Kennedy's fries, Maddie could see where the tan on her arms ended just under the edge of her sleeve. A farmer's tan. No makeup. Just a girl who apparently worked outside with animals.

But when Tori heard Josh's name, her smile softened, and her voice took on a dreamy note. Like she was madly in love.

"Josh is a great guy," Maddie said. "Probably my favorite Landry, to be honest."

Kennedy snorted. "Bullshit."

Maddie looked at her. "I mean, I like Sawyer a lot, too. But he always backed Tommy up when he was telling me what to do and not to do. And Ellie's great, of course, but she doesn't let you get away with anything. Leo is probably my second favorite. He's funny and sweet."

"He's cantankerous and full of shit," Kennedy said of her grandpa, but her smile was nothing but affectionate.

"Well, there's that, too," Maddie agreed with a laugh.

"But no way any of them are your favorite," Kennedy said. She got a sly smile on her face. "You never burned anything down for any of *them.*"

Maddie sighed. "I'm never going to live that down."

"Are you kidding?" Kennedy said. "It's a fantastic story. Especially since it's Owen."

Tori nodded. "Owen is so laid-back and charming and friendly. I can't imagine someone getting that worked up over him. And vice versa."

Yeah, well, she and Owen had always created sparks. Figuratively and literally.

"Crazy," Maddie said. "It's someone getting that *crazy* because of him."

Tori grinned. "Yeah. I mean, he's awesome and the girls seem to really like him. And I get it. He's hot. And the charming thing," she added.

Maddie sighed. Oh, she was *sure* the girls liked Owen. She had no trouble at all believing that Josh and Owen were the main attraction for a lot of the swamp boat tours. They did a lot of bachelorette parties and groups of girls in town for spring break, Mardi Gras and St. Patrick's Day and…hell, most major holidays. Even girls who came with groups of friends or their families would, no doubt, find the view at the front of the swamp boat even more enticing than anything they'd see in the bayou. From her rare phone calls with her brother, she knew that Tommy had been the more serious, business guy. He'd led most of the fishing and hunting parties. Sawyer tended to take the families with kids out. He liked to take more of an educational angle, teaching the kids about the animals and plants and history. Josh and Owen were the party guys.

"But he's just so easygoing," Tori said. "I'd assume he'd be pretty great at apologizing and talking you out of a snit if he did something wrong."

Kennedy laughed. "She didn't burn the shed down because of something *Owen* did."

"No?" Tori turned wide, interested eyes to Maddie. "Then why?"

"She was *defending* him," Kennedy said.

Tori's mouth formed a little "o." "Tell me," she said pleadingly to Maddie.

Maddie shrugged. Looking back, she'd gone over-the-top, but she still remembered how she felt when Owen's mom told her that Wade had shown up on their front porch. "My ex-boyfriend threatened him after we broke up."

"Did you break up with him because of Owen?" Tori asked, softly, almost as if she was hoping that was the answer.

Maddie nodded and Tori let out a happy sigh.

Maddie wasn't sure if she should laugh or roll her eyes. Clearly Tori was one of them now. If she was into big huge displays of this-is-mine-and-you'd-better-back-off, then she was in the right place.

The story was public knowledge. Maddie had no doubt it had grown a little over the years, but it didn't have to grow much to be pretty entertaining. Twelve years later she could look back and mostly just roll her eyes. She was a little embarrassed by the whole thing, of course, but in Autre, where over-the-top was a way of life, she was a bit of a celebrity because of her overreaction on Owen's behalf.

Of course, outside of Autre was something else altogether. She wouldn't want anyone outside of Autre to know about her past actions. The owner of the art gallery where she worked thought she was a sophisticated, composed, intelligent woman. So did her few girlfriends, the men she dated, her co-workers, really everyone. Because that was exactly who she was. Outside of Autre.

Tori leaned her elbows in on the bar and looked at Maddie eagerly. "What did he do? What did you do? What did *Owen* do?" She glanced over to where Owen was helping set up for the "partner meeting".

Maddie reached out and swiped one of Kennedy's fries and popped it in her mouth. She chewed for a moment, regarding Tori. She was involved with Josh. Josh was the least intense of the Landry guys. He was fun and friendly and flirtatious, but that didn't mean he didn't have a little larger-than-life in him. Tori had also been around these people now for three months. Nothing Maddie was going to say would shock her. In fact, it almost seemed that she would be delighted.

Maddie swallowed and brushed her hands together. "Okay, here's the story. Wade was being an asshole at the Valentine's Day party we went to. He kept saying that the only present he wanted from me was sex. I kept telling him no, he kept drinking and the more drunk he got, the more insistent he got. Finally, I'd had enough and called Owen to come and get me. He, of course, came right away. I didn't tell him what had happened until we got to my house but after I did, he dropped me off and went right back to find Wade. I wasn't there for that but there were lots of witnesses. Owen pretty much threatened to rip Wade's dick off if he ever said anything inappropriate to me again."

Tori's eyes were predictably wide and Maddie felt herself smiling. She should *not* enjoy remembering or telling this story. But dammit, she kind of was.

"I found out about it pretty much as it was happening and I went straight to Owen's house."

"To yell at him?" Tori asked, leaning in.

"To kiss him," Maddie said.

She grinned at Tori's delighted, "*Yes.*"

Maddie lifted a shoulder. "I'd wanted to kiss him for a long time and that seemed like a good reason."

"Very good reason," Tori agreed. She leaned in further, clearly anticipating the rest of the story.

Maddie laughed. "Well, Wade wasn't happy about the breakup or Owen's threats, but he was especially pissed off to find out that I'd spent the night in Owen's room."

Tori gave a little gasp.

"Yep. But we didn't have sex. That night. I just slept there. In his bed, while he took the floor."

"Aw, he's a good guy," Tori said.

He was. He always had been. One of the best. Owen was everything she'd grown up thinking she wanted. He was loyal, hardworking, funny, and cute. At age seventeen, he'd been very, very cute. That cute had turned into hot. But she'd always been attracted to him.

Part of it was his blue eyes and his I'm-mostly-full-of-shit grin and his willingness to jump into any situation where one of his family members needed him. He'd reminded her of her dad. Danny Allain had been a great guy, always willing to help anyone out, plus steady and protective. Which was good, because Maddie's mom had not been steady. She'd been fun. She'd fit right in with the Landrys. She'd loved the always-a-little-chaotic environment around the Landrys.

Maddie hadn't fully realized it until she'd lived with her mom's parents and understood what a stifled atmosphere her mom had grown up in. It had been a relief to Maddie after all the craziness surrounding her mom's death and her dad's imprisonment. But it was easy to believe that Molly Allain had left California and found a lifestyle that was fun and loud and boisterous and so different from the way she'd been raised, that she'd jumped right in.

Owen was wrong. Maddie wasn't worried about being like her dad. She was worried about being like her mom. And making Owen like her dad.

"What happened next?" Tori asked.

Maddie shook off the thoughts of her mom's love of a good party and the way she'd yell at football games and do shots at the bar and argue politics with the old men. She was always loud and in the middle of everything and happy and fun. Everyone had loved her.

Danny had been the steady one. The quieter one. The one

who smiled indulgently watching his wife pull a wallflower out onto the dance floor or call for another round.

Danny Allain plowing his truck into a living room wall, trying to kill the guy who'd killed Molly in a drunk driving accident, had been a shock to literally everyone who knew him. Put simply, he'd snapped.

If that could happen to him, it could definitely happen to a guy like Owen, who hadn't hesitated to put Wade up against the wall with his hand on Wade's throat, or who'd gone crashing through a plate-glass window with her brother.

Maddie cleared her throat. "Well, Owen and I got together and our exes didn't like it. Wade tried to start something by showing up at Owen's house one night, threatening to take his dog since Owen had stolen me."

"Noooo," Tori gasped. "Not the dog!"

Maddie glanced at Kennedy who gave her a nod and a wink. "Yep. His dog. That pissed me off, so I went to Wade's house."

"And...the fire?" Tori asked.

"Yep." Maddie nodded. "I took his football jersey, a T-shirt he'd given me, a teddy bear, and a photo of us together. I threw them on his front lawn, doused them with lighter fluid, and tossed in a match." She felt herself grinning, remembering. She quickly made herself *stop* grinning. That wasn't a good memory. She never should have done that. It was a huge overreaction.

But damn if she didn't clearly remember the feeling of satisfaction that washed through her when she'd struck that match. And when the football jersey started to burn. And when Wade had come thundering out onto his front porch.

"I thought you set a shed on fire?" Tori asked, glancing at Kennedy.

"Wait for it," Kennedy told her, tossing another fry into her mouth.

Maddie shook her head. "I set Wade's stuff on fire. But their grass was really dry, which I didn't notice or even think about, and the fire took off. It ended up at the shed and...it took a bit to put it out."

Tori stared at her for a moment, then she grinned, and started laughing. "Wow."

Maddie nodded. "Yeah. Wow."

"What happened after that?"

"Firefighters showed up, including my dad." Danny had been a volunteer firefighter in Autre for as long as she could remember. "They put it out, but there was a lot of damage. Wade and his dad were furious. The police chief took me downtown and asked me a bunch of questions and my dad had to pay a fine and then Owen and I had to rebuild the shed."

It had been okay. No one had gotten hurt, she'd made her point, and she and Owen had been able to spend a bunch of time together. Owen without his shirt on. And her kissing him and touching him and flirting with him the entire time, especially whenever Wade was around. Right in his backyard.

That had been fun. The kissing and touching for sure. But the revenge, too.

Maddie shook her head. No, she had to quit thinking that way. Normal people didn't burn things down when someone said something mean to their boyfriend. Wade had had a reason to be jealous. She and Owen had definitely started a hot and heavy relationship immediately after she'd broken up with Wade.

They'd been sixteen and seventeen. Kids. Dumb, hormonal, crazy kids. And they'd acted like it. Even more, they'd acted like Landrys in love.

She'd grown up with a steady guy who had been quietly romantic, indulgent, and supportive, but she'd also been raised around a family that believed in big gestures and that when you fell in love, you made sure *everyone* knew it without a doubt. That was what she'd believed falling in love was like.

Big, loud, bold, and yeah, crazy. She'd been led to believe that her father was the exception rather than the rule. In Autre, Louisiana he was. But not in the real, normal world.

She knew better now. She knew that she should feel bad about the shed. Sheepish.

Maybe she did. A little.

But not enough to reassure her that she'd grown out of all of this.

Kennedy had finished off the fries and now sat forward, reaching for a bottle of beer. "Ask her about the car she stole," she said to Tori.

"You stole a car, too?"

Maddie frowned at Kennedy. "Not exactly."

"That's not what the cops said," Kennedy said with a smirk before tipping her bottle up.

Maddie sighed. She was right. "I...took back the parts that Owen had put in Sarah's car. He paid for them with his own money. They were technically his."

"Sarah was his ex?"

Maddie nodded.

"How many parts did he put in her car?" Tori asked, her mouth twitching.

"Just three. Like the wipers."

Kennedy snorted. "The four tires count as just one thing?"

Tori grinned and Maddie felt the corner of her mouth twitching, too. "Yeah."

"Hard to drive a car without the tires," Tori said.

"Maddie could have left the tires alone," Kennedy said. "The missing transmission was probably enough."

"You took her transmission out?" Tori asked.

Maddie nodded.

"You know how to do that?" Tori asked to clarify.

"Know how to put one in, too," Maddie said with a wink. She felt a little surge of pride at that.

"And if she'd just taken the transmission, she wouldn't have gotten caught," Kennedy added.

"You got caught taking the tires off?" Tori asked.

Maddie shook her head. Then she felt a little snort emerge. Then a full chuckle. "I got caught taking the wipers."

Tori's eyes widened. "You got away with the transmission and the tires?"

"Yep."

"You couldn't just let the wipers go?"

"Fuck no. I didn't want her to have anything of Owen's left."

They all looked at each other and then started laughing.

"Oh, wow, you really are a Landry," Tori said.

That sobered Maddie a bit.

Tori shook her head. "I mean, I know you're not, but it's clear there's been an influence."

Maddie took a breath and nodded. She couldn't deny it. "Yeah, well, there's plenty of crazy in my family, too." She'd inherited it from her mom, but it was *her* crazy and she had to lock it down.

"I love this place," Tori said, shaking her head.

"You do?"

"I'm from Iowa. Very regular. Very...normal." Tori winced slightly. "I mean that in the nicest way possible."

Maddie gave her a smile. Normal *was* nice. She knew very well. "Just so you know, it's not an Iowa thing. Iowa is fine. This is an Autre thing. Autre is...not fine." Autre was a tiny village of enablers. It was very easy to start thinking that being impulsive and going with your gut and having *no* filter was normal.

It wasn't.

"I *love* Autre," Tori said with a tiny frown.

Maddie sighed. They'd gotten to her. Tori was her one chance at having a friend who knew what the outside world was like. But they'd already sucked her in. Dammit.

It wasn't Tori's fault. Autre combined with sex with a Landry boy? Yeah, Tori hadn't stood a chance.

But Maddie could survive.

It was only thirty days.

She just had to get a grip and then hold on tight for thirty freaking days.

Unlike Tori, she knew the risks here. Surely that gave her an advantage.

"She scare you off yet?" Josh came up behind Tori and wrapped his arms around her, kissing the side of her neck.

Tori looked at Maddie. "Honestly? She's just made me love it here more."

Maddie shook her head. She was definitely on her own here in the resistance. She opened her mouth to reply, but just then Cora came through the swinging door behind the bar, carrying a bowl. The smell of cheesy grits and shrimp hit Maddie and she swallowed hard.

She had to keep her hormones, her temper, *and* her freaking taste buds under control.

"Well, thank you for making her love it here even more," Josh said to Maddie. He was watching her carefully over Tori's shoulder.

Almost as if he knew that had absolutely not been her intention.

Just then Sawyer called, "Okay, let's get going."

Maddie swiveled on her stool and took a deep breath. *Yeah, let's get going.* She had to convince them to let her sell. The sooner the better. She was already feeling little swirls of nostalgia. She had to spend thirty days here, but if she could prove that her selling was best for everyone, then all of this would be settled, and she'd feel back in control of her plans. Her life.

Maddie made her way to the table where the food had been laid out. Ellie was filling glasses with sweet tea and Maddie was already anticipating the taste.

She wanted Boys of the Bayou to be okay. They had to believe that. She didn't want them to fail or go broke. She just didn't want anything to do with it all.

That's why she'd found them Bennett Baxter. She would never just sell her portion to a random stranger on the internet. She'd researched Bennett. She'd spoken to him on the phone. He knew the history of the business, knew the family, even knew their crazy stories. He'd, apparently, taken three swamp boat tours with the guys. He hadn't let on who he was or that he was interested in the business, but he'd checked them out. He'd even agreed that Ellie's boudin balls were the best he'd ever tasted. He was enthusiastic about the business and, as she'd told Owen, he had cash.

He was a great fit.

She took a seat and Cora slid the grits and shrimp in front of her.

It occurred to Maddie that she should maybe try to resist *all* of this. She shouldn't even risk falling in love with the shrimp. But she had to eat, right? And when in Rome...

She scooped the first amazingly delicious bite into her mouth and at least managed to resist moaning.

Josh and Owen both pulled out chairs across from her, while Kennedy dropped into the seat next to Maddie. Kennedy wasn't technically a partner, but she was the most involved in the business besides the guys. And everyone else pulling up chairs on the outer perimeter around the table weren't partners. They were just nosey. If anyone should be curious about this meeting and deserved to know what they were discussing, it was probably Kennedy.

Sawyer stood at the head of the table and tucked his hands into the back pockets of his jeans. "There's no sense beatin' around the bush. Maddie wants to sell and we don't want her to. So we've got thirty days to figure this out."

Maddie swallowed and eyed her grits. How much more

could she get down before her stomach knotted and she lost her appetite?

See? That was what emotions did. They ruined perfectly good meals.

Among other things.

"Okay, why do you want to sell?" Josh asked her directly.

Dammit, there was a little knot already. "I just don't want to own part of a business that I have nothing to do with," she said.

"You want more of a say?" Josh asked. He glanced at Sawyer. "We could fill you in on plans. We could do a monthly Skype call or something. You can be more involved."

Maddie ran her spoon through the grits, watching it make a track through the cheese, between two shrimp, rather than meeting Josh's eyes. "I don't want to be more involved. It's not that."

"Then what?" he pressed.

She put her spoon down with a sigh. Dammit. One bite. She looked at Josh, then Sawyer. She couldn't quite bring herself to look at Owen. She could *feel* his tension. He'd be pissed that she'd choose California over Autre. That she'd choose a life far from here without any family around to being here in the midst of them. That she'd choose to make a living in a pristine, air-conditioned, quiet building full of works of art—and rich people—over making a living out in the hot sun on the dirty bayou on airboats full of regular people.

Rich people were really easy not to get attached to.

She definitely needed to keep hanging out with them.

But Owen being annoyed was good. *They* could be emotional. As long as she wasn't. The more pissed Owen was, the more he'd stay away from her and the easier it would be to avoid getting sucked into everything here.

She lifted her chin and met Josh's gaze. "I'm not going to own a business that's a couple thousand miles away that I know nothing about. And more—" she said, as Josh opened his mouth to reply, "—one that I don't want to be involved with. I don't know anything about airboat motor parts or fishing lures or—"

"You used to."

Owen's muttered comment interrupted her for a moment.

She'd helped him with car and truck engines but never the boats. Still, she didn't need to correct him. He was just trying to make a point. So was she.

Maddie took a deep breath. This was the hard part. Not wanting this business was a rational decision. It made sense for her. She *loved* stuff that made sense. She craved things that were controllable. This business was none of those things. It was too far away, it was too far out of her wheelhouse, and it was way too tangled up in her past and all of the emotions that went with that.

But they would never get it. This business was a part of them. Part of the family.

So she just had to be tough. Stubborn. Even a little bitchy if needed.

Hell, if she was a bitch, that would only help with them not wanting her around.

"Look," she said, sitting tall on her chair. "I have control over the things in my life and I make choices that make sense. Owning a business I don't care about in a place I never come to, doesn't make sense."

"You could come visit more often," Josh said tightly.

She could tell he was offended. But she couldn't care about that. She couldn't care about any of this. It was going to be hard but it was self-preservation. Maybe even *shed* preservation.

She didn't think they'd appreciate the joke so she just pressed her lips together.

"Hell, you could live here and be involved every damned day," Josh said.

There was the tight stomach knot she'd been expecting.

They couldn't really expect her to *move* back here to help them run a swamp boat tour company. She pushed her bowl back and took a deep breath. "I'm not going to do that," she said. "I have a life in California that I really like. That I'm proud of."

She didn't have to say that she wasn't proud of her past here. That unspoken sentiment hung in the air over the table. It wasn't that she was embarrassed of being *from* Autre exactly. But it wasn't as if she told everyone she met that she'd grown up on the bayou in Louisiana or that her mom had been killed by a drunk driver or that her dad was in jail. When people asked, Maddie said she was from San Francisco. Because for the past twelve years that had been true and those twelve years mattered most. Those were the years when she'd gotten to know herself and become who she wanted to be. That was when she'd really started painting, when she'd gone to college, when she'd decided she wanted to work surrounded by beauty and to express her passions in safe ways—like with paint-brushes.

"I'm...happy," she said. She swallowed. She knew that mattered to them and that made the knot in her stomach tighter. "I just want to keep being happy."

No one said anything to that right away and she snuck a glance at Owen. His jaw was tight and he was staring at his sweet tea. His grip on the mug made her think that he was seconds away from pitching it at the wall. That wouldn't have surprised anyone.

The stupid ribbon of heat she felt didn't surprise her, either. Twelve years hadn't made it any less hot when Owen got worked up about her. *That* was the biggest problem here of all.

Sawyer finally broke the tense silence. "Well, the thing is, before we can change anything in the partnership agreement, there are a few things we have to do."

Yeah, the camping trip. She started to answer that—with a "that is not happening"—but he kept on.

"You have to come to work every day," Sawyer told her.

She frowned. "Work?"

"At the tour company," Sawyer said. Judging by the look on his face, he was either trying hard to stay firm or he was sincerely annoyed with her.

Working at the tour company? Yeah, right. "What am I going to do?"

"Well, Tommy led tours, did repairs, balanced the books," Owen said. He shifted, leaning back in his chair and finally looking directly at her. His entire demeanor had changed. Instead of looking like he was barely holding onto his temper, he now looked nonchalant.

"I can't lead tours or do repairs," she said, also sitting back and crossing her arms.

"You could fill the tanks, hose off the decks—"

"I'm a majority owner," she interrupted. She couldn't hang out with these guys every single day. That was *not* the way to stay emotionally closed off. She looked up at Sawyer. "That means I get a majority vote in all of this stuff."

"You're an even partner with me," Sawyer said with a little nod.

"But I have more vote than Owen. And Josh," she added, so it didn't seem like Owen was getting to her.

Sawyer cast a glance at his brother and cousin. "We've never run things that way," he said. "We're all equally invested with our time and energy and commitment."

"Well, that's very nice," Maddie said, digging deep for some cold I-don't-care-about-this. "But in reality, I have more say than they do."

Sawyer's brows rose but Owen and Josh said nothing. "I guess that's true," Sawyer finally said.

Maddie looked down at her nails, pretending to study her manicure. "So I'll do the books this month and I can help with scheduling, inventory, things like that."

It wouldn't be like doing the work at the art gallery, but it would be away from the guys. She couldn't take watching them all do their thing with the tourists. She knew that they were enthusiastic and friendly and fun and charming. Nope, she had to stay away from all of that. She couldn't watch them with the kids and the little old ladies or even the bachelorette parties. Okay, she couldn't watch Owen with the bachelorette parties. She would have *feelings* about all of that and she needed to avoid those as much as possible.

"But I won't be working full-time. I have work to do remotely for my *real* job." That was actually true. "And I won't be doing any tours, or repairs, or really anything outside." There, they could think she was a spoiled city girl who was afraid of sunburns and bugs rather than knowing she was afraid of liking all of *them* too much.

"I don't want her doin' any repairs," Owen finally spoke up. "God only knows what she'd mess up. The girl works with paintbrushes now, not wrenches."

Maddie looked at him in surprise. He was giving her an out?

"She'd probably make everything too...tight, you know? Or we'd find a stick stuck up someplace it doesn't belong."

Maddie rolled her eyes. Tight. As in uptight. Stick up her ass. Right. Real subtle.

"Exactly," she said. He was trying to bait her into an argument? Get her saying things like, "fine, I'll do it," just to prove she could? That had worked when she'd been a teenager. It didn't anymore. She had a lot more self-control than that.

And frankly, she didn't want to be tightening things or sticking things anywhere down on that dock. He was actually giving her good excuses not to get too involved.

"I could mess everything up," she said.

In fact...if she was really bad at the job, they wouldn't have her keep doing it...

"Don't think that you're gonna go in there and fuck everything up on purpose," Owen said, leaning in, suddenly not as nonchalant. "You don't want to be here. Fine. But you're not gonna mess stuff up for us."

He still knew her. Her heart gave a little stutter. She shook her head. "Okay, I promise I won't." She looked around the table. "You guys, I really don't want the business to have problems. In fact, the opposite is true. That's why I want to bring Bennett in to meet you all."

Sawyer sighed. "We're not ready to talk about all of that."

"He's great," Maddie insisted anyway. "He's excited about the opportunity. He wants to learn to fish and hunt and drive the boats. He's like a big kid—"

"He doesn't even fish?" Owen asked. He scoffed. "Yeah, sounds like a perfect fit."

"Anyone can learn to fish," Maddie said. "Not just anyone can come in here with a quarter of a million dollars on day one."

"Holy shit." That was the first time Kennedy had said anything. "Are you serious?"

Maddie nodded. "I am. He's willing to buy me out *and* make a substantial investment right away."

"Who is this guy?" Kennedy asked.

"Bennett Baxter," Maddie told her. "He's from Savannah. Old money. His great-grandfather—"

"Bennett Baxter?" Kennedy repeated, wrinkling her nose. "He sounds like a dick."

"He's not. He's very—"

"He's from *Georgia*?" Owen asked. "He's not even a Louisiana boy?"

Maddie sighed.

"Oh, fuck," Josh groaned. "Is he a Bulldog?"

Yeah, like who the guy rooted for in college football mattered.

But Maddie had asked him the same thing.

She was still a closet LSU fan. Not that she'd admit that to these guys. They'd think that meant she was nostalgic about home and football Saturdays. She ate nachos and drank beer every Saturday in the fall and was perfectly happy. On her couch. At home. Alone. But it was good. There was no yelling and cussing—except her own—and no risks of things like coffee tables, lamps, or big screen televisions getting broken. All of those things had been victims of LSU football losses in the past.

"He doesn't even like football," Maddie told them as a reassurance.

"Shit, that's even worse," Kennedy said. "What kind of person doesn't like football?"

It was a fair question, but Maddie gave her a look, pretending that being a grown-up meant realizing that there were more important things about a potential business partner than him caring about a college sporting event.

"One who thinks snapping turtles are cool and can't wait for his first crawfish boil."

Kennedy tipped her head back with a loud groan. "He doesn't even eat crawfish? Jesus."

Bennett Baxter had been raised in the lap of luxury and on the phone had been enthusiastic, almost kid-like, about all of the things he imagined were waiting for him on the bayou.

Of course, he wasn't wrong. Not only could he attend a crawfish boil nearly any weekend, if Leo found out about his turtle fascination, Leo would cook one of those up for him, too.

"He's got *money*," Maddie said. "And he *wants* to buy in. That's really the important part here."

"I'm not babysitting some rich asshole who's bored golfing and traveling the world and has decided to come slum in Autre," Kennedy announced.

"Calm down," Sawyer told his sister. "That's not going to

happen."

Maddie hoped he meant the babysitting thing and not the entire Bennett thing. Kennedy spending time with the rich guy who didn't know anything about airboats and alligators would probably not go well. She was clever and, having grown up as the only girl in the Landry family, she'd developed a taste for pranks and one-upmanship. There was very little that intimidated Kennedy Landry.

Bennett wouldn't stand a chance.

"Look," Sawyer said, pinning Maddie with a look. "Our grandfathers started this business and passed it down. They wrote up this partnership agreement to ensure that if anyone walked away, it wasn't without a lot of thought and examining all options and angles."

Maddie nodded, squeezing her hands together. Saying no to the idea of hosing bayou scum off of airboats was easy. Listening to these people talk about their family roots and history and how much this—bayou scum and all—meant to them was way harder to be callous about.

"I said I'd put some time in at the office," she said, coolly.

"Fine," Sawyer said. "But you also do the camping trip with us."

The camping trip.

It meant sleeping in a cabin that had been built sixty years ago, had no running water, no air-conditioning, no WiFi...and held a ton of memories for her.

Like losing her virginity to Owen Landry.

She did *not* look in his direction, but she could feel his gaze on her.

She was absolutely going to pretend that her resistance was about the WiFi. "I will do almost *anything* else," she told Sawyer.

"You can choose from the ten-year-old's birthday party or the bachelorette party tomorrow," Sawyer said. "One is going to squeal and want alligator souvenir cups and will probably puke over the edge of the boat. The other is a bunch of little boys. You're going to have to let both groups touch a gator."

Maddie shivered. She hated alligators. She thought fast. "Okay, I will make green swamp slime and a batch of swamp water for the kids. And I'll put together little hangover packs for the girls. They'll need water, ibuprofen, eyedrops, sunglasses, and iced coffees. But I'm not touching an alligator."

There was a beat of silence. All of the guys were staring at her.

"What?"

"Swamp slime and swamp water?" Josh asked.

She nodded. "That slimly play stuff that you make with glue and water and Borax," she said. "And swamp water is a green punch with gummy alligators in it."

They were still staring. But they looked a little impressed.

"You know about slime?" Owen asked, with a small smile.

She shrugged. Apparently she did. The idea to use it had just kind of come to her. Looked like desperation to avoid the old bayou cabin had brought out her creativity.

Sawyer snorted. "Fine. No camping. I doubt you even remember how to catch catfish and cook over a campfire anyway."

She grimaced. She loved a good salmon fillet at her favorite seafood place at Fisherman's Wharf, but it had been a long damned time since she'd eaten catfish. Even longer since she'd caught her own.

"Poor Maddie," she heard Tori say to Kennedy.

Well, maybe she had one—sort of—ally.

Kennedy laughed lightly. "Hope she brought something other than those heels."

And...crap.

If she was going to be hanging out on the docks regularly, she was going to need to get some new shoes.

4

Owen found Maddie down on the dock in the dark. The moon was up and there was enough illumination from tall yard lights up by the road that she could easily find her way —and he could easily see her—but it was dark down here. It was nearly midnight and when she'd slipped away from the fire pit outside of Ellie's and the music, drinking, and laughter that accompanied her welcome home party, he'd assumed she was headed to Cora's to call it a night. She had to be exhausted.

But when he'd followed her around the corner of Ellie's, he'd been surprised to see her head across the road toward the Boys of the Bayou buildings.

Now she was on the far dock, just watching the water.

She was fine. He should leave her alone. She was safe here in Autre. At least from people.

The snakes in the area were another story. Did she remember to look for those? Were there snakes in San Francisco? Probably not along the streets that ran to swanky art galleries.

At least she was wearing decent shoes and clothes now.

She was now in denim shorts and a tank top. Not that she

looked any less devastatingly beautiful. He'd choked on his swallow of beer when she'd first stepped out of Ellie's, carrying a plate of corn on the cob. In fact, she looked even more gorgeous in denim. Because now she looked like the Maddie he remembered. The bayou girl.

Most importantly, she had Converse tennis shoes on her feet now. Those were far more practical than those fuck-me heels she'd shown up in.

Still, they wouldn't necessarily keep her from getting bitten by a snake if she didn't see the thing coming. Or if she didn't remember what to do if she *did* see one coming.

"Hey," he said softly, not wanting to scare her.

He saw her shoulders rise and fall and then she glanced back to him. "Hey."

"You okay?"

"Um..." She took another deep breath. "Probably not." She focused on the dark water again.

Her answer made his chest tighten. Fuck. He moved from the path onto the dock. "You want to be alone?" He really hoped she wouldn't want to be alone. Leaving her alone when she was two thousand miles away was one thing, but when she was right here? It was going to be extremely hard. But if she was "probably not" okay? Yeah, forget it.

She made a soft sound that was not really a laugh, but not really a sigh. "It's funny. I'm alone a lot. But here...it feels weird."

He took a few steps forward, shoving his hands into his pockets. "I'm not sure I've ever actually been alone here. Not unless I take a boat out on my own or something. Even then, it's maybe thirty minutes before someone's calling."

She nodded. He stopped a few feet away.

"Tommy was out there alone, right?"

His chest tightened further and he felt a cold arrow of regret shoot through him. He cleared his throat. "Yeah."

God, that had been a horrible fucking day. Easily the worst of Owen's life.

They'd all been out on the bayou alone at one time or another. They fished. They just drove the airboats around the way someone might take a drive down a backroad. They headed out to the cabin just to get away. But never without telling someone where they were going and never without their phones. The bayou was home, but it could be a dangerous place. Cottonmouths, copperheads, and alligators were just a few of the things that they learned to live alongside growing up here.

Bull sharks were something else. They weren't common, not like snakes and gators, but they could get into the bayou and rivers from the gulf on occasion. There had been several in Lake Ponchartrain. They were able to live in less saline waters and had even been spotted as far up the Mississippi River as Illinois. Still, people were always surprised by the idea of sharks in rivers and lakes. And in the bayou, they were even more of a problem. They were hard to see in the muddy waters, blending in with the colors and looking a lot like logs until you were too close. They were also aggressive as hell. Even the babies.

The one that had attacked Tommy had been a juvenile. And it probably wouldn't have done much damage, really, if it hadn't hit his femoral artery. He'd managed to call Sawyer, but by the time he'd gotten there, Tommy had lost a lot of blood. Too much blood. He'd been out cold by the time Sawyer got to him and he'd died en route to the hospital. Sawyer had been attacked while he was trying to rescue Tommy, too. The shark had charged and though Sawyer avoided the shark's mouth, its tail had swiped over Sawyer's face and the sharp scales had left a deep laceration. He still had the scar. He always would. It made him look badass, actually. But Owen knew that every time Sawyer looked in the mirror, he was reminded that he hadn't gotten there in time to save his best friend.

Owen scrubbed his hand over his face. He had nightmares about the whole thing. They all did. No one was more agonized over it than Sawyer, though. Tommy's best friend. The guy who blamed himself for Tommy being out there alone. Even though that was bullshit.

"I miss him." Maddie's voice was soft and sad.

Owen felt his fists ball inside his pockets.

"I do, too. Every damned day."

She nodded. "I guess I don't. I mean, I didn't see him every day. We didn't talk every day." She sighed. "We didn't talk at all. Maybe a few times a year." She shifted and wrapped her arms around her middle. "So how can I miss him?"

Fuck.

Owen knew it was probably a bad idea, but he took a big step toward her. It had to be a bad idea to not try to comfort her, too, right? It was just a matter of which was a worse idea.

"You miss him because he was a part of Autre for you," he said.

"Yeah." She took a deep breath. "My mom and dad, too. None of them are here anymore. So yeah...I'm probably not okay."

With a resigned sigh, Owen took the rest of the steps between them.

"You know, I had never wanted to hug someone as much as I wanted to hug you at Tommy's funeral," he told her.

She turned to face him, her eyes wide.

"Until now."

He reached for her. But there was a moment where she hesitated.

"This might be a bad idea," she said softly.

He kept his hand outstretched, his heart banging against his chest. "No worries," he said. "I hid all the matches."

When that sunk in, her mouth curled slightly. "How about the wrenches?"

"Crap, I forgot the wrenches."

"And there are a bunch lying around down here," she said.

"There are. Even a few hammers."

"So, this could be...risky."

Risky. Yeah, that's what this was going to be. But not because of the hammers. He wiggled his fingers. "Come here, Maddie."

She pressed her lips together, but she did finally reach out.

He felt relief wash over him as she slid her hand into his. Then he pulled her in, bringing her up against his chest, wrapping his arms around her. And heat rolled through him right on the heels of that relief.

Maddie fit up against him perfectly. Exactly as he remembered. It took about five seconds, but when she relaxed against him and wrapped her arms around his back, they both sighed simultaneously.

He had to work not to squeeze her too tightly, but holy shit she felt good.

"I'm so sorry about Tommy," he said gruffly. "I'm so fucking sorry."

Her arms tightened around him. "Me, too."

They stood like that for a long time. He could feel her heart hammering against his chest.

There was nothing he could say. There was nothing anyone could do to make this thing about Tommy better. He suspected the hug actually was making him feel better than it was her.

But yeah, it was definitely making him feel better.

Finally, he blew out a breath and lifted his hand to the back of her head, dragging it down the length of her hair. "Damn, girl, you smell so good."

He felt her surprised laugh against his chest. "Well, thanks."

She rubbed her cheek against his shoulder. "You smell pretty good, too."

The feel of her *cheek* against his *shoulder* made his dick hard.

Well, fuck.

He couldn't kiss her. He couldn't *not* kiss her. So he kissed the top of her head. And then started to let go of her.

But she tightened her grip on him. "Just another second."

With a little groan, he pulled her in again, tucking her under his chin. "As long as you need."

They were quiet for several heartbeats.

"I think I've done more hugging today than I have in the past five years put together," she said after a moment.

"You knew that was going to happen," he told her.

Maddie nodded, her cheek rubbing over his chest again and making his body ache.

She's sad. About her dead brother. Give it a rest, he told his dick. It didn't listen.

"You people and your *feelings* always spilling out all over," she said.

"Yep, we're real bastards that way. All loving and supportive and excited about shit all the time."

She squeezed him and then took a deep breath and stepped back.

He let her go, tucking his hands back into his pockets. Because he didn't want to let her go. At all. Ever.

Maddie brushed her fingertips over her cheeks and gave him a smile. "Makes it hard to stay aloof."

He didn't try to pretend he didn't know what she was talking about. She was trying to hold back from them. He fucking hated that. "Good," he said. "This isn't really the place for aloof."

She gave a little laugh, as if that was a huge understatement.

Which it was, of course.

He'd been watching her at the "partner meeting" earlier and then at the crawfish boil. She didn't hold herself back. She let herself lean into the hugs, gave genuine smiles, laughed and talked like she was happy to be here. But she would *pull* herself back. It seemed that she'd suddenly remember she was supposed to be a near-stranger, here on business, annoyed to be here even, and she'd straighten up and take a deep breath and her smile would dim.

It had been driving him crazy all day.

He didn't want it to drive him crazy. It was just as dangerous to *his* emotional well-being to be driven crazy by her long legs in short shorts, and her long sleek hair being mussed by the sticky summer wind, and the lip print she left on the edge of the mason jar she was drinking from.

But add in feeling crazy about how she wouldn't just let herself go...he'd been in a knot for hours.

He was a Landry. He didn't back down from a confrontation. He didn't shy away from emotions. He was respectful of other people's feelings—at least, he tried to be—but he didn't hesitate to push if he needed to.

For some reason, with Maddie, he wanted to push.

For some reason. Ha. That was funny. As if he didn't know why.

He wanted to push her because he wanted her to push back. He wanted her to care enough to push back.

"Thank you for letting me hold you," he said.

She lifted a brow. "Shouldn't *I* thank *you* for that?"

He shrugged. "I'm glad you're not totally scared of me."

She frowned. "Why would I be scared of you?"

"Really?" He gave a short laugh. "The way I was when you...left."

"You mean banged up in the hospital, looking sexy and pathetic at the same time?"

That made him pause. "Sexy?"

"In retrospect."

"Oh?" He felt a smile teasing his lips.

"Not at the time, though," she said. "You both looked pathetic and idiotic."

"They had to put us in separate rooms because we wouldn't stop fighting," he said. "I threw a bedpan at him and they finally split us up."

"Oh my god," she said, shaking her head. Though she didn't seem to be having trouble believing it.

"It was empty. For the record," he said.

"That's something, I guess."

"It was after he told me that he'd hoped we'd end up in a cell overnight. He hadn't been planning on the hospital. But that it was accomplishing the same thing."

"Keeping you away from me until I was on the airplane."

He nodded.

"He was concerned about you, too," she said. "I realize that putting you in the hospital doesn't seem like it, but he was. He was concerned about us together."

"Well, we probably would have just been in a jail cell. I was the one who tackled him by the window."

She pulled in a breath through her nose, closing her eyes for a moment. "I wasn't scared of *you*, Owen. Tommy wasn't scared of you for me. We were scared of *me*."

Her answer didn't shock him. Which shocked him. "What's that mean?" He felt his chest tightening again. He'd wanted to have this conversation for twelve years. He really hadn't intended to dump it all out there on her first night back in town, but that's how things seemed to go around here. And with him and Maddie in particular. Emotions spilling out all over the place, as she'd said.

"My mom talked Bobby Gravier into doing shots with her at the bar. Because it sounded fun and he would do it. Just because it sounded like fun and she *felt* like it. Then she got into his car so he could drive her home because she didn't think through silly things like consequences. Like Bobby hitting the shoulder of the road because he was drunk and the car flipping and her not walking away from it. And my dad losing his mind because what the fuck was she doing with another guy anyway and what the hell was Bobby doing getting behind the wheel. And him driving his F-150 through Bobby's living room and then going after him with a crowbar."

Owen took it all in. He knew the story. Everyone knew the story. "You didn't think that I seemed an awful lot like your dad?" he asked. "Because I did."

She shook her head. "Only because I was an awful lot like my mom." She took a deep breath. "You could get wound up," she admitted. "But only after I egged you on."

"Come on, Mad—" he started.

"You have two scars and a police record because of me. You didn't have any of that before you and I got together."

"Juvie record," he said. "Doesn't count."

"Come on, Owen," she said, mimicking him. "You were not that guy before I called you away from your girlfriend on Valentine's Day, got you into a fight with Wade, and then kissed you."

Okay, that was true. He'd wrestled and shoved and argued with Sawyer and Josh and Tommy growing up. But he'd never punched a guy or put his hand around a guy's throat until he did it that night to Wade. Because of Maddie.

"That doesn't mean you were *bad* for me," he said.

She stepped forward and ran the tip of her finger up the scar on his arm. Heat shot straight to his cock.

"I don't think you can really make that argument," she said, almost sadly.

He captured her hand, holding it but stopping the stroking. "We were kids. Jacked up on drama and hormones and not sure how to handle all of our intense feelings."

She nodded. "But back then, I didn't know that we would

grow out of it. I knew I needed to leave before one—or both—of us went too far."

"But we did grow up. Right? So there's nothing to worry about now?" He was truly asking. Because he wasn't sure. The limits of his self-control hadn't been tested. Because Maddie hadn't been here.

"I...don't know."

"How many California sheds have you burned down?" he asked, trying for light. But his thumb was tracing over the scar on the back of her hand. The burn scar from when she'd tried to put the shed fire out after starting it.

"None," she admitted.

"There you go."

"But you haven't been in California."

"You think it's just me that makes you..."

"Crazy," she supplied with eyebrows up. "And yes."

He couldn't help it. He grinned. He'd always known that Maddie was the only one that made him lose his cool, and he'd liked the idea that he was the only one that did that to her. But he hadn't known if she believed that, too.

She shook her head. "You like that too much."

"Well, let's just say that I haven't gone to jail for any other girls, either."

Before she covered it up, he saw a flash of something that could have been satisfaction. But she did cover it up.

He lifted her hand to his lips and kissed her scar. "Good thing we've grown up, huh?"

She swallowed hard and then pulled her hand back. "Yeah. Good thing."

"And you're happy in California?" he asked. He needed her to be happy. That was just a fact that had never *not* been true. In his whole life. But more so since she'd kissed him, it was true.

Because that's when she'd become his.

Heat and a bit of *oh, shit* went through him at that thought. He couldn't think of her as his. That was just going to make everything so much harder. She was here temporarily. She was trying to keep emotional distance from the family and the town. Wanting her to be his again was a sure setup for heartbreak. Not just when she left, but when she rejected everything that mattered to him—his hometown, his business, and most especially his family.

"I'm...content in California," she finally said.

"Is that good?"

She nodded. "It's quiet. Everything goes at my pace. It's all in my control." She met his gaze directly. "I like being in control. Of my schedule. Of my emotions."

He got it. Loud and clear. She wasn't in control here. They were dictating that she had to work at Boys of the Bayou. They were dictating what she did during those hours. Hell, they were dictating that she had to be here in the first place. She might have put her foot down when it came to camping and leading tours, but that didn't mean she was getting to make a lot of choices here. And, clearly, she was determined to keep her emotions locked down, as much as possible.

"Okay," he said. It wasn't really. All of this meant that he was going to be torn between letting her do what she needed to do to be happy—mainly, sell the business and go back to California—and his family and the business they'd built. Making Maddie happy seemed like an ingrained instinct that he couldn't shake any easier than he could change his eye color.

But Boys of the Bayou had to come first.

So, if she hated being here, was unhappy with all of this, was cold and closed off, it would make it a lot easier to not feel drawn to her.

He didn't think he could be attracted to someone who wrinkled her nose about stepping onto his dock and who didn't want to guzzle sweet tea with his grandmother and tell tall tales with his grandpa.

So the more she did all of that, the better for them both.

"I should probably get to bed," she said after a long moment. "It's been a big day."

He nodded. "I'll walk you."

"You don't have to. It's like three blocks."

Everyone lived within a three-block radius of Ellie's. It was a little like a family compound, but they preferred to think of it as convenient. Convenient to work. Convenient to stopping over to help each other out. Convenient for Ellie to ring the big cast-iron bell that was mounted out behind the bar to signal dinner, or that she was pissed at someone and needed to yell at them. Josh and Tori were the only ones outside of the family radius since they'd bought the farm, but it was on the edge of town, their front door along the last street of Autre and their land stretching out behind nearly to the county line. Which meant about six blocks from Ellie's. They could still hear the bell. At least the pissed-off bell. Ellie rang that thing with everything in her.

"I'm walking you, city girl," he told her.

She knew exactly what he meant and immediately looked down at the ground. She knew she didn't need to be worried about people. Just critters.

"Yeah, okay."

They didn't talk on the way to Cora's or as they climbed the front porch steps.

But Maddie hesitated with her hand on the screen door. "It was sweet of you to come down to the dock after me tonight."

He didn't say anything. There was a big old "but" sittin' there.

"But it's maybe better if we don't...do that again."

"Do that?" he repeated. "Be friends?"

"Be alone. Hug. Talk about the past," she said.

His chest tightened the way it had on the dock, but for a very different reason. Now he was a little pissed. "That all seems like stuff people should do when it's been twelve years and they've lost someone they both cared about," he said calmly. "And when one of them really needs a hug."

She swallowed hard and then said, "I've had enough hugging, I think. I'm good."

"Oh, well, great," he said. He reached up, tucked a strand of hair behind her ear, and then said, "But I was talking about me."

Then he pivoted on his heel and left her standing at her grandmother's door.

Yeah, he'd definitely grown up. Because he didn't punch a hole in any walls and he didn't throw any bottles against the side of his garage.

He also hadn't backed her up against the side of her grandma's house and showed her that she most definitely wanted to be hugging him. And a hell of a lot more.

Being grown-up kind of sucked.

———

MADDIE WAS UP and out of bed the next morning for work.

Not because she woke up naturally at the god-awful hour of six a.m. Or because she'd set an alarm. Or because she was so excited about work that she couldn't sleep.

Nope, she woke up because of the sound of her three business partners clomping into her grandmother's kitchen, arguing about who made the best eggs, and banging her two cast-iron skillets on the stovetop in the process of making said eggs.

Maddie rolled over with a groan and pulled the pillow over her face. What the actual fuck? These people couldn't even make breakfast quietly? Even *semi*-quietly?

"You don't put the Tabasco straight in the eggs." That was Josh.

"Yes, I do," Sawyer said.

"Not when you're making them for someone else. What if she doesn't like Tabasco in her eggs?" Josh asked.

"Who doesn't like Tabasco in their eggs?"

"Probably a lot of people."

She was *not* eating Tabasco in her eggs. Ugh.

Why were they here? Why were they doing this to her?

Because they were trying to sweeten her up. They didn't want her selling her portion of the business and they thought breakfast would make her first day nicer. And *her* nicer.

Well, they were wrong. It wouldn't matter if they showed up with French press coffee and chocolate croissants—the only breakfast worth getting up at six a.m. for, and even that was pushing it—she was *not* going to get all mushy with them.

Last night on the dock with Owen had been close enough. Too close. Being held in his arms had made everything in her... well, mushy was one way to put it. Other words were soft. Warm. Tempted. Hot. Wet.

She cleared her throat and sat up quickly.

She needed to not be alone with Owen anymore, that was for sure. But she also needed to just avoid anything nice and friendly and familiar with *all* of them.

Breakfast in her grandma's kitchen was one of those things.

Maddie had thought she could avoid the whole breakfast thing entirely since Cora had to be at the restaurant to feed the fishermen and others going off to work at the crack of dawn.

Maddie swung her legs over the edge of the mattress. Well, she was awake now. Only twenty-nine days to go. Not that she was keeping track. Except on the calendar in her phone and in her digital planner and the paper calendar she carried in her briefcase.

She stretched to her feet as Sawyer asked, "What the hell is that?"

"Hazelnut creamer," Josh replied.

"Why?"

"Girls like flavored creamer."

"They do?"

"Tori does."

"I think it's safe to say that Tori and Maddie don't have a lot in common."

That came from Owen. So he was here, too. She hadn't been sure. Maddie narrowed her eyes and strained to hear the rest of *that*.

"You don't think so?" Josh asked.

"Seriously?" Owen asked. Then he laughed. "Tori's sweet. Friendly. She's happy with little things like flavored creamer."

Maddie frowned. Geez, you tell a guy you don't want any more of his hugs and suddenly you're labeled as not friendly.

But she *really* didn't want any more of Owen's hugs. Because they made her want a whole lot more.

And this "not friendly" stuff was coming from the guy who, for just a second last night, had almost backed her up against the wall and been *super* friendly? She'd seen it plain as day in his face. And her entire body—mind, soul, *pinky toe*—had reacted to it. And he knew it. He *knew* that she would have been super happy with his...okay, not so *little* things.

Maddie put her hands over her face and groaned.

Not even twenty-four hours. She hadn't even been in Autre for twenty-four hours and she was already feeling hot and bothered. Not just by the weather—though it had taken forever to fall asleep last night in her grandmother's hot upper level. Fucking Louisiana in June. Who built entire towns on *swamps* anyway? In what scenario did someone say, "Hey, it's hotter than the devil's ball sack. Let's live here!"

"Maddie's not that easy to please?" Josh asked.

Maddie could practically hear the smirk on his face. She rolled her eyes and stomped over to her suitcase, making sure they could all hear that she was up.

She grabbed her toiletry bag, the lightest sundress she owned, and stomped down the hall to the bathroom to shower. With cold water.

Forty minutes later, she wondered why she'd even bothered. She was out of the shower, dressed, deodorized and perfumed, and sweating like she'd just gotten back from a run. Well, a run in San Francisco. A run here would probably kill her.

She absolutely could not even think about pulling out a blow dryer and applying hot air to her hair on purpose, so she left it damp and curling around her shoulders. In this humidity it would take a miracle to get it to lay sleek like it should anyway.

Then she stomped down the steps and into the kitchen.

It smelled like coffee, eggs, and yes, Tabasco. Sawyer was sitting at the table, reading the paper. Josh was leaning against the counter, flipping through his phone. Owen, the last one she looked at, was *lounging* at the table. His long, denim clad legs stretched out, ankles crossed, his big hands cradling a mug against the Boys of the Bayou T-shirt that covered his hard abs.

She realized that she'd done a thorough inventory of Owen's body while she couldn't have even said what color Josh's shirt was.

She stomped to the coffeepot. "I'm doing the books today and don't be surprised if your snack budget gets cut."

"We can't be expected to work without beef jerky," Josh said, looking up. "And M&M's. I'm no good without my M&M's fix."

"Then stay the hell out of this house until nine a.m. from now on." She could smell the chicory as she poured the coffee into her cup and she grimaced. She'd never developed a taste

for the chicory coffee that was a staple down here. She hadn't
been much of a coffee drinker when she'd lived here and she
now had a taste for medium roasts. And yes, with a splash of
flavored creamer, thank you. She reached for the bottle of
creamer Josh had apparently brought from home and poured
three servings worth into the strong brew in her cup.

She shot Owen a glance as she stirred. He was watching
every move and gave her a small smile when she caught his eye.

"I stand corrected," he said. Clearly he knew she'd overheard him. "One thing in common."

She flipped him off.

He laughed. "Yep, maybe just one."

Maddie hid her smile behind her cup. This was all far too
familiar.

The first morning and her plan to stay unattached was
already going to hell. And she was smiling about it.

Typical.

5

_____

"Yeah, I'll take care of it."

Owen watched as Sawyer pocketed his phone and climbed up out of the boat.

"Folks, it's just gonna be a second," Sawyer told his boat full of tourists. "Sorry about the delay, but we'll head out soon."

"What's up?" Owen asked as he joined Sawyer on the dock. He had a tour loaded and ready to go out, too, and he'd just been waiting for Sawyer to move his boat.

"Need to talk to Maddie."

Sawyer didn't look happy as he headed for the office. Owen told his boat the same thing and followed Sawyer. Though he wasn't sure who he was going in to protect.

Maddie had been working in the office every day for eight days now. She'd taken the inventory and books seriously. She'd been going through all kinds of records and she'd already negotiated a new contract for shipping with one of the parts dealers they worked with in Mobile.

She'd also put her foot down with Leo, telling him that he had to stop offering moonshine to the passengers on his bus. Leo and their cousin Mitch drove the buses back and forth between New Orleans and Autre, picking tourists up at their hotels and then delivering them back after the tour. Leo thought that the moonshine gave them a taste of the local area and also loosened them up so they had more fun—and tipped better. He wasn't wrong. The people loved it.

Maddie didn't.

She didn't like the liability that went along with getting people drunk or offering food in general to people in light of all of the food allergies out there in the world. Not to mention the fact they didn't have a liquor license, and there could be a case made that they shouldn't be serving drinks without that.

Owen knew better, though. She was being a stick-in-the-mud on purpose. She was coming down on the fun so that they'd all get annoyed and not want her to be a part of all of this. She was wily. But he wasn't going to let her get away with it.

They stepped into the office and were met by the unusually cool air. She'd put a window air conditioner in on day three—and yeah, she'd literally put it in herself, which meant she'd used tools and she'd threatened to take Josh's truck engine apart if he didn't stop teasing her about it. She'd also had to order some new clothes—clothes with less material—after nearly passing out day two when she'd worn pants and a shirt that she wore to the art gallery. That was both a blessing and a curse. Owen really did love looking at her in less clothing. So did a lot of the other guys who came through the office. Including the guys who stocked the drinks and snacks for the tourists to purchase.

One of them, Brody Carson, was leaning on the front counter at that very moment, as a matter of fact. It might have been that he was taking a break from the hot sun, but Owen was pretty sure that it was more because of the gauzy yellow material of Maddie's sundress than the AC. The *short* sundress. It was so light it was nearly see-through with the sun coming in the window behind her. He couldn't really *see* anything, but Owen scowled at the whole situation anyway. Of course, it probably didn't matter what she wore. She'd had her hair up in ponytails to keep it off her neck the past few days, and she'd said she was done with makeup considering it was melting off by noon. She was now, after only a week, the perfect picture of a sweet, sun-kissed, southern girl.

Until she spoke.

"That is a ridiculous price for candy anyway," she was telling Brody. "And now I have to keep the stupid candy bars in the fridge to keep them from melting, which means they're costing me more than if they were on the shelf."

Not only did she sound like a Yankee, she sounded like a cool Yankee businesswoman.

"You think I should make up the difference of what you're spending on electricity on a fridge that's running anyway?" Brody asked her. But he was grinning. And not as if he was making fun of her but just as if he was...having fun sparring with her.

Owen knew the feeling. At least he had at one time. Maddie had been pretty much avoiding talking to him much and when she did, there wasn't much flirtatious about it. It was very straightforward and always about business. She'd been avoiding family dinner at night, too. He swore she was doing it to make him crazy, but that was just a knee-jerk reaction. She didn't want to be here and she didn't want to get too close to any of them. Family dinner would have made that hard. He knew she cooked for herself at Cora's and then worked on stuff from San Francisco rather than coming over and joining them all at Ellie's. But Cora had said she'd gone to New Orleans two nights ago. That was making Owen super itchy. He wanted to know what she was doing. And who she was doing it with. And it was definitely none of his damned business.

"I think you should give me a fair price on the candy,"

Maddie said. "Or I can find another way to feed our tourists. I mean, sending them over to my grandma's place for pie and bread puddin' sounds like a better idea than selling them over-priced Snickers bars anyway."

Had she just dropped the 'g' on pudding? Owen was distracted for a second. But only one. Because Brody reached out and put his hand on top of Maddie's. "Well, maybe if I had some of this...pie, I'd agree with you and we could just toss the Snickers bars. How about we head across the road and you can introduce me to it?"

Owen felt Sawyer's hand on his chest, pushing him back before he'd even realized he'd taken a step forward. "Whoa. Jesus. They're talking about candy bars," Sawyer said low enough for only Owen's ears.

Yeah, no they weren't. Brody's emphasis on *pie* had been all full of innuendo. "You know that's not true."

"And I know she can handle it," Sawyer said. "Cool it. I don't need you gettin' wound up just because he smiled at her. We can't afford new windows in here."

It wasn't Sawyer's hand that kept Owen from crossing the space between him and Brody. It was how satisfying Owen knew it would be to actually throw Brody through one of the windows. *Fuck.*

"But then I wouldn't get to see your smiling face once a week," Maddie told Brody, pulling her hand back from his.

"Oh, we could figure out a way for you to keep seeing me."

"I couldn't do that to you," Maddie said, feigning disap-pointment.

At least she'd better be faking it.

"I can't have...pie...with a supplier," she went on. "It would be a conflict of interest to keep buying from you and you'd lose this contract."

"I think I would be okay with that," Brody said.

"We need to talk." Sawyer finally interrupted them. "I just got a call," he told Maddie. "And I've got a tour waiting."

She gave Brody a little smile. "Sorry to cut this short. But thank you for understanding and for taking that ten percent off our bottom line."

Brody straightening with a frown. "Now I don't know if we agreed—"

"A verbal agreement doesn't mean anything down here anymore?" Maddie asked.

"I didn't *say* that we were going to have a discount, either."

"Cookies," Maddie said to him with a big smile. "We should sell cookies in here. That's perfect. My grandma makes amazing cookies." She looked at Sawyer. "Shaped like alligators and turtles."

"Love it," Sawyer said.

Brody frowned, looking between them. "Fine. Five percent. That's the best I can do."

"Oh, I don't want melted Snickers bars anymore," Maddie said. "It's cookies." She said it to Sawyer rather than Brody.

"We gonna sell them or just have it available?" Sawyer asked, looking mildly amused.

Maddie wrinkled her brow. "I'll have to think about it."

Brody sighed. "Fine. Ten percent."

Maddie shook her head and came around the counter. "No."

"No?" Brody asked, letting her lead him to the door.

"No." She pulled the door open for him. "That wasn't a negotiation technique. I really want to sell alligator cookies instead."

"But..." Brody scratched his head. "Are we going to have pie then?"

She nodded. "You should totally go have pie at Ellie's. The huckleberry is my favorite."

"By myself?"

She smiled up at him. "Don't worry. With Ellie, Cora, Jerry, Leo...you'll have lots of company."

With a resigned sigh, Brody headed out of the door. Maddie's smile dropped as she shut the door and turned back, returning to the front counter.

"So now we're not going to have any candy for sale?" Sawyer asked.

"Two weeks of us selling cookies instead and Brody will come back and give me twenty percent off our bottom line," she said. "Of course, by then the cookies will be a huge hit and we won't buy as much from him. But that's his own fault."

"I've known Brody since we played football against each other in high school," Sawyer said.

Maddie nodded, her attention on her laptop screen. "Yeah. He should have paid more attention in math class. Or maybe you shouldn't have hit him so hard in the head."

Owen could see that Sawyer was fighting a smile. That in and of itself was nearly a miracle and he wanted to kiss Maddie for it.

Oh, who was he kidding? He wanted to kiss Maddie period.

"Okay, so we have another similar situation that we need to discuss," Sawyer told her.

Owen folded his arms and leaned back against the wall to watch. Sawyer was a grumpy, intimidating guy who got his way ninety percent of the time. The only time he didn't was when Ellie didn't agree with him. But now Maddie was here and Owen had a feeling that, at least for this month while they were business partners, Sawyer's percent might drop into the eighties.

"What situation?" Maddie asked, typing on her computer.

"Cash Wilks just called me," Sawyer said.

"Who?"

"He owns Shirts and Slabs."

Maddie looked up. "Oh."

"Yeah."

"That has got to be the worst name in the history of business names," Maddie said, taking her hands off the keyboard.

"It was supposed to be a T-shirt shop...and a meat shop."

"Supposed to be?" Maddie asked.

"His girlfriend was in charge of the meat and...they broke up."

"His girlfriend was a butcher?" Maddie asked.

Sawyer lifted a shoulder. "Yeah."

She gave Sawyer a you-have-to-be-kidding-me look, and Owen had to cover a chuckle with a cough.

"So now it's just a T-shirt shop with a horrible name," Maddie said.

"He does embroidery and screen printing," Sawyer said, in Cash's defense. "And he does hats, too."

"Yes. I know," she replied. "And tote bags, and pens, and little tiny T-shirts that fit on stuffed alligators."

"Exactly."

"And he charges you twice what you should be paying for those things."

Sawyer sighed. "He's a friend, Maddie."

"I know. Which makes it disgraceful that he's overcharging you the way he is."

"Don't you mean the way he *was* overcharging me?" Sawyer asked. "He said you fired him."

"I gave him the chance to meet the other company's price." Maddie shrugged. "He said no. So technically, he quit."

"Hire him back."

"No."

"Maddie, hire him back," Sawyer said firmly.

"Sawyer," Maddie said, calmly, and also firmly. "No."

"Mad—"

"Look," she said, twisting on the stool, putting her hands on her thighs, and looking Sawyer directly in the eye. "You have me here to convince me not to sell my portion of this business. In part, because you don't have enough money to buy me out. I'm not going to sit here and let you throw money away on stuff because you played football with one of the guys and the other's been over for a few barbecues. You can use the money you save to pay *me* so that I can go back to my nice, peaceful life in San Francisco where people have actually heard of central air-conditioning."

Sawyer opened his mouth. Then snapped it shut. He blew out a breath. Then he turned on his heel, shot Owen a glance that said, "well, shit," and headed out the door.

As soon as the door shut behind him, Maddie rolled her eyes and turned back to her computer.

Yeah, Sawyer's chance of getting his own way might even get into the seventies.

"Wow."

She looked up. "Wow?"

"Cash is a long-time friend."

"Everyone here is a long-time friend," she said. "That's what happens when people never leave a fifty-mile radius."

Uh-huh. Owen moved to the counter. "Cash is actually a long-time friend of Tommy's. Tommy helped him get started. The butcher thing was his idea."

She swallowed, then said, "I know."

"You do?"

She looked up. "Yeah, I know. Dad told me about the whole thing. The name, Tommy getting them started, the breakup. All of it."

"You talk to your dad?" He hadn't been expecting that and he was totally thrown off track for a moment.

"I do. Once a month."

Owen stared at her. He *really* hadn't been expecting that. "Are you okay with that?"

She stared back. She looked surprised that he'd asked that.

"I'm...not *not* okay with it. I like talking to him. But it usually takes me a day to get over missing him and being pissed that he made the choice to go to prison instead of being my dad."

Owen felt like she'd hit him in the gut. "You feel like that was a *choice*?"

"No one turned the key on the truck for him," she said. "No one told him to go after Bobby. And there's no way he didn't know that he'd end up in a cell no matter what happened after he got to Bobby's house that night."

Owen had no idea what to say. She was...right.

He, like most people here, had chalked Danny's actions up to grief and passion over his wife's death. Most people had been shocked initially but then they'd started nodding their heads, saying they understood where he'd been coming from. Or at least forgiving him for his actions because of what he'd been through.

But Maddie was right. Danny had had two kids to still take care of. Getting in his truck that night had been a choice.

She sighed. "Anyway, he told me about Cash and Tommy. And I thought the idea was dumb even then."

Owen shook his head. He didn't quite have his head around her talking to her inmate dad on a regular basis, and that she felt her dad had betrayed her by choosing to go after her mom's killer instead of staying and taking care of Maddie. It made his chest ache and he really wanted to hug her again.

Maddie lifted a brow. "Owen? You okay?"

He really wasn't. But he shook his head, clearing his thoughts. "Cash isn't...a great businessman. Sawyer's wanted to fire him for a while."

Maddie nodded. "And he won't do it because he feels guilty about Tommy dying. Tommy was the only guy to give Cash a chance and encourage him. And Sawyer feels, at least partially, responsible for Tommy not being here, and so it makes it difficult to put pressure on Cash and impossible to fire him."

Owen blew out a breath. "Yeah."

"So I just did Sawyer a favor."

Owen studied her. She wasn't saying that flippantly. She actually meant it.

"You did that for Sawyer? To help him out?"

"Of course. I can be the bitch for the business. I get that sometimes it's hard to make tough choices. You guys know everyone and feel like everyone is your friend and because you're a small-town local business, you want to support everyone else in the same position. So I can make the decisions that you guys can't and then take the blame. Sawyer's excuse to everyone who's pissed can just be that I'm an equal majority partner and there's nothing he can really do."

Again, she was right. And that really did let Sawyer—and him and Josh—off the hook for some of the bigger, tough decisions.

"So you didn't really mean that you're doing it so we have money to buy you out."

"Of course not."

"I mean, that's not a bad point."

"Snickers bars and overpriced T-shirts are not your main problem," she said.

"What is?"

"Losing Tommy."

Owen felt his gut tighten. "Yeah."

"He was another body that could be taking tours out and dealing with stuff in the office so that Sawyer could take more tours out. Sawyer is awesome. But he's better with people than books."

Owen nodded. "He used to be, anyway."

"What do you mean?"

"He doesn't like doing the tours anymore."

"Why?"

"He...worries. He can't get past the idea that he's responsible for all of these people. If something happens, it's his fault. A guy reached his hand out to a gator the other day, even after being told not to, and Sawyer lost his shit."

Maddie's eyes widened. "Oh, no."

"Yeah. He launched into this big lecture about safety and listening to people who know more and are experts and what the hell did the guy think was going to happen and on and on. People were pissed when they got back to the dock." Owen shoved a hand through his hair. "And it takes him twice as long to get his fucking boat out on the bayou in the first place because he triple checks everything and his safety instructions take forever. He sucks the fun out of it from minute one. Once they're out there, he doesn't get too close to anything, just points stuff out from a distance. Especially the animals. People bitch about that, too."

"Oh, crap." Maddie looked genuinely concerned.

"So, Josh and I are taking as many tours out as humanly possible. Kennedy knows to try to keep Sawyer's stuff light and to give him the older crowd, who doesn't care as much about getting up close with gators and stuff. But we can't always do that."

She nodded. "Right. Well…that sucks."

"It does. I wish he'd go talk to someone. But then again, I can only imagine what it was like for him getting that call from Tommy and then going out there and—" He cut himself off, but far too late. This was Maddie's *brother* he was talking about.

She was a little pale.

"Fuck. I'm sorry, Mad."

"It's…okay. It's not like I haven't pictured it all myself."

He pulled in a deep breath. Dammit. "Well, thank you. For looking out for Sawyer. And all of us."

She nodded. "I don't want the business to fail. I really don't. And this is all another reason you need Bennett. He can do some of the tours. He's very charming and—"

"I'd better get back out there. I've got a boat waiting," Owen interrupted. He liked feeling like Maddie was on their team and had their backs. Bringing Bennett up was just a reminder that all of this was temporary.

"Yeah. You should." Maddie turned her attention back to the computer.

He felt like maybe he should say something else. But he had no idea what that would be, so he started for the door. He felt unsettled and baffled. Maybe it was just that he was surprised to find her working like she was. She didn't want to be here, didn't want the business, yet she was actually diving in. She wasn't just doing inventory or straightening out the file cabinet. She was fixing things. She could have sat behind that counter and done her nails all day or worked on her art gallery stuff on her laptop instead of actually helping Boys of the Bayou, but she wasn't.

He turned toward the dock but he noticed Brody talking to Kennedy at the end of the path. He knew he shouldn't go over there. He knew he should let it all go.

But he was wound up and restless. So, of course he wasn't going to leave it alone.

"Brody."

"Hey, Owen."

Kennedy excused herself, leaving the guys alone.

"Don't ever touch Maddie again," Owen told the other man without preamble.

Brody's eyebrows rose. "Excuse me?"

"Maddie Allain is off-limits."

"Oh, really?"

Owen moved in closer to the other man. "I'm serious. You touch her again, I'll break every bone in your hand. Your jerking off hand."

Brody frowned. "What the hell, man?"

"Just leave her alone."

"Okay, fine, fuck."

"Good." Owen turned away. Then he pivoted back. "And tell your brother, too." Byron worked with Brody and was better looking than his younger brother.

"Holy shit."

Yeah so Brody and Byron were going to think he was nuts.

And he didn't care at all.

Which was exactly how everything had started before.

————

THREE DAYS LATER, Maddie clipped a green band on the wrist of the last guy for Josh's next tour as Kennedy worked on checking in the group for Sawyer's boat.

Typically, Kennedy handled all aspects of getting the tour groups checked in and organized, but Maddie had started helping after a few days of observing. The faster they got people out of line in the main office area, the more time they had to spend browsing souvenirs and snacks. Their sales in the little gift shop had gone up by fifteen percent simply by having Kennedy taking the payments while Maddie supervised signing the consent forms and fastened wristbands onto people.

And directing them into the gift shop, of course. Especially the families with kids. Hey, it was simple business economics. She'd reorganized the shop so that the shelves with the things like the toy tackle boxes, stuffed alligators, and swamp flashlights were at eye level for the average six-year-old, while the little Louisiana history books and real fishing lures were up higher for the adults. The alligator cookies were also a big hit, and it didn't hurt that she'd figured out a way to draw the kids' attention to the display. All it took were a couple of aquariums filled with real fish, a couple of frogs, and two turtles.

"Okay, head out that door," she said pointing. "That will

take you through the gift shop. The restrooms are on the right and the dock is to your left. You can wait on the benches for your captain."

The group with the green wristbands moved off and she turned to the group that needed yellow wristbands.

She clipped four bands on and explained how the day-long and weekend fishing trips worked to a guy and his brother who were already interested in coming back. Then she looked for the next wrist.

But the last two for Owen's group were hanging back, pretending to look over the map they held, while watching the two fishermen. As soon as the men exited, they moved up to the counter.

"Ladies," Kennedy greeted. "Names?"

"I'm Lacey and this is Natalie," the very pretty, twenty-something blonde said.

"Great, I've got you right here," Kennedy said.

"Well, we were wondering..." Lacey glanced at Natalie. "Is there a chance that we could split up and I could go on Owen's tour and Natalie could go on Josh's?"

Kennedy shook her head. "We've got you booked with Sawyer. Is there a problem?"

Maddie moved in behind the counter, curious about the request.

"Well, we were down here Christmas before last," Lacey said. "We went out on Owen's tour and then..." Again she glanced at her friend. "We invited Owen and Josh up to New Orleans to party. They brought their friend Tommy and we had a ton of fun."

She giggled and Maddie's eyebrows rose. Fun, huh? She could only imagine. But she didn't want to. At all. Tommy was her brother. Josh was practically a brother. And Owen was... Owen. And the main reason she wanted to slap this girl.

"So we were hoping to see them again and hang out," Lacey said.

"Or maybe they could give us a ride back to New Orleans," Natalie inserted. "We could hang out at the bar across the street until they're done."

Lacey, clearly having decided that Kennedy and Maddie were their confidants, leaned in with a big smile. "Maybe you get these requests all the time. But, between us girls—and I'm sure you know this since you work with them—Josh and Owen and Tommy are amazing. We could *really* use just a night to kick back and...relax...with them."

Maddie did *not* want to know how the three guys-two-girls-relaxing-thing had gone down. Definitely not. In fact, she felt a little ill.

"You met them this past Christmas?" She'd been under the impression that Josh had met Tori last Mardi Gras and had been waiting on her the entire year in between then and now.

"Christmas before that. Like a year and a few months," Lacey said.

Ah, so they would have met about two months before he met Tori. Got it.

They did, actually, get a good number of people requesting certain captains on return trips to Boys of the Bayou. But it came equally from all age groups and both genders. Okay, maybe not exactly equally, but it wasn't just the young, pretty tourists making requests.

"That trip was the *best*," Natalie said. "We came down to see Lacey's grandma—she lives in Mandeville. So we decided to go to New Orleans for the weekend, saw an ad for swamp boat tours and came down for the day. And—" She sighed. "Had the *best* time."

Lacey nodded. "So, you can help us out, right? Come on. There's just one of each of us. Surely we could squeeze onto their boats."

Maddie didn't think the girl had said "boats" with any innuendo, but Maddie heard it that way and curled her hand into a fist. She couldn't slap a customer. That would be really bad.

"Yeah, their boats are nice and *big*," Natalie agreed with a giggle.

Okay, so she *had* meant the innuendo. The strength of the jealousy that ripped through Maddie shocked her. But there was no denying it. The idea that one of these girls had even touched Owen made Maddie see red.

In the back of her mind, it registered that maybe she should feel weird about their intimate knowledge of her brother as well, but really her desire to punch someone in the nose was all about Owen.

Punching her would still be bad, but Maddie wasn't going to be here in a couple more weeks, so maybe the harm wouldn't be that great...

"Well—" Kennedy looked at Maddie. "Do you want to tell them or should I?"

Maddie saw the twinkle in Kennedy's eye. Kennedy was going to keep these girls off of Josh and Owen's boats, but she was giving Maddie the chance to be the one to come up with how. She really loved this girl.

Okay, maybe she didn't need to punch anyone.

Maddie sighed and nodded, trying to look sorry. "We can definitely book you on one of their tours, but I think we should be honest with you—you know, between us girls."

Lacey looked at her. "Honest about what?"

"Well, for one thing, Tommy isn't here anymore," Maddie said. Her heart clenched as she said it.

"Oh, he quit?" Natalie asked, with a tiny frown.

Maddie nodded. That was a lot better story for them. She wasn't going to tell these girls what had really happened. "Yeah, he's not with the company anymore."

Kennedy shifted on the tall stool and Maddie knew she was

uncomfortable.

"And Josh is married," Maddie said, rushing to change the subject from Tommy's absence.

"He's *married*?" Lacey asked. "Really?"

Well, close enough. Maddie nodded. "Madly in love. Met her about two months after he met you and she just erased all other women from his heart and memory."

All completely true.

Lacey frowned and looked at Natalie. "Sorry, Nat."

Ah, so Natalie was the one who'd been friendly with Josh. Which meant Lacey had been Owen's "friend" for the weekend.

Maddie hated her.

It was sudden and an overreaction and kind of ridiculous. She had no claim on Owen. But...she didn't want him to be with anyone else, either. At least until she went back to San Francisco and could pretend that he wasn't with anyone else. And where she definitely didn't have women requesting she make it easier for them to entice him back to their hotel rooms.

"What about Owen?" Natalie asked.

"Oh, Owen." Maddie gave Kennedy a look and they both shook their heads sadly. "Well, you *could* hook up with Owen but I would *definitely* not go back to his place," she said, thinking quickly.

"Why not?" Lacey asked.

"Rats," Maddie said.

Lacey's eyes grew round. Maddie nodded. "Yeah, he's got a rat problem. It's probably because he never does dishes or anything. Total pig."

"Oh...wow."

"Thankfully he's now symptom-free."

"Symptom-free?" Lacey asked. "What symptoms?"

"From the typhoid fever."

Kennedy had just taken a drink of her soda and immediately started coughing.

6

"*Typhoid fever?*" Lacey repeated.

Kennedy hit herself in the chest trying to stop coughing, and Maddie struggled to keep a straight face. She knew nothing about typhoid fever. For all she knew, it had been eradicated with small pox. But she was gambling on Lacey and Natalie not knowing anything about it, either.

"Yeah. From the rats," she said. "But he's better now. He'd probably be up for some fun in New Orleans."

"Oh, wow, I don't know," Lacey said quickly. She straightened. "That's all too bad. Him getting sick and stuff. He was a great guy."

He was. Still was, in fact. And Maddie knew she should feel guilty about all of this. But she didn't.

Of course, she had to hope that Owen wouldn't find out about this. Which meant keeping Lacey and Natalie from seeing him until their tour with Sawyer left. The girls might just avoid him. But he might recognize them. If they'd spent the kind of time together Lacey and Natalie had implied, Maddie sure as hell *hoped* he'd recognize them. And what if he did? What if he invited them to stay or invited himself to New

Orleans for a repeat? And then the girls would have to turn him down. Which would make no sense unless they told him *why*. Then not only would he want to know why Maddie had lied about the illness, but he might convince the girls it wasn't true and still end up in one of their beds. Or in a bed with them both since Josh wasn't an option. Or he might figure out why she'd lied. Because *she* wanted him.

Maddie forced herself to take a deep breath. She was freaking out over nothing. Owen was out with another tour and should be back after these boats left. Then she'd either send him out on another before they got back, or she'd find something for him to do in the office. Or at Cora's house. Yeah, he could...clean the gutters at Cora's house. Gutters always needed cleaned out. And those gutters were several blocks from here.

Was she actually coming up with ways to *hide* Owen from other women?

Yes, yes she was.

"Okay, so I guess we're with Sawyer?" Natalie asked.

"Oh, Sawyer," Maddie said, putting a little gushing into her tone. It wasn't hard. Sawyer was great, too. Of course, he was not really himself right now. He hadn't been for almost nine months. But maybe a couple of pretty girls flirting with him would help. "Now *he's* amazing."

"Yeah?" Lacey asked.

Sawyer was a big guy. Bigger than the others. Taller, broader, bigger hands and feet. She could only assume the rest of him matched. "Talk about a big...boat," Maddie said with a nod.

Kennedy started choking again, whacking her chest.

Oh yeah, he was her brother. Maddie grinned. Oops. "Sorry," she muttered.

"Is this Sawyer?" Natalie asked, pointing to a photo of the four guys, their arms around each other, that hung on the wall next to the computer.

"Yep."

"Nice." Natalie studied the photo for a moment, then turned back to face Lacey. "Yeah, very nice."

"Okay, then. We'll go with Sawyer," Lacey said.

Maddie resisted rolling her eyes. Great, Sawyer had passed their test. "Great." She held out the wristbands and the girls presented their arms. She clipped them on and pointed. "Right through there. You can wait out on the benches. Should just be a few more minutes."

They had just stepped through the doorway into the gift shop when Kennedy started laughing. "Oh my God, that was hilarious."

Maddie grimaced. "Pathetic is the word you're looking for, I believe." She covered her face with her hands. "Why did I do that?"

"Because you were super jealous and wanted to stake your claim but couldn't just come out and say 'he's mine', so clearly you had to give him a communicable disease to keep the women away instead." Kennedy nodded. "Makes total sense."

"Is typhoid communicable?" Maddie asked.

Kennedy shrugged. "I mean...probably?"

Maddie glanced toward the door the girls had gone through. "I guess as long as *they* think so." Kennedy started laughing again and Maddie groaned. "Ugh, why does he make me crazy?"

"Hey, there was no lighter fluid this time. I think you're getting better."

Maddie shook her head. "Still."

Kennedy's laughter faded but she was still grinning as she leaned in. "You're not crazy, you know."

Maddie gave a short laugh. "Oh, I don't know that at all."

"If I had the one and only bowl of Cora's jambalaya in the world and someone came walking in here and tried to take it away from me, I'd grab it out of their hands and yell 'mine!' too. That's not crazy."

Maddie felt her heart flip but she teased, "You're comparing Owen to a big bowl of jambalaya?"

Kennedy widened her eyes. "Excuse me? I'm saying he's like the *only* bowl of the *best* jambalaya in the world."

Maddie laughed. "Okay, I apologize."

"And," Kennedy said, sitting back on the stool and propping her feet on the counter. "If I hadn't had Cora's jambalaya in *twelve years*? I'd be diving into it headfirst and not coming up for weeks." She grabbed a magazine off the stack to her right and flipped it open. As if she hadn't just essentially told Maddie that she should be diving into *Owen*.

Maddie swallowed hard. "You're making jambalaya a euphemism for sex?"

She shook her head. "Owen is the jambalaya. The idea of stuffing yourself full of it is the sex euphemism."

Maddie started choking and Kennedy started laughing.

"Oh my God, that's your cousin!" Maddie said, her eyes watering slightly.

Kennedy nodded. "This is what happens when you grow up around all guys. I'm very inappropriate and slightly disgusting a lot of the time."

Maddie leaned over and hugged Kennedy around the neck. "You're awesome and I missed you."

Kennedy actually sniffed slightly at that. "Ditto."

Maddie pulled back and took a breath. "I shouldn't claim Owen is mine," she finally said, seriously. "That's not fair. I'm not staying and it's been a long time."

"Well," Kennedy said, laying the magazine on her legs. "The way I look at it is, if I can't have that jambalaya all the time, then I'm sure as hell gonna enjoy it when I can. And…the jambalaya deserves to be appreciated by the person who truly loves it, right?"

"Jambalaya probably doesn't have feelings about the people eating it," Maddie said. But she knew what Kennedy was saying.

"Well, a comparison between a guy and jambalaya is bound to break down at some point," Kennedy told her. "But you don't really want me to go into a whole thing about putting it in your mouth and swallowing, do you?"

Maddie instantly felt her cheeks heat. "Oh my God, Kennedy!" But a second later she was laughing.

"I'm just sayin', you do *not* spit jambalaya out, you know?" Kennedy's grin was huge...and evil.

"You are—"

"It's downright *sinful* to even think about spitting jambalaya out."

They both swung toward the door at the sound of the deep male voice.

"Owen!" Maddie squeaked.

Kennedy smirked. "I knew you'd feel that way," she said to Owen.

"Why the hell would someone think about spitting it out?" he asked as he came into the office.

Kennedy looked at Maddie. "Oh, I'm not worried. She'd swallow for sure."

Owen lifted a brow because, well, yeah, that sounded like they were talking about something else entirely. Which they were.

Maddie's cheeks burned hotter, and she forced her eyes to stay on his face rather than travel over his body. Kennedy was a terrible person. Maddie's head was filled with dirty thoughts now. And she was hungry. For Owen.

That wasn't new. Her thinking about it in so much detail was. She'd been resisting that. Ignoring it. Distracting herself from it.

Now Kennedy had put it all front and center. Along with a

reassurance that Maddie feeling *very* much like claiming him as *hers* was completely fine.

She wasn't sure about that. But now she couldn't get it out of her head.

"You okay?" Owen asked her.

Maddie realized she'd been staring at him. She shook herself. Then she truly realized that he was *here*. Shit. "What are you doing here? I thought you were out on a tour?"

"Nope, I was up at Cora's."

Maddie's eyes widened. "Doing what?"

"Cleaning her gutters out."

No. Way.

"Headin' out to the dock now to check on some stuff."

He started for the door and Maddie panicked. He couldn't go out there until Lacey and Natalie left. Her hand shot out and she grabbed his sleeve. "Wait."

He looked back. "Yeah?"

"I, um...need you." Well, that was true enough. But she needed to keep her mind off of jambalaya. At least until she'd really had a chance to think it through and make a decision. One of the things she now prided herself on was being able to make rational plans and *not* act on only instinct and what felt good at the moment.

Owen turned around to face her. "You okay?"

For a second she hesitated, realizing that instead of making the "need you" dirty, he actually looked concerned. She nodded. "Yeah, I just...need to talk to you. Privately. In the office."

He frowned slightly. "Okay, let's go." He took a step toward the door behind her that would lead out onto the dock and around the side to the office door.

Maddie pulled on his sleeve and turned him in the opposite direction. They could get to the office through either door. This was the long way, but it was also the non-Lacey way. Owen didn't resist. He just followed her toward the other door, but Maddie kept her hold on his sleeve for some reason. Maybe it was to keep him from veering off course once they stepped outside. Or maybe it was that she liked touching him and this was a fairly innocuous way to do that. The fact that just having his sleeve in her hand made her feel a little warm and think about the hard muscles underneath that sleeve—and underneath the rest of his clothes—was ridiculous, but undeniable all the same.

She cast Kennedy a glance as they passed the counter and got a thumbs-up in response.

Yeah, she wasn't sure it was a thumbs-up situation. But she didn't want Owen to see his fling. Period. She wasn't going to analyze it or worry about it. She was just going to keep him distracted until Sawyer's boat left.

"Dammit, Owen!"

Speak of the devil. Sawyer banged into the office, clearly pissed.

Owen sighed. He didn't seem surprised. He turned. "What's up?"

"You were *fishing* on the north bank last night?"

"I...was," Owen said slowly. "How did you know?"

Sawyer crossed his arms, his biceps bulging. "I found the poles and tackle down under the far dock."

The far dock was the least used one. The boats tied up there were mostly those that friends and family used personally.

"Oh, shit, sorry," Owen said.

"What the fuck? At night?" Sawyer demanded. "There are cottonmouths down there."

Owen nodded again. "You're right."

"Who was with you?"

"No one. Just me."

"With *three* poles?" Sawyer asked.

"Yeah," Owen said. "But slow night. Didn't catch much."

"Well, you're lucky you're not in the hospital with a snake bite or that you didn't drown. Tell me the empty tequila bottle I found wasn't full when you took it down there."

Owen took a deep breath. "Nope. 'Course not. Just had a couple of shots."

"Well, for fuck's sake, use your head," Sawyer said.

"Yep. You got it. Sorry."

Sawyer stomped back out, slamming the door behind him.

Kennedy gave a low whistle. "Damn. Good thing you've got those broad shoulders."

"Don't know what you mean," Owen said as he started for the door again.

"The Benson kid and his two buddies were down there last night," Kennedy said.

"How do you know?"

"I'm guessing, but I found his hoodie on one of the benches outside."

Owen frowned. "Well, when he comes in to get it, tell him that getting drunk in the dark where a bunch of cottonmouths live is pretty fucking stupid."

Kennedy nodded. "Will do."

Maddie was still frowning over the exchange as she pulled Owen out the door, around the far corner of the building, and into the office before she asked about it. She nudged him inside and shut the door behind them. Then, after only a second's hesitation, she turned the lock. She didn't want Lacey or Natalie getting lost and thinking this was the restroom or something.

"Why do you do that?" she asked Owen, turning to face him.

"Do what?"

"Take the blame with Sawyer for stuff you didn't do? That's the third time I've seen it."

She hadn't thought that much about it the first time. Sawyer had found one of the boats had half the amount of gas in it that it should have. Meaning someone had taken it out after hours. Owen had said it was him, and Sawyer had bitched about it, then they'd both gone on their way.

The next time, she'd taken more of a note. Sawyer had been pissed about someone using the cabin and not cleaning it up—as evidenced by the empty beer cans and the trash that hadn't been taken out when he'd gone out there to grab some boots or something. She hadn't paid a lot of attention to the details, but she'd definitely noticed that Owen had again apologized for it, and Sawyer had again lectured him about safety and reminded him that he didn't like the guys going off by themselves without anyone knowing where they were.

Owen sighed. "How do you know it's all stuff I didn't do?"

"You weren't at the cabin the night he blamed you for leaving beer cans all over," she said. "You were at Ellie's when I went in there to get stuff from the kitchen."

"I could have gone out after that," he said, tucking his hands in his pockets. And not making direct eye contact.

Maddie crossed her arms. "Did you?"

Owen blew out a breath. "No."

"So why did you tell Sawyer you did?"

"Because it lets him bitch at someone, but keeps everyone else from being bitched *at*."

"I don't understand."

"Ever since Tommy," Owen said slowly. "Sawyer needs to... take care of people. He gets all knotted up when someone might be doing something that could be dangerous."

Maddie nodded. "That makes sense."

"It does. But he goes way overboard. Ever since it happened, no one can really have any fun. He wants to know where we all are at every moment, he makes us always have someone with us, he constantly harps about being careful and using our heads."

"He's not...wrong," Maddie felt compelled to say. "Going out to that cabin alone is more dangerous than having someone with you."

Owen nodded. "But we all know what we're doing. We've all done it a million times."

"So had Tommy," she said, softly. "I see where Sawyer's coming from."

"Yeah. I know. But you can't live your life that way." Owen took a step toward her. "If you're afraid of something happening every damned minute, life is going to get really boring and sad really quick. People are just havin' fun. Takin' the boats out, fishing after dark, going out to the cabin to party."

"So you're protecting Sawyer by letting him think that's it's just you who isn't being careful and listening to him?"

"I'm volunteering to be Sawyer's punching bag so that everyone else can still have fun."

Maddie lifted her brows. "You're taking the blame so that Sawyer gets to yell at someone and everyone else can keep doing their thing without getting yelled at?"

Owen shrugged. "Pretty much."

"Are you doing it to protect him? Or them?"

"Both."

"And you don't think that Sawyer's getting suspicious that it's always you and only you doing this stuff even after he chews your ass?"

Owen gave her a half smile. "I think Sawyer knows that it's not always me. But he gets to vent his frustrations while not pissing *everyone* off."

"You think he *knows*?"

"Deep down, I think so. And I think he kind of appreciates it. I'm like his therapist. He can't *not* worry and bitch and lecture—that makes him feel better and gets all of his frustration and fears out—but he's also aware that he's being unreasonable some of the time. Believing that it's always me and making me the one he chews out, means he's not upsetting everyone else."

"So he can't help but lash out, but you're a safe person to lash out at?" Maddie summarized.

"Pretty much."

She watched Owen for a moment, taking all of that in and studying the face that she knew so well, yet was actually new in a lot of ways. This wasn't the boy she remembered. That boy had been hot and fun and protective of her and his mom, but not all that self-sacrificing. He'd been a teenage guy. Most guys that age were pretty focused on their own wants and needs. *This* Owen was a man. A man who was loyal and loving and protective but focused on the other person and what *they* needed more than what he needed. A man who would let his cousin berate him, repeatedly, just to make Sawyer feel better and keep the peace with everyone else.

It was a strange gesture, but it worked. Owen didn't take what Sawyer was saying seriously. He knew Sawyer was grieving and this was Owen's way of helping him through that process.

"Why do you always take the bachelorette parties out on the tours?" she asked, as something occurred to her. She'd been noticing some patterns in the schedule and she wanted to confirm her suspicion. At first, Owen being assigned all the bachelorette parties and other all-girl groups had seemed obvious. Owen liked girls and he was charming and good-looking and would keep them happy. But as she'd studied the patterns in scheduling, she'd started to wonder if there was more to it.

"Pretty girls who like to party are kind of my thing," he said. Predictably.

Maddie dropped her arms and stepped forward. "I don't think that's it."

"You don't think I like pretty girls who like to party?" He

quirked an eyebrow. "I think you know *personally* that's not true."

"I think you're doing it to protect Josh."

Something flickered in Owen's eyes and she knew she was right.

"You think poor Josh needs protected from a bunch of bridesmaids?"

"I think bachelorette parties and other groups of girls come down here for a good time. And I think that includes drinking Ellie's Hurricanes, and driving fast on airboats, and flirting with hot guys. And I think that they tip better and give better reviews when those hot guys flirt back. And I think that now that Josh is with Tori, he doesn't want to flirt with other girls, and he definitely doesn't want to be in the position of getting phone numbers or having girls rubbing up against him, but that if he turns them down or pushes them away, it might make him seem like a jerk. So you save all of that from being an issue by taking the girls out yourself."

She watched Owen swallow.

"That's me. Always willing to do that hard stuff for my buddies."

She smiled. "I didn't say you didn't like it. But yeah, I think that's it even more than you liking that the girls show up in high heels and short skirts."

"Wow, you've been giving this a lot of thought," Owen said.

"I have. I also think that you and Josh also try to keep Sawyer from taking out groups that include kids." She tipped her head. "Is he even more over-reactive when there are kids on board?"

Owen blew out a breath, as if finally giving up. He nodded. "Definitely."

Maddie shook her head slowly and took another step closer to him. "Wow. That's pretty great."

"We're just looking out for the business," Owen said. "If

Sawyer snaps at little kids and ruins their trip, it's bad for business."

"Uh-huh." She took the final step until she was standing right in front of him. "I'm not buying it. I think you're looking out for Sawyer and Josh and that you would do anything for either of them way before you'd worry about the business."

Owen swallowed. "He's worried about scaring the kids."

Her eyes widened. "What?"

He nodded. "The scar. He's worried it will scare little kids. So we've been trying to keep those tours with me and Josh."

"Oh no," Maddie said softly, her heart breaking a little for Sawyer. He loved kids.

"I think he doesn't want to get asked what happened, too," Owen said.

"You and Josh are taking *a lot* of the tours."

He shrugged. "We're doing what we need to do."

"I really like that about you," she said, her voice a little husky.

Owen's gaze got hot and lifted his hand and cupped the side of her face. Instantly everything in her went soft and warm.

"Is this what you needed to talk to me about?" he asked.

She hadn't really needed to talk to him about anything in particular at all, but she wasn't ready to confess that she was hiding him from a past one-night stand—and she really hoped it had only been one-night—because then she'd have to tell him why.

She nodded. "Yeah."

"You're okay?"

Well, with him standing this close and his hand on her, she was feeling a strange combination of very-okay and this-is-going-to-complicate-everything. Still, she said, "Not quite."

"Okay, what can I do?"

She took a deep breath and said, "Just hold still." She put her hand behind his head, leaned in, and kissed him.

Her kissing him didn't last long. Within seconds, Owen was very much kissing *her*. His mouth was hot and hungry on hers. He ran his tongue along her bottom lip, demanding entrance, which she happily gave with a little moan.

His hand slipped to the back of her head, his other coming up to cup her jaw, holding her in place as he stroked his tongue deep, tasting her and letting her fully taste him.

Every stroke sent furls of heat through her stomach and down between her legs. Her clit tingled, as if his tongue was *right there*, *almost there* and Maddie arched her back, pressing against his fly.

Owen gave a low groan and said against her mouth, "Not sure I can do the hold-still thing, Mad."

Her breaths came in little pants as she asked, "No good?"

"It would be a hell of a lot better if I could put you back on that desk and move. A lot."

The heat in her belly flared even hotter and she nodded. "Scratch the holding still thing."

"Awesome." He scooped his big hands under her ass and lifted her, carrying her to the desk a few feet away.

He shoved some papers out of the way, and she heard what sounded like one of the coffee mugs hit the floor before he deposited her on the desktop.

She immediately slipped her hands under the soft, warm cotton of his T-shirt. She'd been wanting to get her hands on these abs for a long time. She ran her palms over them, loving the rumble of a groan from him as she did it along with the tightening of those firm planes. God, she wanted to run her tongue over every single one of these ridges. She pushed his shirt up, determined to see—and taste—it all.

Owen didn't lift his arms, though, and she looked up at him in confusion.

"Windows," he said simply.

She glanced at the one to her left. There was one behind

him, but it was blocked by a file cabinet. There was another behind her, but it faced the storage shed, built after the office window was already there, with only a narrow space between the two buildings. It would be unusual for someone to be back there to look in the window.

"Pull the blinds down," she said, nodding at the one window that could expose them.

Owen pulled a breath in through his nose, then pinned her with a serious look. "If I do, I'm stripping you naked."

Hot lava seemed to shoot through her from her core. "You better," she answered.

Because if she was naked, *he* was going to be naked. And she really wanted him to be naked.

With a muttered curse, he stepped to the window and yanked the blinds down covering most of the window. The cord tangled, not having been pulled on for decades likely, and he gave it another hard jerk. It wouldn't budge.

"Fuck."

"Doesn't matter," she told him. Only a few inches were exposed at the bottom and someone would have to lean over and purposefully peer through that portion of the window. "Come here."

Owen gave the blinds another yank and Maddie shook her head. She reached up to the buttons that fastened the front of her dress and began undoing them. When the fourth one was freed and the dress began to gape, she said, "Owen."

Just his name, but he looked over. And froze.

"Come here," she repeated, continuing to unbutton.

"Fuck, you're gorgeous."

She felt her smile spread. "Thanks. Come. Here."

He shoved a hand through his hair. "You should know, once I do, you're not leaving this room without me doing a bunch of dirty things to you."

Heat coursed through her and she freed the last button, spreading her dress open.

"Good." She shrugged the straps off her shoulders. The dress was much better without a bra so she was now completely exposed except for her panties. In fact, she hadn't worn a bra much at all since coming to Autre. It wasn't a matter of fashion, really. The heat down here just made her not care as much. Her nipples certainly didn't get hard from the cold. Only from Owen, actually.

They were beaded and aching right now, as a matter of fact.

"Like dirty beyond what we did in my truck or out at the cabin," he said, one hand still in his hair, the other in his back pocket. His eyes were firmly on her, though, his hot gaze scanning her body.

Yeah, well, that didn't really narrow it down a lot. Things had been pretty straightforward in his truck and at the cabin. They'd been kids. Much more eager than experienced. They'd had sex with him on top on both the lower bunk and the couch at the cabin, and with her riding him in the front seat of his truck. She'd taken him in her mouth once. That had been okay—though she hadn't swallowed, actually. He'd put his fingers inside her and played with her clit but when she'd orgasmed, it had been because of *her* fingers and previous experimentation to know what to do. It had been better with him inside of her, but that hadn't caused the orgasms. The sex between them then had been hot because it had been new and they'd had to sneak around and because she'd been madly in love with him. Being connected with him that way had been enough without anything dirtier.

But she wasn't opposed to dirty.

And with an Owen who was twelve years older and more experienced? Yeah, she wouldn't mind seeing what "dirty" meant to Owen now.

"So why are you still standing way over there?" she asked.

He blew out a breath. "Yeah?"

She nodded. "Yeah."

"Thank fuck." He moved toward her swiftly. But in spite of her naked breasts, he cupped her face in both hands and kissed her deeply.

She leaned into the kiss, opening her mouth and meeting the strokes of his tongue with hers. But after several long, hot moments, she moved her hands to cover his and then dragged them down, over her neck and shoulders and to her breasts.

Owen gave a soft growl as her breasts filled his hands, her nipples poking into his palms. She gasped as he squeezed slightly and then ran his hands back and forth, lightly abrading her nipples. Then he took the tips between his thumbs and first fingers, tugging and rolling them.

Her clit pulsed and she moaned, "Owen."

He moved his mouth to her neck, his beard brushing over her skin and sending goose bumps skittering down her arms and tightening her nipples and making her wiggle on the desktop.

"I need to taste you," he muttered against the base of her throat.

"Yes," she encouraged. "Please."

"I want to suck on your nipples until you're squirming on this desk and then I want to lick your wet pussy until you scream my name."

Her breath caught in her chest. Already the dirty was turned up from high school and she wanted every bit of it. "More," she told him, breathlessly.

He pulled back and gave her a naughty grin. "You're not shocked?"

"If I say no will *you* be shocked?"

"Yes. In the best possible fucking way."

She laughed. "Not shocked."

"That's perfect." He dipped his knees and took one nipple

in his mouth. He swirled his tongue around the tip and then sucked gently. He nipped her lightly with his teeth, then sucked harder.

"Oh my God, Owen." Her hand went to the back of his head and her fingers curled into his hair, her nails scraping over his scalp.

He groaned and sucked even harder. Her pussy pulsed with the pressure and she did, indeed, squirm on the desk.

"That's my girl," he told her gruffly as he felt her hips moving. Then he switched to the other breast, while he plucked the one he'd just left wet and aching.

She knew the squirming was going to get him to move that hot mouth and magical tongue down between her legs, and she would have gladly done it on purpose to get him down there, but she couldn't have kept still for anything.

"Owen, yes."

"Yes? You want me to stay right here?" He ran his hand down her side to her hip, cupping her butt and pulling her to the edge of the desk. "Or do you maybe want me to put my fingers somewhere else?" He ran his hand over the top of her thigh and brushed his knuckles over her panties between her legs. He groaned. "So hot and wet, Mad."

"I know. I know." She reached for the top of her panties. "I need to get them off."

He chuckled softly. "God, I remember how eager you always were. Such a fucking turn-on."

Maddie wiggled, pushing her panties down her legs. The lace caught on one of the rhinestones on her sandals and she gave an irritated growl as she reached down to pull them free. Finally she kicked them off.

She looked up to find him watching her with an amused-but-turned-on expression. "I would have helped," he said, gesturing toward her shoes.

"I'm impatient."

"I love that."

"I'm only ever like that with you."

Owen froze for a moment, his gaze snapping up to hers. "Really?"

Okay, she was bare naked except for her sandals now and, while she appreciated eye contact and him not being *all* about her naked parts all the time, at the moment, she needed his attention down a little lower. "Really. I'm usually pretty cool and confident. Except around you."

He cleared his throat. "I know what you mean."

"You do?"

"Yeah. I mean, I don't get *nervous* or anything. And I like the women I sleep with, but—"

"Okay, enough of that." She reached out and snagged the front of his shirt, pulling him in between her knees. "Take your pants off."

He gripped her thighs in his hands, spreading her knees further and pulling her ass right to the edge of the desk. He looked down at her, his gaze hot. "I was going to finish with, 'everything is different with you.'"

She gave him a soft smile. "That's sweet." Then she frowned. "But don't talk about sleeping with other women when you have one naked on your desk and so wet that it's going to take like one lick to set her off."

His eyes widened in surprise, but his mouth curled into a naughty smile.

"Because the more you talk like that, the more licks it's going to take," she added.

Her body was humming and she felt completely surrounded by him and she felt a sense of comfort even as she felt like she was burning up from the inside out. Comfort. She didn't typically feel that with guys. And if she ever thought about Owen and sex, it was images of sweaty bodies and hot kisses and trying new things and...laughter. There had been laughter, all the time, every time. They'd *enjoyed* each other. They'd liked the sneaking out together and having a shared secret and making new memories and talking about the future as much as they had liked the actual sex. Maybe more in some ways. They'd been kids. She'd been a virgin. He practically had been. They hadn't really known what they were doing at all. But the sex had been the best of her life. Because of everything that went with it.

Maddie took a deep breath and blinked rapidly. She wasn't going to *cry* right now, for God's sake. Even if the tears would be happy and nostalgic tears, this was definitely not the time. For one thing, Owen would stop. He would want to know what was wrong and he'd want to fix it.

She didn't think he could actually *fix* anything here. They couldn't go back to that time. She couldn't change the past. She couldn't go back and decide to stay in Autre instead of going to California. It was like catching a rerun on TV. You watched, it made you smile, it brought back fond memories, but then it was over. It wasn't something you could have all the time anymore. But that didn't mean you didn't stop on that channel and absorb every minute while it was on.

"Well, it's a really good thing that I *love* licking and have absolutely no trouble giving you as many as you need," Owen told her, his voice rough.

That certainly worked to snap her back into the moment. And the heat.

She wiggled again. She was completely exposed right now. She was naked and he had her legs parted, her ass on the edge of the desk with very little leverage, but instead of feeling vulnerable or shy, she felt hot and needy. Owen did that to her. Nakedness, sex, talking about licking each other—none of it was awkward or embarrassing. It was raw and real and honest. She could see in his face that he was feeling everything she was. "Yeah, we might be inching up to needing *three* licks now."

He chuckled, letting his gaze roam over her. "Maybe I'll wait a little longer, say a few more stupid things, just so I can push that number higher."

He ran a big hand up her thigh. He worked outside, with his hands, all day long every day and the roughness of his skin against hers not only sent sparks of pleasure along her nerve endings, but it made her heart clench a little. He was a hard-working, rugged, strong southern man who loved the outdoors and would rather be out in the sun and fresh air than almost anywhere.

"You don't have a single tan line," he said, looking up at her. "But this isn't your usual color. You sunbathe nude out there in California?" he asked, a little gruffness in his voice.

She nodded. "My grandmother had a pool. And a high fence around it," she added with a smile.

"You swim naked or just lay in the sun?"

"Both."

"Little different than skinny-dipping in the bayou." His hand ran up and down her thigh again.

"Well, I can see the bottom of the pool," she agreed. "And the bottom doesn't squish."

His hand kept moving and he continued to study her, his gaze touching every inch of her. His eyes even tracked down her legs to her sandals.

"You still like having water all over your bare skin, though?"

"Yeah."

His gaze settled back between her legs and he moved a hand. He traced over her mound with one rough index finger. "With all this waxing, you gotta be diligent with the sunscreen."

She laughed lightly but it ended abruptly as she sucked in air when he skimmed the pad of his finger over her clit.

"God, you're pretty," he said, almost as if to himself.

"Owen, please. More." Her voice was breathless and she

knew that sounded needy and almost like begging. And she didn't care. She needed him to touch her, to stop this ache.

"How many licks are we up to?" he asked with a half smile.

"Maybe five." That she could still tease about it was amazing. She needed his tongue on her like she'd never needed anything. And she wasn't all that into oral sex. She wasn't that into foreplay, actually. All of this touching and teasing and just *looking* was driving her nuts.

Especially since she wasn't getting to look at anything.

"Five." He nodded. "I can do that."

He went to his knees and Maddie suddenly had a hard time swallowing.

"We never got to this back in high school," he said.

"Nope."

"So I don't actually know what you taste like." He ran the tip of his finger over her clit again and then lower, dipping into her wetness.

"I guess not," she said, her voice tight as she felt pleasure rippling through her from even that simple touch.

"So it's strange that I've been dreaming about it since you walked onto my dock in those high heels, huh?"

He pressed his finger into her, just to the first knuckle and Maddie's head fell back. She had her hands flat on the desk on either side of her, keeping her upright. She could lay back and spread her legs wide and just let him go at it, but...she wanted to watch. She wanted to watch Owen's tongue on her clit, watching him licking and sucking. She wanted the visual of his head between her legs so badly that she was stunned. That hadn't occurred to her until this moment, but now she wanted it so much she was barely resisting grabbing his hair and saying some very raunchy things.

Her head came back up and she looked down.

He looked really good down there.

7

"**M**ore," she said quietly. She was sure he could hear the pleading tone in her voice.

And, if she was the manipulative sort, she would have outright *begged*. Owen Landry would do anything for her. It might have been twelve years, but she knew that for a fact. Of course, he'd do anything for anyone he cared about. He'd do *almost* anything for *anyone*. That was becoming more and more clear the longer she was here in Autre. But she also knew that she was special and that if she *needed* something he could give, he would. And if she needed something he couldn't give her, he'd find someone who could. And if it was something as straightforward, and awesome, as an orgasm—and yes, she knew he'd given out many of them, she just didn't want to think about it—then she knew he'd be *all* in.

But she wasn't going to manipulate his good guy side here.

She wanted his bad boy side.

"Tell me if I taste like you imagined," she said.

His gaze snapped up to hers, then he gave a little growl and leaned in, putting his mouth on her. He gave her a long, firm lick from slit to clit and then he sucked lightly.

Her legs tightened and her lungs froze. She let it all wash over her and just reveled in it. Like the water of the pool gliding over her naked body, like the sun touching every inch of skin, the feel of Owen's mouth on her most intimate part was equally decadent and liberating. She felt warm and cool at the same time, free and sexy and uninhibited while also like she was doing something secret and naughty.

He licked again, and again. "That's three," he said, his voice husky. Then he flicked her clit with his tongue before sucking hard.

She lifted her hips, trying to get closer. "Let me see," she heard herself say as she grasped his hair on top of his head and pulled him back a little.

He looked up at her. "What do you want to see, Mad? My face when I taste you? When I'm in absolute heaven? Or you want to see your wetness on my beard?" He turned his head and ran his chin over her inner thigh.

Feeling that wetness from his beard to her skin made her pussy clench and she sucked in a breath.

"Or do you want to see me spread you completely open and feast on you like I'm a dying man with his last meal? Because, baby, that's exactly what I'm about to do. I'm going to fuck you with my tongue and make you come, drinking it all in like it's the fucking elixir that will make me immortal."

She was panting and her fingers tightened in his hair. She nodded. "Yes. All of that. I want to watch your tongue even as I feel it and I want to see myself all over your face."

He stared up at her, his eyes burning, his nostrils flaring. "Holy shit, Mad."

She laughed lightly and shook her head, covering one hot cheek with her hand. "I know. I never talk like this. What are you doing to me?"

He was making her crazy. That was the answer. That was always the answer.

"I'm making you wanton," he said with a predatory grin. "And I fucking love it."

Her heart flipped. The thing was…if she was going to be wanton, he was the only man she'd do it with. For. Because of. She was safe with him. She could let go. She could just do whatever felt good, say whatever came to mind, and not worry about shocking him or scaring him off. If she could burn down a shed and have him show up to rebuild it with her, she could easily tell him that she wanted him to tongue fuck her right now on this desk.

"You are," she said with a nod. "And I love it, too."

"You need to get a better grip on the edge of that desk," he told her, nodding at her hand.

She grinned. This. The sexy teasing, the being totally open, the *enjoying* it all while also getting all the physical pleasure from it, was what she'd never found with anyone else. She hadn't looked hard. She hadn't slept with many guys over the years. Like four. Okay, exactly four. In twelve years. Only one had been a one-night thing. The others had been relationships and even then, the sex had been…okay.

For sure, none of them had gone down on her, talked about her being an immortal elixir, or mentioned getting his beard wet with her. Simply put, none of them had come even close to Owen Landry, and she suspected that might be the case for the rest of her life.

She swallowed hard, but thankfully Owen leaned in again just then, completely distracting her from what she'd be missing by, well, giving her exactly what she'd be missing.

He spread her open with his thumbs and then licked. A nice, long slow one. And she saw every bit of it. Her fingers tightened in his hair, and she gave a little whimper as he sucked on her clit, swirling his tongue around it. Then returned to licking again. Over and over, with perfectly timed sucks and little nips that sent sparks of hot, electric pleasure through her. Then he dipped lower, thrusting his tongue in and out of her. She felt the knot of need tightening and when he slipped two fingers in and again sucked hard on her clit, she shot over the edge, her orgasm erupting from so deep inside, she felt like it was coming from her *soul*. Her knees tightened around his head and she cried out his name. If someone was standing right outside the door, there was no way they wouldn't hear. The chances of that were slim, but even so, she didn't care. Hell, she was fine with the whole world knowing how amazing Owen Landry was at oral sex. She might take out a billboard.

She drifted back to earth slowly, satisfaction spreading through her like the warmth from a big shot of her grandpa's moonshine. Owen pulled back, sliding his hands up her body, over her stomach, breasts, and up the sides of her neck as he rose. He cupped her face and kissed her, making sure she tasted herself on his tongue and that the wetness from his beard also covered her chin. When he lifted his head, he dragged his thumb over her chin and then lifted it to his mouth.

"Thank you," he told her, his gaze burning into hers. "Thank you for letting me do that."

She gave a little puff of laughter. "My pleasure."

He gave her a sexy grin, then kissed her again, before straightening and actually lifting the front neck of his T-shirt and swiping it over his beard and mouth.

Her eyes widened. "You're going to walk around all day with *that* on your shirt."

He nodded, lifting it to his nose and taking a deep breath. He gave her a wink as he let the shirt drop back into place. "Fuck yeah."

Damn that was...hot. And very intimate to think about him walking around able to smell her like that all day. She squeezed her thighs together. "But we're not done."

He took a step back and let out a breath. "We are."

Now her eyes went really wide. "Excuse me." She dropped her gaze to his fly. "You sure about that?"

Owen reached down and adjusted the front of his jeans over the very obvious, very hard erection he had going on. "I'm sure."

Maddie frowned. There was something in his tone and expression that made her believe him. Her dress was still pooled around her hips on the desk and she reached down to pull it back up, then gripped the front, covering her nakedness.

Owen bent and grabbed her panties off the floor. He looked at them for a second and she wondered if he was thinking about keeping them. But he just sighed and tossed them to her.

"You're serious," she said as she caught them one-handed. They really weren't going to have sex.

"Yeah."

"But...later then?" Maybe he wanted a bed. And all night long. She could be okay with that.

He shook his head and her heart dipped into her stomach. She pulled her panties on, shimmying them up her legs.

"The thing is," he said, running his hand through his hair as he watched her.

The hair she'd been gripping as he made her come with his mouth in one of the hottest moments of her life.

"I can't," he finished simply.

"You can't? You had an accident or something?" Then her eyes went wide. "You have a *girlfriend*?"

Oh, she was going to fucking kill him. Not just for cheating with her, but for *having* another girlfriend and not telling Maddie. For two weeks.

"No," he said firmly. "I don't have a girlfriend. And I did not have any...accidents."

Maddie frowned and slid off the desk. She started buttoning her dress up. "Then what? That wasn't as good as you're used to?" That thought felt like someone had just shoved a hot knife through her heart and she held her breath waiting for his answer. She kept her eyes on her buttons.

"Jesus, Maddie." He took a huge step forward until he was nearly on top of her.

She looked up instinctively.

"You were...too fucking good," he said, almost as if he hated admitting it. He shook his head. "You look and feel and sound and *taste* better than even my dirtiest dreams." He tucked a strand of hair behind her ear in a sweet gesture that was in contrast with the fact he was talking about having his mouth on her pussy just a few minutes ago. Again Maddie had to squeeze her legs together to subdue the tingly ache that was still there, in spite of the orgasm. That had been like a really great appetizer. A *really, really* great appetizer. But she was still in the mood for the full meal.

"If I fuck you, I'll never get over it," he said, letting his hand drop back to his side.

She blinked up at him. Again there was a kind of funny mix of dirty and sweet in that. "What just happened doesn't count?"

He gave a low whistle. "I'm never getting over *that*," he said. "But there's a difference between never going down on anyone else ever again and never doing *anything* with anyone else ever again."

She shook her head. She couldn't believe they were talking about this. "So you're saying that because of that"—she tipped her head toward the desk—"you're never going to...go down... on anyone...again." She definitely stumbled over those words. Partly because she wasn't used to talking so graphically about sex with someone and partly because she felt a little like throwing up when even talking about him hypothetically doing that to someone else.

"I guess not." He actually seemed frustrated by that idea. And serious.

But she still laughed. "Come on."

He frowned at her. "Why would I? It will never be like that with anyone else."

Yeah. She knew what he meant. Fuck. She crossed her arms. "For the rest of your life?"

"I don't eat any jambalaya other than Cora's," he said. "None other ever measures up and it's a waste of time and a sure disappointment to even try. So I'll never eat any other, for the rest of my life."

What was it with this family and comparing jambalaya with sex? Maddie wondered, but she shook her head. She understood what he was saying. It seemed extreme in this case, though. And she told him so.

His frown deepened. "Yeah, well, apparently you still make me crazy, too."

He did not seem pleased by that. That wasn't a teasing or flirtatious statement at all.

"But you don't want to sleep with me so you can preserve the ability to still do *that* with other people?"

He gave her a look. "Come on, Mad. We're both grown-ups. You can't actually be mad that I plan to have sex again in my lifetime."

She *hated* this entire conversation. Because it was clear she wasn't getting laid. But also because it seemed clear he would be. By other people. At least, she could hope that he'd keep it in his pants while she was here.

"I can't believe you did *that*"—she thrust her finger at the desk—"and are *now* cutting me off!"

For just an instant, the corner of his mouth curled up, then he sobered. "I'm cutting you off? At least you *got off*."

"And whose fault is *that*?" she asked, pointing at his cock.

He cleared his throat. "You should be flattered that I'm afraid your pussy will ruin me for life."

She lifted both brows even as a bolt of heat went through her. How could she be so annoyed with him and jealous of all the other potential future women that would be in his life, and still turned on at the same time?

"You should have kept your mouth to yourself," she said, lifting her chin. "That was really mean to go that far and not all the way."

He stepped close, leaning in slightly, and ran a hand over the top of his head. "I can still feel you pulling my hair because you wanted it so much and came so hard. There is *nothing* mean about what I just did to you."

"It's not *mean* to raise the oral sex bar so high for everyone else?"

The second she said it, she regretted it.

He gave her a cocky grin. "That was mean of me," he agreed. "Wonder why I don't feel bad about it."

Well, two could be cocky. And mean. "I can't even imagine how many guys I'm going to have to go out with in my search for someone with a better tongue than yours," she said, stepping around him and smoothing her dress as she headed for the door. "I'll have to sleep with them on the first or second date to get through them all." She grabbed the doorknob and looked back. "I suppose I could get lucky and find a Master Tongue right away, but the odds are against it, if I'm being honest."

Owen was scowling darkly. "You should *not* sleep with a bunch of men."

"Oral sex," she said. "I'm just talking about him going down on me."

She was pleased to see Owen looking furious. Even if she was childishly goading him into it.

"I mean, the sex thing...you're right...if we don't do that, I don't have to change my standards there. So...thank you, I guess."

"You should just avoid oral sex forever. Like I'm going to do," he said.

She sighed. "Come on, Owen. We're both grown-ups," she said, mimicking his words from a minute ago. "You can't actually be mad that I plan to beg a guy to make me come on his tongue again in my lifetime."

Maddie could see how her dirty words, and the idea of her being with another guy, affected Owen. Good. He was the one who'd kept his fly zipped.

She turned and pulled the door open.

"Maddie."

She stopped. Owen's low, deep voice sent goose bumps skittering down her back. "What?"

"You could just stay here. You can have my tongue every night. Right here on this desk every day, if you want. And I'll happily fuck you senseless whenever you ask."

Damn him. He knew the effect his words had on her. It was why he was talking that way. He knew she was still wound tight and could still feel the wetness between her legs because of him. He knew she liked the dirtier side of him she'd seen today. He knew she liked knowing that she pushed him to the edge of what he would normally, rationally, do and say.

She squared her shoulders, but didn't turn around. "Sure, I'll just move my whole life from California to Autre for your tongue and cock."

But the thing was, it wouldn't just be those things. It would be Owen. She could have all of him. Sure, his cock, too. And that was no small thing. Literally. But she would also have his friendship, his loyalty and protectiveness, his laughter and humor, his big heart. He would take care of her even when she didn't realize she needed it, like he did with Sawyer and Josh. Being here would also mean a big, crazy family, and lots of laughs, and a business that was making her feel surprisingly creative and competent and appreciated. The art gallery made her feel all of those things but, yeah, Boys of the Bayou was different because this wasn't just making a *business* better, it was about making a group of people she knew and cared about better. She was helping them. She was lightening the load around here. And that felt unexpectedly good.

She pulled in a deep breath. She couldn't really stay here. Could she? Could she come home?

"Huh. I think I'd move to San Francisco for your sweet pussy."

She whirled around. He hadn't really just said that, had he? Of course, she knew that *he* knew it would be more than hot sex. But that wasn't what shocked her. "You would not."

He shrugged. "Don't underestimate pussy power."

He was being crude on purpose. He was clearly still irritated. Which was funny, since the entire reason he was hard and unsatisfied was *him*. But underneath the words about her pussy, she knew he meant the power of their connection. Yeah, it was as strong as ever. It was crazy.

Which was exactly the problem. Owen Landry moving to San Francisco would be crazy. But that's what they did to each other. They reacted based on emotion and didn't think through the consequences until afterward.

She frowned. "You would never leave the bayou. Your family. The food and traditions. The water. The boats."

"Ask me again after I've had you on my tongue and am smelling you all day long," he said. "You might be surprised what I'd do for y...that."

He'd almost said "you." *You might be surprised what I'd do for you.*

As that shock bumped around in her brain—and heart— Maddie also realized that she wouldn't actually be surprised at all. There had been a time when he would have done *anything* for her. And that didn't seem to have changed much no matter how long the time or distance had been between them.

She swallowed hard. "You should grab a new shirt from the gift shop. Wouldn't want you doing anything...crazy."

Then she pulled the door open and stepped through, shutting it behind her and between her and the man that made her want things...lots of things...that she had thought were far behind her.

———

OWEN GRIPPED his hands into fists as he watched Maddie leave the office and shut the door between them.

What the *fuck* was he doing? He shoved a chair away, causing it to crash into the desk on the other side of the room. He hadn't fucked her? She'd been begging him for it. She'd been bare fucking naked, spread out, ready, wanting him. He'd never been harder in his life.

But *not* shoving his pants down and thrusting deep had been pure self-preservation.

Maddie had shown up just over a week ago and had tipped everything on its side. She was in *everything*. Everywhere he looked.

She was making the business better. She even seemed to be enjoying it. Cora was glowing lately, telling him that having Maddie there with her meant the world to her. Apparently they watched the evening news and then *I Love Lucy* reruns every night together. Maddie was helping Kennedy in the office and giving his cousin an ally against all the testosterone Kennedy was swimming in every day. Maddie had reorganized everything, cut their costs, dealt with suppliers, essentially making everything easier for Sawyer, too. Dammit, she was putting her mark on everything. And it was a really good mark.

If he just wanted to fuck her—because she was hot, because they had chemistry, because they had a past, whatever—that would have been one thing. He would have done it. And enjoyed the hell out of it.

But it was more than that. He *liked* her. He appreciated her.

He respected her. And he felt a connection that went deeper than the physical. He saw her making things better for the people he loved, the people *he* tried to help whenever and however he could, and it made him feel like they were teammates, partners, something.

It wasn't as if he didn't like the women he slept with. He *definitely* did. But they didn't work together. They didn't share incredibly important people in common. He wouldn't expect any of them to step up to protect his family members.

And it wasn't as if this was all just a blast from the past. He and Maddie hadn't been quite this...empathetic and outwardly focused—yeah, that was a nice way to say it—when they'd been together before. They'd been dumb, fun-loving, selfish, wrapped-up-in-their-own-little-bubble teenagers.

Now they were all grown-up. They were both a lot less selfish and a lot smarter, and he loved the way she saw the situations and people around her and reacted in a confident, firm way, with her heart clearly in the right place.

Dammit. He was falling for her again.

And if he'd fucked her just now, he would never recover. He hadn't been overreacting or being dramatic. Flat out, if he ever wanted a chance to move on and have a relationship with another woman, he had to avoid letting Maddie get any further under his skin and mixed up in his life.

Blowing out a breath, Owen started for the door. Thankfully, his cock had calmed down, too, and as long as he didn't think about what had just gone down in this room, it would stay that way. But as he pulled the door open, he caught a whiff of her. Yes, the sweetness he'd transferred to the front of his shirt as well as the lingering scent of her perfume. That was probably absorbed into his shirt, too, if not his very skin.

He might never wash this shirt again.

Resigned to being in a semi-hard-mostly-horny state for the

next couple of weeks, Owen rounded the corner of the building.

He immediately saw that someone had Josh cornered. A very pretty someone with long red hair and wearing white short shorts. Exactly Josh's type. Before Tori.

Owen knew he needed to go save Josh.

His cousin was a good guy. He was Ellie's sweetest grandson, according to her. And most everyone who knew her three grandsons. He was charming and funny and flirtatious, but he was *nice* and he'd never been able to hide that. Owen, on the other hand, could turn on the bad boy just enough that most girls didn't mind him stealing them away from Josh. In fact, he'd been doing it to mess with his cousin even before Tori had come along and he'd started rescuing Josh. Not every girl chose him. Plenty of girls went for the true good guy. The gentleman. But Owen probably swayed about sixty percent of the ladies. Maybe sixty-five if he was feeling especially mischievous.

But as he considered approaching Josh and the redhead, he felt less roguish and more resigned. He needed to help Josh out here, but with the scent of Maddie soaked into his pores and the taste of her still on his tongue, it seemed...wrong. He supposed before he approached the girl, he could go brush his teeth and change his shirt. But the only thing that was really going to help was getting over Maddie and well, he was pretty much screwed there.

Owen took a breath and a step in Josh's direction. He was out on the end of the dock, his escape blocked by a gorgeous woman with her tits jutted out and her hand on his arm. *He* didn't have time for Owen to go brush his teeth.

He opened his mouth to say something charming and cute, but before he could make a sound, he saw Maddie approaching from the other direction. She was focused directly on Josh and the girl and she didn't look happy.

She must have seen them through the window.

Owen thought he should maybe try to get there before she did, but a bigger part of him really wanted to see how this was going to go down.

Maddie was easily as protective of these people as he was, whether she saw it—or liked it—or not. Maybe she'd dump the girl off the end of the dock. That would be hilarious.

Maddie pasted on a huge, too bright, very fake smile as she stopped next to the girl. Josh looked relieved and the girl looked annoyed. Perfect interruption then.

Owen needed to hear what was being said. He moved closer as Maddie managed to peel the girl away from Josh with a, "This is important."

Yeah, she was moving her closer to the edge of the dock.

He stopped a few feet away. He wouldn't keep her from pushing the girl over, but he'd probably have to be the one to jump in after her.

Suddenly the girl gasped and her hands went behind her to cover her ass.

"I just know if it was me, I'd want someone to tell me. We girls have to stick together," Maddie said.

The girl nodded. "I *really* appreciate it. Oh, wow, how embarrassing." She glanced over at Josh. "Do you think he saw?"

Maddie looked sorry. "Yeah. He was definitely checking you out."

The girl groaned. "Oh, God. Well, now I just need to get out of here."

"If you go that way, the dock wraps around and will take you right up to the sidewalk that will take you back to the bus."

"Thank you." The girl looked genuinely embarrassed but grateful.

"Like I said, I'd want someone to tell me."

The girl started in the direction Maddie had pointed, but strangely moved around Owen keeping her front facing him.

Once she was around the edge of the building, she took off running and Owen turned back to Maddie.

"What was that?" he asked, advancing on her.

Josh had already gone into the office.

"I was getting her away from Josh. Did you see her?" Maddie asked.

"I did."

Maddie narrowed her eyes.

"Not like that. I saw her leaning in and Josh looking super uncomfortable."

Maddie nodded. "So I fixed it."

"I thought you were going to shove her in the bayou."

"I considered it."

Owen grinned. "What did you do instead?"

"Told her that her butt had a huge brown streak across it. Said she probably sat in something on the boat but that it looked pretty bad."

"Wow. Nice."

"She's the type who loves to have guys checking out her ass. I knew that would do it."

"What about when she gets back to her hotel and realizes you lied?"

"What's she going to do? Come down here and yell at me for breaking up her chance to get laid?"

"Well..."

"Why doesn't Josh just tell them that he's got a girlfriend, anyway?" Maddie asked, clearly irritated. "Why can't you guys turn these girls down?"

"It's just a part of the job," he said, lifting a shoulder. "It can be fun for us, too, you know."

She narrowed her eyes further. "Got it."

"I just think...it's kind of part of our reputation, if you want to really know. Hot guys who are a ton of fun to flirt with...and more," he said, quoting a review he'd read recently. "It's on a few of the travel review sites."

"Travel review sites?"

"Those websites where people review their trips and the places they go and things they do while on vacation," Owen said.

"And women review *you guys*? Not just the tour?"

"Oh, they definitely review us," Owen said, nodding. "We had a huge contest going on for a while between the four of us. Whoever got the most stars each week got all their beer paid for Friday night."

Maddie rolled her eyes. "Nice marketing plan."

Owen grinned. "Ask me who won the most free beer."

"No." She turned on her heel and started toward the office.

"Come on, ask me!" he called after her.

She turned back at the doorway, looked him up and down, and said, "Sawyer, right?"

He laughed. "Yep."

She nodded. "The serious brooding guys always make us girls want to take care of them and kiss it all better."

The stab of jealousy shocked him. "That right?" he said with a little growl in his voice.

"Yeah. And if we could just get him to stop yelling at people about wearing their life jackets and keeping their hands inside the boat, he could lock that top spot in for good. Chicks really dig scars." Then she disappeared into the office.

He watched her go with a smile. He was relieved, and happy, that they were back to joking around after what had happened in the office.

And he wasn't jealous of Sawyer. Much.

8

"Are you aware that alligators in the swamp are attracted to the scent of Old Spice?"

Maddie stepped into the front office the next morning to find Kennedy on the phone. She was lounging with her feet propped up on the counter and twirling a piece of her hair, but she looked annoyed.

"Seriously," she said to whoever she was talking to. "And they hate Armani." She paused. "I don't think Armani makes hip waders, sir."

Maddie was amused, but she gave her friend a curious look.

"You seriously have a money clip that looks like an alligator?" Kennedy asked into the phone. She rolled her eyes. "They also go for the pretentious ones first, just so you know."

Maddie stepped forward. "Who are you talking to?"

Kennedy swung her feet down off of the counter. "Hey, Maddie's here now." She paused, listening. "Well, yes, I do still feel like you would make a terrible swamp boat tour company owner." She listened again as Maddie's eyebrows rose. "Email? What's that?" She again rolled her eyes. "Nope, we don't have all those new-fangled inventions down here on the swamp. Sorry. I guess you should have taken better notes."

She held the phone out to Maddie.

"Who is it?" Maddie asked, afraid of the answer.

"Bennett Baxter," Kennedy said with mild disdain in her voice.

"And you were giving him notes about living down here?" Maddie asked. Bennett actually had a decent sense of humor, so she wasn't too worried about Kennedy insulting him, but...it was Kennedy. And Kennedy did not want Bennett here.

"I was giving him notes about why he won't last two days down here," Kennedy said.

Maddie nodded. "Right. Okay." She took the phone and lifted it to her ear. "Hey, Bennett."

"Maddie," the bayou-crazy billionaire greeted.

Maddie found his obsession with the swamp endearing, actually. And convenient, of course. Along with his huge bank account.

Maddie moved out onto the dock. "Kennedy was giving you some...tips?"

He chuckled and Maddie smiled. He was a nice guy.

"She's trying to scare me off."

"Yeah she is," Maddie agreed. "Is it working?"

"From the company, no," he said. "From sharing an office with her? Yes."

Maddie laughed. "You won't have to share an office with her."

"There's another office space?" he asked.

She thought about the crowded, dusty "office" that was supposed to be an office. And that had worked very well as a place to have almost-sex with Owen. She felt a flush rush over her skin and she cleared her throat. "No, the one Kennedy's in is pretty much the main one. But there's no way she'd share with you."

He laughed. "Good thing I'm not easily intimidated. Especially by teenage girls with bad attitudes."

Maddie lifted a brow. "Kennedy has an attitude for sure, but she's not a teenager. She's twenty-four."

There was a pause on Bennett's end. Then he coughed lightly. "Oh?"

"Yeah." Maddie smiled thinking about Bennett and Kennedy meeting in person. That could be interesting. "How did you not meet her when you were down here for tours in the past?" she asked as the thought occurred to her.

"I don't know," he said. "The first time, one of the guys checked me in. The second time it was a brunette with piercings and tattoos..." He trailed off. "*That's* Kennedy?"

Maddie chuckled. "That's Kennedy."

"Wow. I guess...when you said the guys' younger cousin worked for them part-time while going to school, I assumed you meant she was in high school and filled in on the weekends or something."

Maddie shook her head, even though he couldn't see it. She was enjoying this for some reason. "Nope. She's an integral part of everything down here. She's taking classes part-time from Loyola, but I think she plans to stay here." Maddie frowned. "Actually, now that I think about it, I'm not sure what her plans are."

"Hmm," was all Bennett said to that.

What did the bachelor billionaire think of Kennedy? Maddie wondered. She'd love to know. But she couldn't ask. They weren't that close. They had a professional relationship.

"So how are you?" she asked, changing the subject.

"I was calling to ask you the same thing," Bennett said.

His voice was deep and smooth and Maddie knew this man was very used to getting the answers he wanted and talking people into things. He had taken over his father's business, but he'd grown it significantly in the time he'd been in charge.

They'd only met in person once, but he'd been in an expensive suit and while he'd been friendly—and very enthusiastic about the bayou—he'd come off as sophisticated and commanding. Actually, all of that made his interest and excitement about the bayou and the tour company even funnier.

"I'm fine," she answered. "Everything is good."

"Great. Glad to hear it. Especially with the typhoid and everything going around."

Maddie opened her mouth to reply, then shut it. She frowned. Then she said, "The what?"

"The typhoid fever," Bennett said. "I'm glad to hear everyone is okay. I was, obviously, concerned to read about it."

"You *read* about it?" Maddie asked. "What are you talking about?"

"On You Travel," he said.

"What's You Travel?"

"A travel review site," Bennett told her. "One of the best. Though I check on Travel Time and World Wide, too."

Maddie sighed. "Which one rates the bayou boys?"

Bennett chuckled. "I've seen comments on all three, but You Travel is the one with the star rating for each guy."

Maddie rubbed a hand over the middle of her forehead. "There's no typhoid fever, of course," she said. "I can't believe someone put that in a review."

"Yes, imagine my concern, and probably that of the Louisiana Department of Health, when I read that," Bennett said dryly.

Maddie dropped her hand. "The Louisiana Department of Health?" Crap, she hadn't thought about that. Of course she hadn't. She hadn't thought for even one second that the girls from yesterday would write a review, not to mention one that included *that*.

"Don't worry," Bennett said. "I've contacted the woman and asked her to take the review down."

"Oh good." Then Maddie paused. "Wait, you did what?"

"I put a call into the woman and asked her to take it down. She did last night. So we're fine."

"You…how did you get a hold of her?" Maddie asked.

"I have ways," Bennett said. "But in this case it wasn't hard. People have to register with You Travel in order to post."

"And that information is public?"

"No."

"So you got it from You Travel?"

"I did. Well, my lawyer did."

Maddie knew her eyes were wide. She was used to working with guys like Bennett. Guys who had the money and resources to do almost anything they wanted. But they were usually customers buying art from her. She'd never had one that was a…partner. Or an ally. Or whatever Bennett was. In other words, she'd never had someone who used that money and those resources *for* her. Her grandparents had had money. But they were more in the "we're very wealthy for Northern California" income bracket than the Bennett Baxter income bracket. Because of their money, Maddie had been given a number of opportunities—the best education, credit cards, the ability to choose a profession based on her passions rather than what her paychecks would be—but she'd never had the ability to track down a virtual stranger and get them to do whatever she wanted.

"And she just agreed to take it down. No questions asked?" Maddie wanted to know.

"Yes. And no. She took it down, but there were questions. About typhoid. Which we, of course, explained was a joke— one made in poor taste—and that there was absolutely no risk of the disease in Autre. We convinced her to take it down because it was untrue and she realized it would make her foolish to have posted it. But," he went on, his tone firmer, "I'm not going to convince people to take down *true* bad reviews.

Like the one about Sawyer yelling at someone about a life jacket."

Maddie knew that he *could* get rid of all the bad reviews. He was just more ethical than that. Maddie grimaced. It was harder to pin down which group might have posted that review about Sawyer and the life jacket. Sawyer was in general grumpy and not uncommonly stern with his tour groups. "I appreciate that."

"I'm also not going to address the one about the blonde who runs the company lying about a woman's shorts getting dirty," Bennett said.

Good lord, did *all* of their customers post reviews? Maddie needed to keep that in mind. Generally, that was a good thing for businesses, and if this percent was any indication of how many usually left reviews, that was impressive. Unless the reviews were less than stellar, of course.

"Was it a bad review?" Maddie asked.

"It was strange. She said the tour itself was five stars. The woman lying about her shorts was a one star."

"So an average of three then?" Maddie quipped.

"Maddie," Bennett said firmly, in a very I'm-usually-in-charge tone. "Is everything okay down there?"

"It is," she assured him. "It's been...an adjustment. But things are fine. We'll keep the reviews in mind." She shook her head. That wasn't fair to the guys. Clearly *they* were aware of the review sites and somehow had set up a system that encouraged reviews. *She* was actually the problem. Well, her and Sawyer. "I mean *I* will," she corrected. "I'm the one who didn't think that all through."

"Online reviews are really important. We're in a competitive business. Tourism is something people definitely research online."

She didn't miss that he'd used "we" in his comment. She smiled. Bennett was already mentally invested even if he hadn't signed any documents yet. He was already using his influence to help them.

But she didn't want to have to keep asking people to remove bad reviews. They'd—she'd—probably deserved those. She needed to use her head and not just react.

Wasn't that supposed to be kind of her mantra down here?

She sighed. "You're right," she told Bennett. "And I'm sorry those happened. Thanks for your help."

"Of course," he said easily. "And I'm here if there are any issues you need more help with."

Maddie smiled. She knew the guys and Kennedy weren't enthusiastic about the idea of bringing Bennett on, but they could really use him. He not only had money to invest and resources that could help them at times, but he was a very successful businessman. She was certain he'd never taken an engine apart or handled a snapping turtle with his bare hands, but he could still be a great addition to their team.

"Thanks, Bennett. We'll talk soon." They were scheduled to meet on the Tuesday before she returned to San Francisco.

She ignored the pang in her chest when she thought about the plane ticket she had tucked into her daily planner.

"Looking forward to it," Bennett told her. "Take care."

They disconnected and Maddie blew out a breath, thinking about the call.

She would never have lied to a customer—twice—at the art gallery.

The art gallery doesn't matter as much to you as this business does.

She acknowledged that truth. She had no personal stake in the art gallery. She liked working there, but she didn't feel *invested* in it. She was invested in her own art, of course, but if people came through the door of the gallery and didn't buy, she didn't take it personally. If there was ever a bad review of the gallery online—which would never happen since their customers weren't really the online-review-site type of people —she wouldn't care. Art was subjective. What one person loved, another might hate. That was fine and nothing to get upset about.

But someone not liking a swamp boat tour?

Yeah, she cared about that.

Even though she would have scoffed at that idea three weeks ago.

She wanted people to have a good time down here. She wanted them to think the guys were hilarious and fun. And if they thought they were sexy, too, that was fine. Kind of. She wanted to hear the little kids piling off the boats, gushing about how fast the boat went and seeing the turtles and gators, and running into the gift shop to buy books about the swamp and the animals that lived here. Not just for the money that generated, but because that was what travel and adventures were all about—learning and seeing and experiencing new things that opened minds to parts of the world that were different from what people were used to.

Maddie felt her heart flip at that.

Damn, she was getting invested here. Not monetarily, but emotionally. And not just with the Landry family and her grandmother and all the people of Autre as she'd feared—and expected—but with the business and what it did beyond making money.

It wasn't just the kids, either. She loved watching everyone disembark, with huge smiles, their hair tousled by the wind, having just had a unique experience, no matter who they were or where they were from.

The Louisiana bayou was unlike anywhere else and the history and culture in the area was, too. She understood why the guys liked to show it off. She really did.

And that was going to be a problem.

She'd intentionally tried not to get attached. She'd thought it would be the people who would present the biggest problem. The people she already knew. And loved.

And she'd been right. They were a problem.

But she hadn't been expecting the business itself to matter, and she definitely hadn't foreseen starting to care about their customers.

They didn't have a lot of repeat business. That was how tourism worked. People came for a visit, you showed them around, and they went home. Yet, even though they were new every time, Maddie cared that people had a good time here. Sure, she also wanted them to keep their hands off the actual boys of the bayou, but she was starting to understand that the guys were kind of playing a part. The hot, happy, fun-loving Cajuns who worked with their hands and got dirty on the bayou...and loved it. It wasn't a big stretch of course. Which made it all the more appealing. They were actually the guys people saw when they took the tours or went out fishing with them. Maybe with the charm and flirtation and I-once-wres-tled-a-gator-like-that-one turned up a notch.

She knew it all drew the male tourists in, too, actually. Even if it was subconscious. Josh, Owen, and Sawyer were the types of guys that women were attracted to, but that men liked, too. They were the guys men wanted to grab a beer with. They wanted to hear their crazy stories—ninety percent of which were true. They wanted to be *like* the bayou boys a little even. The tough, pure male, alpha types.

So she probably needed to stop lying to the women about typhoid and brown stains on their shorts just to keep them away.

Maddie blew out a breath and headed back into the office. She needed to redesign their brochure, help Kennedy process about twelve tours today, and somehow stop thinking about how it would all work if she actually stayed in Autre. Because that was ridiculous.

———

UNBELIEVABLE.

Two nights later, Maddie stared at the blank canvas in front of her.

Blank.

Still.

Again.

What the hell was happening?

She sighed and tossed her brush onto the counter next to her.

Cora had been great with Maddie setting up her painting stuff in the third bedroom on the second floor of the house. During the day the light was perfect. Of course, Maddie was at Boys of the Bayou during the day. Still, she should be able to at least sketch at this time of night. Or *start* something. Swipe at least one stripe of paint across the canvas.

But no.

She was feeling feelings. Lots of them. Mixed-up ones. Lust, and longing, and confusion, and irritation—mostly at herself, but also at Owen for keeping his pants zipped up the other day —and confusion, and worry, and confusion.

She should be able to paint. These were the things that fueled her. Being in the very midst of Autre and all the memories and emotions that she'd poured into her paintings over the past few years should have yielded some of her best work.

That wasn't happening.

Maddie pushed her hair back out of her face as she regarded the canvas with a feeling of betrayal. "Fine. I guess I'll go *talk* to people then instead."

She'd seen a therapist for a few years after moving to California. She'd lost her mom tragically and her dad was in prison. Yeah, she'd needed therapy. But she hadn't needed someone to tell her that she painted as a way to express emotions she didn't have another way to express.

She didn't have anyone she could talk to in California. Not at first, anyway. And come to think of it, she didn't really have any close friends in San Francisco even now. Work acquaintances were about it. A couple of women she knew from college. But no one she'd spill her guts to.

So she painted. Got it all out that way.

Here...well, she had people to talk to. Did her subconscious know that? Was that why she couldn't produce anything?

Well, great. If she couldn't create here, that was just another reason she couldn't stay.

She twisted her hair up into a messy bun and pulled a thin knit top over her tank. She checked her legs and the baggy white shorts she wore for paint. But how would they have gotten paint on them? It wasn't like she'd actually been painting.

Huffing out a frustrated breath, she headed downstairs and out the door, then turned left to walk the block to Ellie's. She hadn't spent a lot of time there in the evenings. She'd been going back to her grandma's house after the tours were done. They did do an evening tour three times a week, but she and Kennedy took turns being there for that. Maddie had used the time at Cora's to catch up on work in California—the two-hour time difference helped there—and to just have some time alone. She wasn't used to being with people all day long. The gallery was quiet and when she did have customers come in, it was one or two at a time. She wasn't used to constant conversation, phones ringing, people shouting and laughing and stomping. Seriously, the Landry boys all stomped and the wooden dock made it all the louder.

Maddie pulled the door open to the bar and was met, as expected, with laughter and conversation and the amazing smell of Cajun cooking. She took a deep breath and felt herself smiling as she stepped inside. She also had to admit that she loved that she was not underdressed. She loved her dresses and heels that she wore to work in San Francisco. She loved her sundresses and sandals that she wore here. But she also loved the comfort of the loose-fitting shorts and baggy top and, even more, the idea that Ellie's was a come-as-you-are kind of place. That wasn't just in regard to clothes, either. Everyone who came in here could just be who they were—with the exception of complete assholes, of course—and that was just fine.

"Maddie!"

She looked up to see Kennedy and Tori waving at her from the far end of the bar.

Maddie grinned and started in their direction. She did a quick inventory of people. Cora was probably back in the kitchen and Ellie was leaning on the end closest to the door, talking to Leo—Maddie could swear that Leo was going to have his ass permanently shaped as one of Ellie's barstools—and a guy she didn't know. Josh was next to Tori, of course, and Sawyer came through the swinging doors from the kitchen carrying a to-go box as Maddie slid up onto the stool next to Kennedy.

So everyone was accounted for.

Except Owen.

Not that she was looking for him. But didn't he eat dinner here every night? Maybe he was already done. But by the time the boats were cleaned up and everything stored and the guys headed home for showers before dinner, there was no way he'd already been here.

Maybe he was still coming over.

Her heart flipped and she rolled her eyes. Good lord. She'd seen him all day on and off. Did she feel a little flutter when she heard his voice outside the office just before he walked through the door? Maybe. But she ignored it. Did she peek out the office window at the dock more often when she knew he was out there? Possibly. But she ignored that, too. Just like she was going to ignore any flips and flutters that occurred at the idea of him walking in while she was here.

"What are you doing here?" Kennedy asked her. "Not that I'm not happy to see you, but Cora said you've been eating salads for dinner at her house." Kennedy's tone made it clear how she felt about salad. Pretty much how most people felt about liver and onions.

Maddie nodded. "I have. The pastries for breakfast and the fried food, grits, rice, cheese, etc. for lunch need to be balanced out."

Kennedy gave her a look. "It's not the spices?"

Well, she had started taking an antacid before bed. "Okay, maybe that, too."

Kennedy shook her head. "Amateur."

Maddie laughed.

"Hi, sweetie." Ellie appeared, wiping the bar in front of Maddie. "Have you eaten?"

Ellie and Cora would make a lot more money if they didn't feed all of their relations for free, but Maddie didn't comment on that. "I haven't."

Ellie's eyes lit up and Maddie smiled. These women loved nothing more than to feed the people they loved. And ply them with liquor, of course.

"What do you want?" she said. "Catfish? Gumbo?"

"Actually—" Maddie glanced at Kennedy. "Could I have a salad?" She almost winced as she said it.

Ellie sighed. "Salad is such a waste of your grandma's talents."

Maddie had to agree with that. "How about a *small* bowl of red beans and rice with it?"

Ellie nodded. "That's better, I guess. And there's always pie later."

Maddie groaned. Her grandma's pie was a definite weakness.

Ellie heard the groan and gave Maddie a wink. "I just like havin' you in here."

Maddie felt her heart warm as Ellie turned for the kitchen. That was nice. She wasn't sure when she'd been *wanted* like she was in Autre.

And that, of course, made her think of Owen as well. Because that guy wanted her. He'd pulled back the other day in the office, but he'd *wanted* her. Hell, he'd pulled back *because* he wanted her.

She understood it. She knew that if they slept together, leaving would be even harder. She knew that it would complicate things. She knew that it would mean an even bigger chunk of her heart would be staying behind in Autre. All of those things should make her want to stay far away from Owen and his magic tongue.

But it wasn't working that way.

The guy had always made her think "what the hell?" She had a very bad habit of not being rational when it came to him.

His magic tongue was *not* making her want to be any more sensible.

"Hey." Kennedy snapped her fingers in front of Maddie's nose. "You okay?"

She blinked. "Sorry. Tired, I guess."

And frustrated. By her painting. By her thoughts of "what if I stayed in Autre?" By her horniness and the fact that this town sucked away her common sense.

"Oh, good, you're not feeling sick then?" Kennedy asked.

Tori leaned in. "You're feeling sick?"

Maddie shook her head. "No. I'm fine."

Josh leaned in. "You're sure?"

"Yes, I'm sure." Maddie frowned at them all. "Do I *look* sick?" Maybe she was sick. Maybe that would explain her lack of concentration and motivation for her painting. It didn't, of course, explain the fact that she seemed to have plenty of motivation at the tour company. Or that she could concentrate just fine on all things Owen.

"You look beautiful," Tori told her.

Tori was sweet. Very sweet. She and Kennedy together were a funny combination, actually. It was like the angel and devil people sometimes pictured sitting on their shoulders. Tori was a veterinarian and almost any animal could win her affection and attention over most humans. Except Josh. Tori was pretty and kind and funny and had a tendency to overreact when she was showing affection. But that just made it so she fit in with the Landrys perfectly. It was definitely how much she loved Josh that made Maddie like her so much, though. Tori adored him. And vice versa.

"Thank you."

Kennedy was studying Maddie with one eye narrowed. Maddie gave her a questioning look. "Yes?"

"You do look beautiful," Kennedy agreed. "You look a lot more relaxed than when you got here."

"Do I?" That actually surprised her. She didn't feel more relaxed. She felt...frustrated. Except that feeling had really just started two days ago. Since Owen had wound her up and then walked away.

"You do." Josh reached for his beer. "I'm glad Owen didn't give you whatever he's got."

For just a second, Maddie's mind went dirty and thought about the things Owen had that he hadn't given her. And how much she wanted them. But then the words really sank in. "Owen's sick?"

Kennedy nodded. "At home tonight all by himself. Didn't even come in for dinner."

Maddie was up off her stool before she even thought about it. "No one's been over to check on him?"

Kennedy looked over at Tori and Josh. "I didn't go."

"Me, either," Josh said with a shrug. "But he just went home a little bit ago. And he's got all our numbers."

Tori nodded. "And I'm sure Ellie will check on him later, right?"

Maddie, Kennedy, and Josh all laughed at that. Tori looked at each of them. "No?"

Josh shook his head. "She stayed away when we were sick. Didn't want to catch it. She has to run this place and she's never missed a day for illness."

Tori's eyes widened. "Seriously?"

"She cleans this place top to bottom with some powerful stinky cleaning solution that she mixes up herself, and she bitches at anyone who comes in here with so much as a sniffle," Kennedy said.

Maddie nodded. "There were always other people around to watch us if we were sick and needed to stay home from school."

"Ninety-five percent of the time it was Callie," Kennedy said. She glanced at Tori. "Owen's mom. She did daycare for all of us from the time we were born until we were old enough to take care of ourselves after school. She was a single mom and everyone just grouped around her and figured out that they could take care of her by paying her to take care of all of us."

Tori's eyes went soft—Maddie swore she looked like those stuffed animals with the huge, round, sweet eyes—and she sighed. "Oh, that's nice."

The thought of Callie Landry made Maddie smile. Callie had been the stay-at-home mom for them all. If they were sick, she was there. She greeted them with cookies after school. She showed up for their school programs and always went along on school field trips. She was actually the complete opposite of Ellie, her mother, in nearly every way. Which amused everyone. Including Callie and Ellie.

"Anyway, if none of *you* are going to go check on Owen, I guess I will," Maddie said.

Ellie carried her food over just then.

"I'll have to take it to go, Ellie."

Ellie sighed. "You couldn't tolerate these three even long enough for a meal?"

"Your *grandson* is sick and I think someone should check on him." She hadn't noticed that Owen seemed sick but maybe it had come on suddenly. Or maybe he'd just pushed through it. It probably wouldn't be good for business for the tour guide to act ill. Maybe he'd faked it for the sake of the tourists. Owen would totally do something like that. And that made her even more concerned. How bad was it?

"He's a grown man," Ellie said, studying Maddie as she said it. "You don't think he can take care of himself? Let us know if he needs something?"

Maddie scowled at her. She actually *scowled* at Ellie Landry. "You know, I get the tough love thing and I know you actually care about all of your kids and grandkids, but once in a while it would be okay for you to show it. If you're not going to hold hands and wipe brows, you could at least, I don't know, make chicken soup or some damned thing, couldn't you?"

Ellie simply waited until Maddie was done, lifted a brow, pulled a take-out box from under the counter, and dumped Maddie's food—the salad and the rice and beans all together—into the box. She shut the lid and slid it across the bar.

Okay. Point taken. "Thanks." She grabbed the box and Ellie turned and headed back down the bar.

Maddie blew out a breath. "Shit."

"Wow," Kennedy said. "So that was—"

"Yeah, I know," Maddie snapped. "I keep telling you all that I do things and say things here I wouldn't and don't anywhere else." She sighed. "I'll apologize to her."

"Tomorrow," Josh inserted. "I'd wait 'til tomorrow."

Crap. She didn't want to insult anyone. Least of all Ellie. Her second grandmother. She ran a hand through her hair. "Okay, well, I think she'd like me to leave and I get it, so I'm going to go check on Owen."

"Yeah, good idea," Kennedy told her.

Maddie thought she saw Tori elbow Kennedy in the side, but she couldn't be sure.

"And don't worry about her too much," Kennedy said. "She's kind of pissy tonight for other reasons, too."

Maddie frowned. "Like what?"

"She and Trevor had a big fight and he's been staying at his place in New Orleans," Kennedy said.

Oh. Maddie wasn't a huge fan of Trevor's, mostly because she was a fan of Leo's and it was weird to her that Ellie and Leo weren't together. Even though they were kind of together. They saw each other every single day, fought like, well, an old married couple, and clearly cared a lot about one another. Maddie was positive they were still in love and she resented the younger man being in the way. But that was coming from a girl who'd missed their divorce and didn't know Trevor at all. She'd met him once.

"What did they fight about?"

Kennedy shot Josh a grin. He rolled his eyes.

"Trevor was trying to talk her into going to the Grand Canyon with him," Josh said. "He's never been."

"And Ellie has," Kennedy said. "Told him she was there in 1972 and she was certain it hadn't changed much."

"To which Trevor stupidly commented that he wasn't even born in 1972," Tori added.

Maddie shook her head. "That really was stupid."

"Yeah, and then he tried to talk her into going so they could do one of those mule rides to the bottom," Kennedy said. "Ellie informed him that she was surrounded by asses every day and she didn't need to go clear to Arizona to ride one."

Maddie's eyebrows shot up. "But she didn't mean that like... it sounded."

Josh nodded. "She pointed right at Leo when she said it."

"Oh, no," Maddie groaned. "That's terrible."

"Well, anyway, Trevor's been sleeping at his apartment for the past few days."

"And he's pissed about not going to the Grand Canyon?" Maddie asked.

"He's still going. With some buddies," Josh said. "Leaving next week."

Maddie didn't know if the fight would lead to a true breakup or not, but she felt bad that Ellie was upset and that she'd been a bitch to her on top of it. "I will definitely apologize tomorrow," she said. "But I might ask one of you to gauge her mood for me first."

"Good plan," Kennedy agreed.

Maddie picked up the box and started for the door. She'd just passed the end of the bar when she heard Ellie call to her and she turned back.

Ellie was holding out a bottle of whiskey and two cans of ginger ale. "This is good for sore throats and coughs," she said handing over the whiskey. "And this is good for upset stomachs." She passed Maddie the ginger ale. "And they're not bad mixed together if he's extra whiny." She shot a look at Leo. "He might have inherited that from his grandpa's side."

Maddie hugged the bottle and cans to her stomach. "So mix them for him if he's just whiny?"

"Mix them for *you* if he's whiny," Ellie said.

Maddie gave her a small smile. "Got it. Thanks." Ellie loved them all. It was very obvious. Maddie had been out of line. Owen did that to her. "I'm just..." She blew out a breath. "Protective of him."

"I know." Ellie held her gaze for a moment. "Take good care of him."

Maddie swallowed. Ellie didn't mean just tonight. She didn't mean soothing his sore throat—or whatever. She wanted Maddie to not break his heart.

She simply nodded and turned on her heel before she made any promises that she couldn't keep.

9

Once outside on the front walk, Maddie took a deep breath of sultry June Louisiana air. It frizzed her hair and made her feel like she was constantly sweating, but she'd already gotten used to it and had to admit that feeling the air touching her bare skin, almost soaking into her, felt better...or at least more real...than the air-conditioned air of the art gallery.

Wow. She was getting used to everything, adapting, even *liking* things here. Exactly as she'd feared.

She looked down at the bottle of whiskey in her arms. She could just take that back to Cora's and medicate *herself*.

But Owen was sick. That truly did concern her. She was going to go check on him because the only other person who might was Sawyer. He worried about everyone. Which probably meant that Owen, and everyone else, was keeping his illness a secret from Sawyer.

Maddie turned in the direction of Owen's house, thinking about all of the people in his life. His mom, Callie, would check on him, of course, but she was living in New Orleans with her new boyfriend, according to Kennedy. She'd apparently started dating again after Owen graduated high school. As a kid, rather than wanting Callie all to himself and scaring potential suitors off, Owen had always encouraged her to date. He'd wanted her to fall in love, not because he wanted a dad—he truly had several awesome men in his life, including her own father—but because he wanted Callie to have someone who doted on her like he saw all the other men doing with their wives. Josh and Sawyer and Kennedy's mom and dad were a true love story and it was clear even now how crazy they were about each other. Maddie's grandpa had been Cora's soul mate. Maddie and Tommy's mom and dad had been, obviously, a wild love story, too. Love—big, crazy love—was all around them here and Owen had wanted that for his mom.

But she'd never even looked. Not until he was older. Maddie smiled thinking about Callie finally finding someone. She was happy for her. And for Owen. Kennedy said Owen really liked the guy and that made Maddie happy. Owen was as protective of his mom as he was everyone else and her being happy would make him happy.

Maddie found herself standing on the sidewalk in front of Owen's house a few minutes later. Nothing was very far from anything else in Autre, and nothing Landry was very far from Ellie's at all. Maddie took a deep breath. She was just here to check on him. This wasn't anything more than that. It wasn't a booty call.

He was sick. He couldn't very well booty call with her while he was hacking and coughing. Or puking. She didn't really know what was wrong with him, but whatever it was, if it was enough to keep him from Ellie's, it was enough to keep Maddie's clothes on.

"You comin' up here or what?"

His voice came to her in the darkness and she jumped, gasping out loud. "Holy shit, you scared me."

"What are you doin' just standin' out there?"

She headed up the walk. "What are *you* doin' out here?"

"Sitting on my porch, having a beer, and enjoying the night."

She frowned as she climbed the steps to his porch. "You are?"

It was dark, more so on the porch, but she could see he was sitting on the porch swing, swaying gently, one foot crossed over his opposite knee, a beer resting on his bare foot. He was wearing athletic shorts and a T-shirt, looking completely relaxed at the end of a long work day. And not sick.

"You're feeling okay?"

"Yeah. Just enjoying some quiet time."

She propped the bottle of whisky on her hip. "You like quiet time?"

"Well, if you hadn't noticed, the airboats are kinda loud. As are the tourists. And, of course, my family. So yeah, I like quiet time once in a while."

Maddie felt herself smile. She personally loved quiet time and it was a small thing to have in common maybe, but she liked that he appreciated it, too. Or maybe it wasn't so small. In a typical day at the art gallery she had a lot of quiet, but since coming to Autre she'd found herself feeling like she *needed* it. It recharged her and then each morning she was ready to go back to the dock. That was interesting, too—in spite of the hubbub that surrounded her at Boys of the Bayou, she was ready to go every morning. Huh.

"You have to lie to people to get this quiet time?" she asked him, taking a step closer to the swing. Maybe he wasn't sick and was just wanting to be alone. Did that mean she should go?

"Nah. No one uses my front door, so I'm safe up here in the shadows," he said.

"Why don't people use your front door?"

"Usually they're bringin' food or beer or something over so

they come in through the kitchen," he said. "And everyone cuts across the yards. It's closer than comin' around front."

She'd followed the sidewalks so had naturally ended up in front, but what he said made sense.

"Everything okay?" he asked when she didn't say anything for a few seconds.

"Yeah. I—" She looked down at the stuff in her arms. "I brought you stuff."

"Stuff?"

"Yeah. Depending on what you need. I've got whiskey and ginger ale."

"What's in the box?"

"Uh...red beans and rice. And salad."

"That for me, too?"

She shook her head. It wasn't really for anyone now that it was all mixed together. "My dinner."

"So why whiskey and ginger ale?" He seemed amused.

"For your throat, cough, or stomach. Again, depending on what's going on."

He stretched an arm out along the back of the swing, angling his body more toward her. "What would be going on?"

"Kennedy and Tori said you're sick. I came to check on you. Your grandma gave me this stuff to help."

There was a beat of silence and then he chuckled softly. "Ah. Well, I guess I don't know what best treats typhoid."

Maddie froze. "Wait. What?"

"Typhoid is kind of a stomach thing from what I understand."

Typhoid. Right. He had typhoid. Supposedly. Maddie groaned. "Those bitches," she said softly. She shook her head. "So everyone knows about that? *You* know about that?"

"That you told some girls that I had a very contagious, and kind of disgusting, disease to keep them off my boat?"

He said boat with the same inflection the girls had used and Maddie felt herself frown.

"Yes, I know about it," Owen said. "I also know that you don't get typhoid from rats. That's bubonic plague. Or rabies."

"You looked it up?" she asked.

He grinned. "I just knew it."

Thankfully those girls hadn't.

"And rats? In my house? Really, Maddie?"

She tipped her head back. "Oh my God. Kennedy and Tori and Josh knew I'd come over to check on you if I thought you were actually sick. They totally played me."

He chuckled again. "Well, I'm not gonna deny that you showing up to make sure I'm okay makes me feel a lot better. But then, so did you getting jealous enough to scare some girls off."

She could argue. She could insist that it wasn't jealousy. That she'd been concerned for some other reason. But he wouldn't believe it. Because it wouldn't be true. "Why did I come up with a stupid story like that, though?" she asked. She set the box down on the floor of the porch but carried the whiskey and ginger ale to the swing. She sat next to him. "Because you make me crazy," she said, answering her own question.

"I hope you're not looking for an apology," he said, his voice a little gruffer.

She sighed. "No. It's not you. It's me."

He gave a noncommittal grunt at that.

Maddie popped the top of one of the cans of ginger ale and leaned over to pour about half of it over the edge of the porch and into the bushes. Then she unscrewed the top of the whiskey bottle and poured whiskey into the can until it was full. She swirled it, mixing the two, then took a drink.

Not bad.

"It's why I pulled you into the office the other day, too," she said after she'd swallowed. "I was hiding you from those same girls."

He didn't say anything.

"I mean, that was kind of an overreaction, too. It's not my job to decide who you flirt with or date or hook up with."

"Nope, not your job."

For some reason that made her feel worse.

"But I still like that you did it."

She glanced at him. "Yeah?"

"Mad, you're not going to find me helping you *not* be crazy about me. I like it too much."

And that made her stomach flip.

"I also insulted your grandmother tonight. Because of you."

He looked interested in that. "Oh?"

"I was pissed that no one was coming over to check on you. And I told her that it would be okay for her to show some love and affection once in a while."

He winced. "Ouch. And on top of her breaking up with Trevor."

"Yeah." Maddie sighed. "I feel like shit. I never talk to people like that."

Owen didn't actually shift position, but for some reason she felt like he was leaning closer. "I wouldn't worry too much about Ellie, if I was you," he said. "She can take it. We all do stupid shit here. Emotional shit. She does, too. Like telling Trevor she prefers *wet* heat in Louisiana to dry heat in Arizona."

Maddie groaned. "And she said it with all that innuendo?"

"Of course."

"Why? Why is she doing that?"

"I think she wants to break up with him, but doesn't realize it. Think it hit her when Leo took Caroline Trahan to dinner the other night."

"Who's Caroline Trahan?"

"Mother of a couple of friends of ours in New Orleans. It was nothing really. Caroline needed a date for some charity thing. But it ruffled Ellie up."

Maddie rolled her eyes. "Is someone going to say something to her about it? Point that out?"

Owen tipped his beer up. "Actually, we were all just talkin' earlier that maybe you could do it. Kind of like firing Cash. Easier for you to do it than us." He gave her a little smirk.

"Well, I want her back with Leo—just so you know before you send me in there."

Owen nodded. "I want her back with Leo, too."

"Yeah?"

"Of course. They belong together. So you can talk to her tomorrow."

For some reason Maddie smiled. "I can probably do that." She'd be gentle, but yeah, she could be the one who said and did things that were hard for the rest of them to say and do. She could help out that way. She'd be helping Leo, too. And Ellie, too, really.

"Anyway, Ellie isn't going to be mad at you for snapping at her about me. She gets it. We don't filter and we don't suppress things. You know that."

Maddie did. It was what had worried her about coming back here. But now it felt...freeing. Like she could just feel things and not worry. Not analyze those feelings, not redirect them, not think about what they were really about. They were just what they were. If she was frustrated, or worried, or jealous, or happy, that was just what it was.

Maddie took another drink and pushed against the floor with the toe of her shoe, making the swing move.

"I can't paint here," she said quietly after they'd rocked back and forth twice.

"What?" Owen asked.

"I can't paint here." She glanced over at him, but then

focused on the dark yard in front of them. "That's what I do. In California. I'm a painter. I run the art gallery, too, but I got into that because the gallery has been displaying my work for a couple of years."

"Wow, I didn't know that. You any good?"

She smiled, then took another drink. She nodded after she'd swallowed. "Yeah, I'm good. I've sold several pieces."

"Wow," he said again, almost as if he wasn't sure what else *to* say. "How did I not know this?"

She shrugged. "I sketched as a kid and teen but I didn't start painting until I went out there."

"I didn't even know you could draw."

She looked over at him and held his gaze this time. "When I was here, it was just a hobby. A little thing I did sometimes. Doodling almost."

"Still seems like something I should have known." He was frowning now, as if not knowing this really bothered him.

"We dated for a month," she reminded him. "Before that I was really just your friend's little sister. You wouldn't have known then. Not many people did. And when we were together, it was so short. So...crazy. We didn't spend a lot of time talking about our hobbies and stuff."

He took a deep breath. "I guess."

She frowned, thinking back now. "And you know, I probably didn't draw much when we were together."

"Oh? Why's that?"

Well, she'd been busy with other things. Like losing her virginity and burning down sheds. But she didn't say that. Because that wasn't really it—and she was just realizing it.

"Like I said, I didn't draw a lot of important things back then," she said. "But when I do—did—draw, it was always because I was emotional about something, really *feeling* something. I drew whenever I was pissed at one of my friends or after I failed a math test or when you started dating Sarah."

That clearly surprised him.

"You were emotional about that?"

"I had a huge crush on you and I was super jealous," Maddie said with a nod.

"Huh." He looked almost smug.

"Anyway, my art is always inspired by emotion and that's why it really came out when I was in California. I was feeling *a lot*—grief, anger, loss, heartbreak, guilt, fear—and it all came pouring out."

"What do you paint?" he asked.

Stupidly, Maddie felt her cheeks heat. The subject of her art was very telltale. But she blew out a breath and said, "The bayou and Autre."

Both of his eyebrows rose. "Really? All the time?"

She nodded. "The paintings are all different. It's different parts of the bayou. Sometimes the cypress trees. Sometimes the old cabin. Sometimes alligators and turtles. Sometimes it's stormy—okay, a lot of the time it's stormy—sometimes it's at night or at sunset. And I paint different perspectives on Autre. Sometimes just a building, sometimes a street, sometimes a bird's-eye view over the whole thing. Anyway, it's always about something down here. And I think that's why people in California like them—they're so different. It's actually how I met Bennett Baxter. He was in San Francisco for business and walked by the gallery, and the painting of the bayou stopped him. He came in and we started talking about the bayou and where we were both from and the tour company and everything."

Owen was just staring at her.

"You paint the bayou stormy and at night a lot," he finally said.

She nodded.

"How about the town? The same thing?"

She nodded again. "I paint the cemetery. Our old house.

And yeah, it's dark a lot." This didn't take a PhD in psychology to understand, and Maddie watched Owen work through it.

"That makes sense," he finally said.

"Does it?"

"If it's all about your emotions, then yeah," he said. "It was pretty dark and stormy down here when you left."

He meant figuratively, of course, but he got it.

"I saw a therapist when I first moved out there. She encouraged me to draw and paint to get it all out. It really worked."

"I'm glad." He voice was husky. "But fuck—" He sighed. "I hate that those are your feelings about everything here." He looked genuinely unhappy about that.

She wet her lips. "I don't know if that will keep being the case."

"What do you mean?"

"The dark and stormy stuff was obviously my last impressions. Not just the bad stuff that happened with my mom and dad, but how I felt about it all. The fear, the wanting to get away and yet missing everything like crazy once I was gone, the anger that I had to make that decision in the first place."

He watched her, gently keeping the swing going with his foot.

"But now...my impressions and feelings about everything here are a lot nicer. Brighter. Happier."

Maddie realized he'd been holding his breath when he breathed out in relief.

"I'm glad to hear that," he said with sincerity.

She was, too. Kind of. Would happy paintings of the bayou and daylight images of the little fishing village sell like the dark and stormy paintings? She didn't know.

"Is that going to ruin your rep?" he asked, as if reading her mind.

She shot him a smile. "Not sure." She focused on the floor of the porch. "I don't even know if all of this will change my painting. I haven't been able to paint anything at all since I've been here."

"Why not?"

She shrugged. "I think it's because this place, and all of the people—all of you—suck all the emotions out of me. I'm expressing them out loud and by *doing* things." She paused, frustrated even with trying to explain it. "The drawing and painting are my way of getting my feelings out," she said, starting over. "I channel it all onto the canvas. I don't talk it out. I don't...fire people, or make up stories about communicable diseases to keep girls away from my crush, or snap at a woman I care a lot about. I keep all of that kind of stuff inside and then I put it onto a canvas that will fit inside a frame." She lifted her eyes to his. "I contain it. I literally put it into a box where it just sits and doesn't change or grow. Or get out of control."

Owen's expression was hard to read. He looked concerned, which made her feel warm. He also looked pissed and she knew, somehow, it was on her behalf. Whether it was because she was feeling all of these things that he didn't like her having to feel, or because she clearly hadn't had people she could talk to or who would comfort her, she didn't know.

"Dammit, Mad," he finally said, his voice rough. "You're killing me."

"Sorry." She looked down at the can in her hands. "I shouldn't have dumped that all on you."

He reached out, wrapped his hand around the back of her neck. "Mad." He waited until she looked up at him. "Not what I meant."

There was an intensity in his eyes that she knew not many people saw from him. He was the laid-back, fun-loving playboy. He didn't do intense. At least, he didn't let people see it.

"I want to know all of this. But, babe, I can't help also wanting to fix it all. So, I'm just...struggling. I'm not a very good listener."

"Not true," she said softly.

"I'm not very good at *just* listening," he amended. "I want to *do* things."

"You can't fix this."

"I can't fix the past, no. I can't change what happened here. And seems that making new, better memories is...maybe not all good." He frowned as if confused by that.

"I didn't say that," she protested.

"But you love to paint," he said.

"I do."

"And you can't do that here. You need to control your emotions, channel them, put them someplace safe—like on a canvas."

Her throat felt tight. "That's what I've always thought, yes."

"And you still *want* to paint. You still want to make a living from your art."

"That's always been my plan," she admitted, rather than saying yes. Because lately she wasn't sure what she wanted exactly.

He just sat quietly, the swing rocking, for nearly a minute.

"So, I can let you...help you...go," he finally said.

She frowned. "Help me go?"

"You can't paint here. And you want to paint. So I can help you get back to California where things work the way you want them to."

His voice was tight and he sounded pained, but Maddie knew that he meant what he said. "How would you do that?"

"I'll talk to Sawyer and Josh," he said. "I'll tell them that I think Bennett is an okay option and we should let him buy you out."

Maddie's heart thudded at that. Owen was torn between wanting to keep the business as is, not risk bringing a stranger in, and making her happy by sending her back to California.

And he was choosing her. Her happiness. Helping her be happy in the only way he could.

She didn't know what to say. The idea of the guys getting together and deciding to let her go and bring Bennett in made her chest feel tight. She certainly didn't feel relieved. And shouldn't she? This was what she wanted. And the sooner she got back to California, the sooner she'd stop falling deeper and deeper in love here. With the town, the business, the people...Owen.

But the idea that she'd be leaving it all behind, have no further say in where they got their Snickers bars, couldn't look out for Josh and Sawyer, couldn't watch Owen's face light up every damned time he stepped onto one of the boats as if it was his first time...

Her stomach twisted a little thinking about not walking into Ellie's every day and being greeted like she was one of them, about not counting how many empty creamer tubs were in the trash each morning to judge how many cups of coffee Kennedy had had—it was safest not to talk to her before she was into her third cup—not watching kids run excitedly to the railing to look over into the water and ooh and ahh at the airboats, not listening to Tori's stories about how she'd saved a hawk with a broken wing or how her new litter of piglets was doing. Not having the chance to lean over and kiss Owen.

She was done thinking and worrying. She'd realized how good it felt to just *feel*. To just accept her emotions for what they were and to express them.

With that as her last thought, she leaned over, set her can down, and then turned to Owen. She opened her mouth, but she didn't really have anything to say. He'd figure out what was on her mind quickly, she was sure.

She shifted to one knee and then moved onto his lap, straddling him. The foot that had been propped on his knee thunked to the floor and the hand not holding his beer went to her hip. She took his face between her hands, leaned in, and kissed him.

———

SHE FELT SO FUCKING GOOD.

Owen tossed his nearly empty beer bottle over the edge of the porch so it would land on the grass and not break. He'd pick it up later. Right now, he needed both his hands free.

He gripped Maddie's hips as she wiggled on his lap, pressing the center seam of her shorts against his. Her very loose, thin, cotton shorts. They didn't mold to her ass like her denim ones did. They didn't cinch in at the waist like her sundresses did. These were just lay-around-the-house-relaxing shorts. But he'd been turned on from the second he'd watched her come to a stop at the end of his front walk. Because it wasn't about what she wore. It was just Maddie. She turned him on just by *being*. She'd come to his house to check on him. She'd snapped at his grandmother for not taking care of him. She'd just told him about her painting. All of that made it completely impossible for him to set her off his lap and out of reach the way he should. He needed to hold her, touch her, give her more good things to think about Autre. She wasn't able to paint here. She wanted to paint. So he had to let her go. That seemed obvious to him. If there was something he could do to make Maddie happy, he'd do it. Period.

But he didn't have to let her go *yet*. It wasn't like she could get on a plane yet, tonight. He hadn't talked to Sawyer and Josh yet.

So he had tonight. He had right now. And yeah, he was going to make the most of it. Saying goodbye to her was already going to suck. He might as well have this to remember when she was gone. And hope that she'd remember it, too.

His cock was already rising to the occasion and he was both

grateful and annoyed by the thin material of his athletic shorts. Lightweight was great when he was running or doing yardwork in the middle of a Louisiana summer. It was not so great when he was trying to take his time and soak up every minute of being with Maddie. He could feel every bit of her heat against him, and it made him want to rip both of their clothes off and fuck her until the swing pulled loose from the ceiling.

He tried to pull his mouth away, to talk, to say something that would slow this all down. But she wouldn't let him go. She pressed closer, squeezing him with her thighs, tightening her hold on his face. He loved that. He loved that she wanted this and was losing herself in the moment. But he wasn't going to let her rush through this. They were going to take their fucking time.

Owen slid his hand to the back of her head and grasped her bun, pulling gently. She simply moaned and kept kissing him so he tugged a little harder.

"Maddie," he said firmly as her head tipped back. "Slow down, babe."

She tried to shake her head, but with his hand in her hair she couldn't. "No. I want this. Please don't stop again."

Fuck. There was nothing he wouldn't give this woman. Walking out of the office the other day had been a freaking miracle, and it was a display of willpower that he knew he would not be able to repeat. Especially if Maddie was going to beg him for something he could give her. Something he *wanted* to give her. There were so many things that he couldn't fix for her. If she needed something in his power, he'd do whatever he could. And if what she wanted was to be kissed from head to toe and a hard, cry-his-name orgasm, he was absolutely the right guy for the job.

"I'm not stopping," he told her. "Just want to savor you."

She gripped his other wrist. "I *really* need you," she told him, looking him directly in the eyes. "Please touch me."

"Happily."

"And I want you inside me, Owen," she said, her voice soft and husky. "I really want..."

He squeezed her hip, fighting to not just flip her over his shoulder and carry her to his bed. The "inside me" had made him granite hard, and he really wanted to hold this together and make it amazing. But God, this woman grabbed him and shook him and didn't let go. His reactions to her were primal and he had to work to not just beat his chest like a caveman and strip her bare.

"Tell me what you want," he said firmly.

"You."

"More."

"I want you to make me come hard," she said. "I want you to suck my nipples like you did the other day. I want your big fingers stroking my clit until I come and then I want to ride you right here on this swing until I come again."

His heart raced and blood pounded through his body, and all he could think was *fuck, yes*. Man, he freaking loved dirty-girl Maddie. She'd always been eager and vocal before, but now she was a woman with more experience—that he didn't want to think about too hard—and she knew what she wanted. And was willing to tell him.

She blew out a breath. "I can't believe the things I can say to you. It's like I really don't have any filter down here and everything just comes out."

It was because she trusted him. That knowledge humbled him even as it turned him on. It made him harder than even the way she was grinding against him now. Because here she could be real and unfiltered because she knew that he would take care of her and not judge her and would do anything she needed him to do.

With his hand still in her hair, he brought her in and put his mouth against hers. "I fucking love it. Don't you keep one thing from me, Maddie. Tell me every single thing and I'll give it to you."

"Promise?" she asked, breathlessly.

"I swear I'll give you anything you want." He wanted nothing more.

"The other day you said it would mess things up for you...in the future. With other women."

Yeah, he'd said that. Because he'd been trying to piss her off so she'd stomp out of the office and he wouldn't completely lose his mind. And it had worked.

But he couldn't lie to her again.

"There's never been a woman that can compare to you, Maddie, and I know there never will be," he told her sincerely. "And I *have* to feel you. I have to be inside you. Even if it's just one more time."

She sucked in a little breath at that, and he was glad that the idea of it being the last time got to her, too. He hated the idea of it, but he had to be realistic. Not only had she always planned to leave and had never said anything else, now that he knew that being here was messing with her art—her passion and livelihood—and that it was actually a problem, he couldn't do anything other than find a way to help her go.

"I want you, Owen."

"I'm all yours."

She sat back on his lap and stripped her top off, followed by her tank, and then her bra.

He was grateful for the streetlight about a block down and the clear night sky that allowed the moon to beam down. He could see enough. And the dark would definitely not keep him from touching. He pulled his own shirt over his head and tossed it on top of hers on the porch. Then he cupped her breasts, thumbing the already hard nipples, plucking and rolling and enjoying every torturous moment of her grinding her sweet pussy against him.

He could easily conjure how she tasted and felt and sounded from when she'd been on the desk in the office, and his tongue tingled with the memory. He couldn't get his head between her legs out here. For one thing, there wasn't a soft enough surface to spread her out on and for another, the way she was gripping his hips with her knees, prying her off of him would be a feat.

He fucking loved that.

He took her ass in his hands and squeezed, pressing her against his aching cock.

"I don't need a lot of foreplay," she told him, rubbing her breasts against his chest. "I'm so ready."

"You wet for me, Maddie?" he asked, his voice rough. "Is your pussy dripping, just waiting for me to thrust deep?"

She moaned and tipped her head back. "Yes. Holy crap yes."

He kissed her neck, then trailed down, bending her back and sucking on one nipple then the other. She was wiggling on his lap, grinding against his cock, making the most amazing noises he'd ever heard within just a few seconds. She gripped the back of his head, holding him close as he swirled his tongue over the hard tip and then sucked hard, then added a scrape of his teeth before looking up at her.

"Lose the shorts and panties."

10

She immediately pushed off his lap and stripped. He was a little slower, his eyes locked on her and not thinking about his own shorts until she tried to climb back into his lap. He quickly shucked his shorts and boxers off, letting them drop at his feet.

Maddie froze, staring at his cock.

"Mad?" he asked, partly amused, partly curious what was going through her head.

"I don't remember it being that big."

He chuckled. "You okay?"

"Very," she said nodding, still staring at his cock and not even trying to pretend not to. "Damn, you look good sittin' there."

"I'm gonna feel even better when I'm buried deep in you." He reached out, grabbed her wrist, and pulled her forward.

She climbed up eagerly, a knee on either side of his thighs. She wrapped a hand around his shaft and squeezed.

Owen felt like she'd just squeezed all the air out of his lungs. He groaned from deep in his belly and gritted his teeth. Even her hand around him was magic. He couldn't wait to be in her mouth and pussy. Of course, sliding in and out of her sweet, hot mouth was going to have to wait. But he needed another tight grip like he needed to gulp in his next breath of air.

He moved his hand between her legs as she stroked up and down his length, nearly causing his eyes to cross. He needed to be sure she was ready for him because he wasn't sure how gentle he was going to be. He was going to give Maddie whatever she could take. And maybe just a little push beyond. He slid his middle finger into her tight heat. She clenched around him immediately, and he barely kept from throwing her on the floor and pounding into her, hard wood and possible splinters be damned.

Then she rose on her knees slightly and then lowered herself again, sliding up and down his fingers. "Owen," she mumbled softly.

She was fucking his fingers while stroking his cock. It was hot as hell, but they could do better than this. He started to shift her forward, then remembered something very important.

"Fuck. Condom," he said tightly. He wasn't sure he was going to be able to walk, but he thought he had some in the downstairs bathroom. That was a shorter tortured walk with a raging hard-on than running upstairs. "Be right back."

"I use the patch," she said. She ran her hand over her lower back just above her left butt cheek. "I'm good to go. I'm clean and..." She swallowed. "I haven't been with anyone in a long time."

He couldn't say the same, but he could for fuck sure say that he was clean and had always used a condom before. His fingers stroked around to her lower back, feeling the thin patch she'd indicated. He hadn't noticed it before, but then again, he'd been focused on her *front*. The idea of taking Maddie bare nearly made him erupt right then and there, and he had to suck in a deep breath and slowly peel her fingers away from his cock.

"Owen?" she asked, clearly confused.

He blew out the breath and said, "I'm clean. I always use protection."

"Oh." She looked hurt for a second, but then started to move back. "That's totally okay. Just tell me where they are. I'll get them."

He quickly grabbed her hips and pulled her back against him, settling her hot, wet pussy against his cock. "I mean I'm good. Sliding into you with nothing between us might make this a little shorter ride, but I promise it will be sweet."

"And hard," she said, melting into him and putting her lips to his. "Short but sweet and hard."

"Hard I can definitely do." He pressed her down against his cock as they kissed, hot and deep. Then he moved his mouth to her ear. "Take me inside, Mad."

She took a shaky breath and reached between them, again wrapping her hand around him. She stroked him once, then went up on her knees. She positioned him at her entrance and then slowly slid down.

Owen gripped her hips hard, stopping her after just an inch. He was breathing like he'd just run a mile, and he needed a second to, well, not just thrust once and fill her. She was heaven and hell at once and his need for her was shocking. He never felt this way about the women he slept with. Not ever.

"Want you to take all of me," he told her, his voice so gruff he almost didn't recognize it. "You okay?"

"So okay," she breathed. "But you are bigger."

"You're tighter."

She grinned down at him. "Well, maybe not tighter than the first time, but yeah, you kept me pretty loosened up that month."

Heat shot through him remembering. He lowered her another inch. "I don't know. You feel brand fucking new."

She took a shaky breath. "Yeah?"

"Bare. Holy shit, Maddie. You feel amazing. This is where my cock was made to be. I never want to leave."

She half-moaned, half-laughed at that. "Ditto. I mean about the you feeling amazing. I can't believe how amazing, actually."

And he wasn't even moving. Owen had to admit this was all really good for the ego.

"But I want more," she said, wiggling in his hands. "Let me have all of you."

Lord, hearing Madison Allain say stuff like that gave him a shot of adrenaline and lust like he'd never felt before. "Oh, you can have all of me," he said, feeling possessiveness grab him by the heart and squeeze. "And I want all of you."

"Yes," she hissed.

He let her drop another inch, and then Maddie spread her knees and sank onto him, taking him fully.

They both moaned at the same time and she put her forehead against his and just breathed, adjusting.

Then she tried to kill him when she started moving. She rose up and lowered herself, at first slowly, then picking up speed.

Owen just let her take over, loving the feel, of course, but also the sight of this blond goddess riding him like his cock was everything she wanted or needed in life. She circled her hips, she rocked forward and back, she rose up almost to the point of losing him, then took him again in a deep, hot stroke.

It was an image he would never forget. And would likely jerk off to about a million times.

He reached up and thumbed her nipples. He felt the resultant clench of her pussy, so he tugged, feeling a harder response and getting a moan. He grinned. "You like that."

"I love it," she admitted. She had a hand braced on his chest as she moved but as he played with her nipples, she moved both hands behind her, bracing them on his thighs. That not only arched her back, but changed the angle of her pelvis slightly, helping him hit a new sweet spot. "Oh," she groaned.

"Dammit, I should have carried you into the kitchen and put you on the table," he said, his jaw tight as he fought not to grip her hips and slam up into her. "I could have spread you out and fucked you good in there."

"You're fucking me good right here," she told him with a playful smile.

"You're fucking *me* good right here," he told her.

Her eyes widened. "I guess I am." She rotated her hips again. "And it's good?"

"So. Fucking. Good."

"Then we don't need the kitchen table."

"No, we don't. But we're gonna need a surface that doesn't move." The swing was keeping him from really being able to brace his feet and thrust. "And I'm gonna have to take over soon if I'm going to fuck you so hard you feel me tomorrow when you walk to work. And sit at the desk. And every fucking time you *move*." He gripped her hips for a moment and drove up into her hard.

She gasped and then groaned. "I want that," she told him breathlessly. "I want to feel you tomorrow."

He didn't ask if she was sure. He didn't hesitate for one damned minute. He gripped her ass and stood. She automatically wrapped her legs around his waist and, still buried deep, he walked them to the solid wall behind the swing. He put her back against the siding and immediately thrust up into her hard.

"Yes! Oh, Owen!"

"Hang on tight, Maddie."

She gripped his shoulders and he held her ass as he pounded into her. He knew she'd feel the side of his house against her back in the morning, too, but she didn't seem concerned as she gasped his name, dug her fingers into his shoulders, and gripped his dick like she was never going to let him go.

It was less than five minutes before he felt the tightening of his impending orgasm and he needed her with him.

"Maddie, I want—"

But that was as far as he got before he felt her pussy clench, her thighs tighten, and heard her cry out his name as she came.

"Fuck, yes." He let himself go then, thrusting deep and exploding.

She was limp in his arms, barely holding onto his waist with her shaky legs by the time he'd caught his breath enough to move. He kissed her forehead and let her slide down his body.

He took her face in his hands and kissed her, long and deep, then linked his fingers with hers and tugged her toward the door. "Let's go inside."

She caught her bottom lip between her teeth and looked up at him. "I can't stay. Grandma will know."

He grinned. "You still have a curfew?"

Maddie smiled. "Kind of."

He understood. Cora would assume Maddie was with him if she wasn't in her own bed, so she'd know Maddie was safe, but it might be awkward. "Well, I'm not quite done with you," he told her. "But I'll have you home before your coach turns into a pumpkin, how about that?"

She considered it for about three seconds. Then she tightened her fingers in his. "Okay."

He glanced at their clothes on the porch as he held the door open for her. He'd grab them later. After he'd taken her again. Or maybe after the third time. Or maybe he'd send her home in one of his T-shirts. He liked the idea of her sleeping in one of his shirts tonight if she couldn't sleep in his arms.

He blew out a breath at that thought. He was in so much trouble when it was time for her to go back to California.

As he followed her inside and realized she was headed upstairs to his bedroom without a single hesitation, he wondered what kind of tour boats they had in San Francisco. After all, they had a bunch of water. And tourists.

He'd miss the bayou. But he knew that he'd miss Maddie even more.

———

"I'M SORRY, a refund is out of the question."

The man leaned onto the counter on one elbow and gave her a smile. "Ah, come on. You can help us out, right? We're just a bunch of fun-loving guys trying to have a good time."

He couldn't have been more than twenty-two or three and he looked the part of the spoiled, rich frat boy. Or maybe it wasn't the matching caps with the dark blue Greek letters they all wore, so much as it was his attitude and smile that said, "Aren't I cute? Don't you want to give me my way?"

He was apparently the spokesman for the tour group that had just come back with Sawyer. After only thirty minutes. They were all pissed off.

Well, she was, too.

Maddie just met his gaze directly, without returning the smile. "Sorry, no."

He pivoted, now leaning with both elbows, focusing on her completely. "Come on, beautiful. Let's work this out."

He was good-looking. She'd give him that. He had dark brown hair and sharp green eyes and just enough scruff that it looked like he *might* be an outdoors type of guy. He was lean but muscular, but he seemed more lacrosse-team muscular than manual-labor muscular. He wore a simple blue T-shirt, gray shorts and white tennis shoes, but the shoes were just a little too clean and the T-shirt and shorts were a little too crisp to believe that he was used to being on any water craft other than a yacht. *Maybe* a sailboat. She definitely knew the type. She sold expensive pieces of art to guys like this all the time.

"Working this out will be really easy," she told him, lifting a shoulder. "You and your friends are going to turn around and leave without giving me any more shit."

His smile dimmed slightly, but he didn't seem offended so much he did challenged.

Great.

"How about half?" he asked. "That's reasonable, right? And I'll even take you to dinner tonight to show there are no hard feelings about you stealing half our money."

Ha. Right. He didn't have nearly enough of a beard or enough calluses or enough grease on his...anything...to even *begin* to get her heart pumping.

"I'm happy to know that *you're* not going to have any hard feelings," she told him.

"Well, I won't if we get our money back. At least some of it."

"No refund," she repeated.

"But, honey, we only got thirty minutes," the man said. He pointed at the brochure for the tour that was spread out between them. "This says it's supposed to be ninety."

Honey? Really? "That's because you're all drunk and your friend wouldn't stay in his seat," Maddie told him coolly. Which was a miracle because she was *fuming*.

"It doesn't say we can't drink on the boat," the guy said, shaking his head. "We were just kicking back and having some fun. We were over at the bar before the tour and *they* didn't think we were having too much. They thought we were hilarious."

Yeah, Maddie was going to have a talk with Ellie and Cora about this, too. It was one thing to serve tourists a couple of Hurricanes on a hot day before a boat tour. That was harmless. But letting people get drunk like this? That was just asking for trouble and it was something they could all absolutely control.

They could do a one or two drink maximum if a person was going on a tour. Or they could at least water the stupid drinks down. Ellie and Cora had to help out here.

Owen had told her about Sawyer's anxiety about safety on the boats and she'd been immediately worried. For Sawyer, for sure. It broke her heart that he couldn't get past what had happened to Tommy and that he felt responsible and that it was bleeding over into other things. But it was also bad for business. Him freaking out and cutting tours short was not good. Refunding all of that money was *really* not good.

But putting drunk jackasses on the boats with a guy who needed everyone to follow his direction and do things by the book was a bad idea, too.

Shit, she was going to have to talk to *Kennedy* about this, too. She needed to screen the tours she assigned to Sawyer better.

"We do not have a policy against drinking on the boats," Maddie told him. Though they *should* and that was going to be on the next partner meeting agenda. They even *served* drinks on the Bayou and Beer tour. That was stupid as hell. There needed to be some changes around here. She could be the bitch that got shit done with the Snickers bar guy *and* with the Landry boys. They wanted her here? Well, she was here. If they regretted that, it was all their own fault.

Just like these guys getting their tour cut short.

"But," she continued, "you have to follow the captain's instructions, and failure to do so will jeopardize your tour no matter your state of sobriety."

"All the reviews say this place is a big party and that you can't miss these tours. Well, we didn't get our tour."

He wasn't smiling anymore. He looked like he was getting frustrated. Seemed that maybe he wasn't used to being told no. Maddie was fine giving him this life lesson. Actions had consequences. Especially when he was messing with someone *she* cared about.

"You need to take that up with your friend. And each other. Him standing up repeatedly on the boat was putting you all at risk. We want you to have a good time, but safety always comes first. You all could have kept him in his seat. Or you could have cut him off at the bar when you saw how much he'd had. So..." She shrugged. "No refund."

"We want our money back," the guy said, his tone firm now. "My sister is a lawyer. You don't really want me to call her, do you?"

Oh, he had *not* just threatened to sic his lawyer on her.

Maddie pushed a piece of paper across the counter and pointed to the bottom third. "These are the rules and regulations you agreed to. Number five states that you will listen to and abide by everything the captain tells you above and beyond what's spelled out in numbers one through four. You signed this when you gave me your money." She slid her finger down. "And right here it says that refunds will not be granted if you fail to follow the above outlined guidelines. I guess your sister might just have to take that up with *our* attorney if she doesn't agree that your signature binds you to this agreement."

The guy squinted at the page.

She really hoped he couldn't read the nine-point font at the bottom of the page because she was totally lying about the refund policy. That wasn't in there. But it would be by the end of the day.

The guy pushed back from the counter with a sigh. "This is crap. We just wanted to see alligators."

She breathed out in relief. "You coming in here demanding your money back after you were all a bunch of asses?" Maddie asked. "Yeah, that *is* crap."

He glanced back at his friends, then looked at Maddie. "How about we leave him here and you take the rest of us out?"

Maddie's eyebrows shot up. "There is *no way* I'm babysitting your drunk friend. Forget it."

"You're being unreasonable," the guy countered. "I'm going to—"

Before she could cut him off, he was lifted off his feet and thrown into his crowd of friends. Owen turned on him, blocking Maddie's view.

"Don't even think about finishing that sentence," Owen told him.

His voice was low and angry.

Maddie's heart started pounding and adrenaline flooded her system.

She told herself it was surprise and alarm, but...it wasn't. Even in that flash of time where her brain was still processing what was going on, her body was responding.

To Owen. And his protectiveness.

Oh boy.

She should stop him. She should tell him she was okay. She should put a hand on his shoulder and calm him down. He was definitely overreacting.

But she didn't.

And that was something she knew she was going to think about—and probably regret—later.

Instead, she leaned to look at the guy on the other side of Owen's wide shoulders.

The guy had his hands up in surrender. "Hey, man, I just—"

"You're not listening to her, but you will to *me*," Owen said. "It's time for you to leave."

"I didn't mean—"

"And because you're being pushy toward *her*, that means *I'm* about two seconds away from getting *really* pushy. You should leave *now*."

Instead of moving toward the door, the guy, stupidly, opened his mouth.

Owen gave a little growl and grabbed the guy by the front of his shirt. He dragged him forward and pinned his back against the front counter. "The only thing coming out of your mouth better be an apology," he said, his nose nearly touching the other man's.

The guy's eyes were wide and he was breathing fast.

Maddie felt herself lean in to get a better look. And still she didn't say a thing. Certainly not, "Owen, stop." Not even, "Hey, calm down."

Like the guy's friends who hadn't said, "How about we drink soda now?" or "Man, sit your butt down," Maddie just let it go.

It was stupid. It encompassed about ninety-five percent of the reason she hadn't wanted to come back to Autre. But she appreciated the way Owen's biceps bulged as he held the guy, the low, gruff quality of his voice that sent tingles through her stomach—and lower—and just the pure fact that he was this pissed off because the guy had been giving her a hard time.

It wasn't as if he wouldn't defend Kennedy or Tori or really any other woman who was being harassed. But dealing with customers was part of this job, and she was sure Owen let it go a lot longer before stepping in with Kennedy. If someone made an actual threat or touched Kennedy, Owen would have reacted this same way. But the frat boy hadn't done any of that with Maddie. He was clearly entitled and used to charming his way out of trouble, but she hadn't felt threatened. Yet, here Owen was protecting her from even the *possibility* of something happening.

And it made her hot.

She'd hate herself for getting turned on by all of this later, but...well, that would be later. At the moment, she leaned onto her forearms and took it all in.

It was a stupid reaction. A dangerous addiction. One that she completely avoided by living two thousand miles away.

"I'm sorry, man. Jesus," the guy said, squirming against the counter.

"Not. To. Me," Owen said through clenched teeth. "Her."

The guy swiveled his head to look at her. "Sorry. Geez. Call your man off."

She gave him a slow smile. "Nah."

A second later she heard, "What the hell is going on?"

Josh had joined them.

He sighed when he saw Owen and the drunk. Maddie sat up, trying to seem as if she hadn't been enjoying the spectacle. Josh pushed through the crowd and grasped Owen's wrist.

"Let him go."

Owen glared at the guy and then dropped his hold.

The guy smoothed his hands over the front of his shirt. "Holy shit," he breathed.

"Get the fuck out of here," Josh told him.

He didn't even know what had happened or if Owen was right—or wrong—to have backed him up against the counter, but he was clearly on his cousin's side.

The guy stalked toward the door, his friends turning and following him out. One of them had an arm around the drunk who had caused all the trouble.

"You're getting a terrible review," the guy called over his shoulder.

"Be sure to mention the new two drink maximum rule!" Maddie yelled back.

The door slammed behind them.

"Two drink max rule?" Josh asked her.

She nodded. "It's new."

"Very."

"Sawyer shouldn't have to deal with *that*," she said. "None of you should."

"People come down here to party," Josh said. "You really think these bachelor parties and sorority girls come for the gators?"

She nodded. "I do."

He gave her a look.

She rolled her eyes. "Okay, the gators are cooler if you've had a couple drinks."

She didn't actually think they were cool at all, ever.

"It's all just fun," Josh said. "We *want* to give them a good time."

"Sawyer's having trouble," she said, glancing at Owen.

He was watching her with a strange look on his face. It was a mix of frustration and...heat. Yeah, it was. There was no mistaking that. She felt her heart flip in reaction and she had to swallow hard.

"I know," Josh said. He sighed. "But that's *our* issue. Not our customers'."

"So what are we going to do about it?" she asked.

Josh shook his head. "Wish I knew."

Maddie glanced at her computer screen, where she had the schedule for the day pulled up. Sawyer had another tour coming in two hours. It was for one of the small airboats. Only five people. A young couple and three middle-aged women.

Josh would already be out and Owen had a tour leaving at the same time. She scrolled up through the previous few days, then down into the next week.

She looked up at Owen. "Do you schedule your tours so you're out there at the same time Sawyer is?" Nearly every tour Sawyer had was at the same time Owen had one. Josh's varied a little more, with him taking most of the longer ones.

Owen nodded. "Doesn't always work, but I try to. That way I'm not too far away if something goes on. Sometimes we even stick right together and take the same route."

She felt her heart flip again, but not because of heat. It was more just...warmth. These guys were looking out for Sawyer as best they could while working to keep the business going. They couldn't afford to keep Sawyer off the boats entirely, but they were there supporting him.

"Can we do that this afternoon?" she asked, making a decision and closing the laptop lid.

"Do what?" Owen asked.

"Stick together and take the same route."

"We?"

She nodded. "I'll take Sawyer's afternoon tour. But we'll stick close to you so I don't get us lost or stuck."

"You're going to do the tour?" Josh asked. "Seriously?"

"I can drive an airboat and I know all the bayou history and stupid facts about the stupid gators," she said, not bothering to fake enthusiasm for any of it.

"You haven't driven an airboat in twelve years," Josh said. "Wait, have you?"

"No. But it's not like it's something you forget."

Airboats didn't operate like most boats. They were flat bottomed and were propelled by a huge fan mounted at the back of the boat rather than a motor. There were no parts below the surface of the water so there was no worry about getting tangled up in the grass and plants in the swampy waters or disturbing any animals that hung out there. The boats were steered by rudders and they didn't have brakes and they couldn't go in reverse, so they took a little practice, but Maddie had been riding on and driving airboats since she was a little girl. It maybe wasn't exactly like riding a bike, but she thought she could probably pull off one tour.

And if she got the fucking thing stuck, Owen would be there. He'd wade into the water and push the boat out. He might even take his shirt off for it. It would at least get wet. It was really a winning situation no matter how she looked at it.

Except for the gators. And the being outside. And the freaking heat.

What was she thinking?

"This tour should be pretty low-key for Sawyer," Josh said. "You don't need to—"

"Let her do it," Owen interrupted, looking at her as he said it. He looked almost proud of her.

That was weird.

"It'll keep her from firing anyone else. For today, at least," he added.

Josh look from Owen to Maddie. "Firing anyone else? What—"

"Never mind," Owen told him. "Let her be a part of this."

A *part* of this. Yeah, she didn't need these guys starting to think that she was getting into this. Or that she didn't hate the bayou. Because she really did.

"I just—"

"You need to go change your clothes," Owen told her, cutting off her protest.

She looked down at her dress. "I do?"

"The wind is gonna blow that skirt up for sure," Owen said with a nod. "And I'd like to limit the audience you're flashing your panties to."

"Well, you're always takin' your shirt off," she said. "Making sure the female tourists remember the ride. Maybe I can help out with that, too."

Dammit. Her voice had just gotten flirtatious. And had she just said "takin'" instead of "taking"? She had also just admitted to noticing him having his shirt off.

But he really did take his shirt off *a lot*. Sometimes he left with one on and came back without it. Twice, one of the girls on the boat—one of the very pretty, just-about-his-age girls— had returned to the dock in his shirt. Twice. In one week. Seriously, they needed cheaper Boys of the Bayou T-shirts just to keep up with Owen's apparent need to strip them off all the time.

"There's no fucking way you're 'helping out' with that."

His firm response snapped her back to the moment.

"I'm just sayin' that the girls on your tours seem to really appreciate the scenery. I don't see why—"

"*No.* Go put some clothes on," he said with a frown.

Maddie felt a little smile tugging her lips. Which sobered her quickly. She was poking him. She was trying to get him all gruff and possessive. And it was working far too easily. She did this without even thinking and she had to stop. She needed to behave. Owen reacted instinctively to her teasing. She needed to control herself. "Fine. I'll change."

"Jeans would be good," he told her.

She shook her head. "No way. I'll die of heat stroke."

"You won't die of heat stroke," he said with a little eye roll. "The wind when you're driving the boat will keep you cool, and once we stop I'll..."

She lifted a brow, waiting.

"I'll be sure we're in the shade."

She laughed. "Don't be ridiculous. You can't keep the tour in the shade."

They both knew that was true and he finally sighed. "Fine."

"What are we going to tell Sawyer?" Josh asked as Maddie came around the counter.

"Tell him..." Owen looked at her.

Really looked. As in up and down her body. And possibly picturing the whole blown-up-skirt-panty-flashing thing.

Maddie felt her nipples pebbling and she crossed her arms. Good grief. Maybe she already had heat stroke and it was making her react stupidly.

"Tell him that I bet Maddie that she'll come back from a tour with me wetter than I do," Owen said.

Maddie's eyes widened. That had definitely sounded intentionally dirty.

Josh coughed and when she glanced at him, she realized that he thought so, too.

"Okay, then," Josh said. He backed up to the door. "I'm gonna go make sure your boat's all ready to go."

"Thanks." Maddie watched him leave, then focused on Owen again. "I'll be back in a little bit."

He nodded and she started to step past him, but he caught her arm in his big hand.

Confused, she looked up at him. Her breath caught at the hot look in his eyes.

He didn't say anything. He just pulled her close and lowered his head.

The kiss took her completely by surprise. That it happened at all, but also how sweet it was. It was just his lips touching hers, lingering there as if he was just absorbing the feel of it. He took a deep breath through his nose and then straightened.

"Wha—what was that for?" She hated that she sounded discombobulated. But she was.

He just looked at her for a long moment, then let go of her arm. "You protecting Sawyer is awesome."

Maddie felt a flutter in her belly and recognized that it was even more dangerous than the heat he caused by setting the drunk customer straight. "I hate that he's having trouble," she said.

He nodded. "Me, too. And we've all been really trying to help him cope. But you're really stepping outside your comfort zone to help. That's...I don't know. Awesome. Very kissable."

"What do you do when Josh or Sawyer does something amazing?" she asked, trying to be glib.

He grinned. "Buy 'em a beer or a shot." His voice dropped a little lower. "Would you rather have a beer, Mad?"

She swallowed. "No. This works for me," she said softly.

Heat flared in his eyes, and for just a second she was sure he was going to pull her in for another kiss. And she was equally sure that she was going to plaster herself against him and kiss him back. Kissing him on his front porch in the dark was one thing. Especially after sharing and getting emotional and everything. But here? In the light of day? Where anyone could see them? As if this was perfectly natural? This was a problem. Because it felt too damned good. And yeah, natural.

But instead of kissing her, he said, "I've got you out there, you know."

She did know that and it made all of the heat swirl even faster. This *was* out of her comfort zone. She didn't like anything about this plan *except* that it might give Sawyer a break. But she was also starting to like how much Owen seemed to like that she was doing this. That was trouble. But she realized that Owen was a big part of why all of this had come to her as a solution. She didn't worry when Owen was around.

She probably should, of course. They were a dangerous combination. She made him do stuff he wouldn't normally do, take risks that he shouldn't take.

She nodded. "I know. I'll be fine with you there."

He looked like he was going to say something more but he finally just nodded. "See you on the dock in a bit."

11

———————

Maddie escaped, taking deep shaky breaths all the way up to her grandmother's house.

It didn't help. She was still jumpy and hot by the time she got back to the dock in tan shorts and a green tank top. Maybe more so. She was going out on the bayou. She hadn't been out there in over a decade. And there was nothing out there that she wanted.

She detoured through the office to grab an overpriced Boys of the Bayou cap from Shirts and Slabs —seriously the worst business name ever—grabbed a bottle of water from the cooler, and then headed out the back door.

Owen was loading his boat with a big cooler as she came around the side of the building. He was bent over, his fine ass in the khaki shorts he wore, tight and hard, his back and arm muscles bunching as he worked.

And she realized it was going to get a lot hotter.

This wasn't about the sun. This was about this man. This rugged, charming, protective man that she'd never gotten out of her system. It was one thing to climb into his lap spontaneously last night. Now they were partnering up because they were concerned about their friend and their business, and the idea that Owen was pleased by that, had *kissed* her because of that, made her hot.

Worst decision ever. Owen and gators. Terrible combination of things she should be staying the hell away from.

"You aren't doing this." Sawyer had come up behind her as she watched Owen.

She jumped and spun, feeling like she'd been caught running her hand over Owen's ass instead of just ogling it.

She looked up at the big man who was frowning down at her. This was her out. Sawyer was bossy and in charge and if he put his foot down, what was she really going to do?

She turned to face him, put her hands on her hips, and said, "Yes, I am."

Okay, apparently she was going to stand up to him.

"I don't need you to do this."

She softened her expression but kept her tone firm. "Yes, you do."

"I'm not losing it."

"I know."

"I'm going to get my shit together."

"I know."

"You hate alligators."

She shuddered. "I know."

Kennedy poked her head out of the office. "Josh is loading up your boat. Everyone is checked in."

Awesome. She forced a smile. "Great." She looked at Sawyer. "I'm doing this."

He sighed. "I'm sorry."

Maddie felt her heart ache. She'd grown up with Sawyer. He was like a second big brother. He'd never been the flirt that Josh was or the prankster Owen was. He was more serious, more responsible, even before Tommy had died. But he'd laughed and joked and given his family crap like they all did. She'd only been here for a couple of weeks and she'd already seen the huge change in him. He was grumpy and was constantly telling the guys to "knock it off" and yes, overdid the safety checks and lectures on his own boats, but she'd also caught him rechecking Owen and Josh's stuff as well.

PTSD. That had to be it. Tommy had been her brother and she missed him, but Sawyer and Tommy had been inseparable since first grade. And he'd been there when Tommy died. No one missed Tommy more than this guy.

"You're sorry about the alligators or Owen?" she asked, giving him a smile.

She was relieved when he returned it.

"Both. Equally."

She laughed. "I'll be okay."

He looked at her for a long moment, then gave her a nod. "Yeah. You will."

"We both will." Then she leaned in and gave him a quick hug before turning and heading for the boats.

Owen was watching as she approached. When she got close, he said, "All good?"

She shook her head. "No. But it's not worse. And for right now, that's probably enough."

He gave her a soft smile. "Yeah. It is." Then his grin grew. "Now let's get you out on that water."

She groaned but followed him to the boats.

The airboats were parked one in front of the other and Owen went to stand between the two.

"Hey, everybody," he greeted. "I'm Owen and this is Maddie. We're going to be your captains and tour guides today."

The tourists returned the greeting with big smiles.

"So we're gonna head out," Owen said. "The airboats are a

lot of fun but they're also pretty loud. You're gonna need to wear those to protect your ears." He pointed to the headsets that hung in front of each seat. "And you won't be able to easily talk to each other or to us until we get out to our first stop. But once we get out there, we'll stop and look around and tell you a bunch of cool stuff and you can ask us questions. We'll make a few different stops and...we'll just have a really good time."

The riders were clearly excited, and Maddie found herself smiling in spite of the fact she was about to get on an airboat. In spite of the fact she was about to *drive* an airboat.

She climbed aboard and took her position on the seat at the back of the boat. She looked around. Everything was very familiar.

"You ready?" Owen leaned in and adjusted the metal box under her seat.

She took a hold of the rudder stick with her left hand and put her right foot on the accelerator. She gripped the armrest of the tall seat with her right hand. "I think so."

Owen reached over and peeled her fingers off the cracked leather. He squeezed them, then put a bottle of water in her hand. "Hang onto this instead. It'll make your passengers less nervous."

She gave him a smile. "Do I look nervous?"

"Yep."

She was. She felt jumpy and like she was losing her battle to not get involved by the minute. But honestly, she'd only lasted about a week before she'd started to feel a part of everything. She wasn't sure why the hell she'd thought that she could fight it and win. Naiveté? A faded memory? Overestimating how much *she* had changed?

Plain old hope?

She'd hoped this would be easy.

It wasn't going to be.

"It's just a boat ride," she said.

And that was just good old lying to herself. And him.

He nodded. "Yep. Exactly."

Owen didn't believe her, either.

"So let's do it."

"Okay."

He leaned in a little further and she realized that he was only pretending to make adjustments.

"Just so you know, you're kickass and even if we only have you for a month, I'm really glad you're here."

Shocked, she stared at him as he leaned back.

He gave her a grin and a wink. "And you look fucking gorgeous right now."

Maddie knew her mouth was open as he turned and started toward the front boat. She looked gorgeous right now? Her hair was a wavy, frizzy mess from the humidity and pulled up under a cap. She'd given up on makeup days ago. She was wearing shorts and a tank top. And she no doubt looked completely uncomfortable—physically and emotionally.

Gorgeous? If so, she'd been trying way too hard for over a decade.

She watched Owen climb aboard his boat and give everyone a huge smile. He said something to the kids sitting on the edges and they laughed. He leaned in and shook an older man's hand and then he went down on one knee in front of the man's wife. She had white hair and there appeared to be a cane leaning against the bench seat next to her. Maddie couldn't hear what they were saying, but she saw Owen put a hand over his heart with a smile that was less bright and charming and more sincere and touched. The woman reached up and patted his cheek, and Maddie, even without knowing what they were saying, felt her heart flip.

He was such a good guy.

It wasn't that it was a huge revelation. Of course he was a good guy.

It didn't surprise her that he was good with kids. He was basically a big kid himself. It didn't surprise her that he was good with guys—and women—his own age. He'd been a flirt and a good old boy his whole life. It didn't surprise her that he was good with older people. He'd grown up laughing and loving with a whole group of the older generation that, while maybe not typical in a lot of ways, had instilled a respect and affection that was clear now.

Crap.

Not only was she already sucked in with the business and worrying about Sawyer, but her attraction to Owen was only getting stronger. He was a man now. He ran a business, he was a wonderful son and grandson, he was a loyal friend, really practically a brother to Sawyer and Josh, and Tommy.

And he was still protective of her, but he was good with her doing this. He was encouraging her. He was going to be there for her, in case she needed him, but he was letting her take the controls here. Literally.

And, this sounded stupid even in her head, but he liked her. He liked how she was handling the Boys of the Bayou business and he liked how she was taking care of the guys. He wasn't a bit jealous. In fact, it felt like they were partners in looking out for Josh and, especially, Sawyer.

It wasn't as if he hadn't liked her before. In high school, he'd liked her. Even before that, before they were a couple, he'd *liked* her. They'd known each other all their lives. Their families spent almost all their time together. There had been nothing really not to like.

But, once they were a couple, in the short time they were together, they'd had a lot of...heat. When they weren't taking ex-girlfriend's cars apart and rebuilding burned down sheds, they were having sex. A lot of sex. It had been clumsy but also enthusiastic and awash with teen hormones and often the risk of getting caught, and a feeling that they'd each won the other's heart away from someone else.

So yes, he'd liked her. But they hadn't really gotten around to sharing deep emotions—regrets and grief—or respect.

In two weeks, they'd gotten to all of that.

He stretched to his feet and looked back at her. She gave him a thumbs-up. She needed him to know she was okay here. He didn't need to worry about her.

In part because when he worried about her, her panties got a little warm.

In part because if he was worried about her, he might not pay attention out there and he might do something dumb.

Owen climbed into his seat.

"Okay, everybody, headsets," Maddie called out as she pulled hers on over her ears.

They both started the boats and pulled out.

Her palms were sweating, her heart pounding, but going straight ahead wasn't really a problem in an airboat in a decent amount of water.

When they got past the docks and out to the wider part of the waterway, Owen hung back and let her pull up next to his boat.

He shouted something to her and pointed to the floor.

She shook her head, indicating she didn't understand.

"Stand on it!" he shouted.

Well, she read his lips anyway.

Yeah, yeah. Okay. She gave a little sigh. Airboats needed a lot of gas so that the boat lifted up and skimmed over the top of the water. The slower they went, the deeper into the water they sunk and the more the boat dragged. She'd been holding back. This was her first time on the water in twelve years. She thought she should ease into it.

But then she looked over at Owen's huge grin, the wind mussing his hair, his arms flexing as he steered the boat. A little thrill shot through her. She pressed on the accelerator and the fan sped up, pushing the boat forward.

"Whoo-hoo!"

She didn't know if she'd heard Owen's cheer or just saw it, but she did feel the adrenaline dump into her blood stream. She didn't love the heat and humidity and the critters out here, but it was really hard to not feel good with the wind whipping past her face, the power of the boat under her, and the hot guy grinning at her like she'd just made him the happiest man in the world.

Damn, she was in trouble.

Owen pulled back in front and she followed him down the waterway. Her heart rate was already up, but her heart kicked hard when he turned down the first narrow bend. She took a deep breath and eased up on the accelerator, then took another one and pressed harder, moving the rudders, and praying a little. The boat jerked hard and she bumped into the thick mess of water hyacinth, but she got it straightened out and after a few minutes, she relaxed and eased into driving.

It only took her three more turns to realize that Owen was leading them on a meandering path way longer than necessary to get to the first stopping point.

He was giving her a chance to practice and get comfortable.

Man, it's going to be so hard to avoid kissing him later.

The thought should have surprised her. But it didn't. Not even a little.

Owen finally turned them into an area that was a little like a cul-de-sac on a street, with a rounded dead end ahead that would require them to turn around to get out. He let up on his accelerator, letting his boat drift to a stop about twenty yards from the bank. Maddie followed, pulling up a few feet from him.

He stood up and moved to the front of the boat, addressing the group. He told them about the vegetation they were seeing and some of the animals and birds they'd seen on the way down. Then he turned and pointed to the shoreline.

"And now you get to meet a few of my friends," he said. "There are three gators that live over in this area. Alligators are very territorial, so they like to be alone, but in this case old Fred is the alpha and he lets Wilma and Betty live over here, too." He pointed and everyone leaned to look. "Right over there was where Wilma built her nest." There was a mound of dirt and grass about ten yards up the bank. "She's got some eggs in there right now." He looked back at the kids on the boat. "Alligators lay eggs like birds, but they don't sit on 'em like chickens. She covers 'em up with mud and grass and then parks herself there to guard them. Raccoons, some birds, even other alligators love gator eggs." Owen pivoted just slightly and said, "And look right there."

There were several gasps and some pointing, and many of the tourists pulled out their phones to record when they spotted the alligator that was basking on the mud at the edge of the water. The thing was eight feet long and blended perfectly into the dirt and weeds. If you didn't know she was there, you wouldn't see her.

Maddie shuddered. That was probably Wilma since she was near where Owen had pointed out the nest, but Maddie didn't care. It was an alligator. That's all she needed to know.

On one hand, this was good. Tourists took these tours to see alligators. That was just a fact. They were happier and gave better reviews when they saw one.

It did make Maddie wonder where Fred was, though. If this was his territory, he wouldn't be far.

Owen continued explaining about how baby alligators make a high-pitched noise when they're ready to hatch and how the mom then uncovers them and helps them and how the temperature of the eggs while they were in the nest determined the sex of the babies.

The kids were fascinated, and Maddie found herself hanging on his every word, too. Not because of what he was saying—alligators were huge, nasty lizards that gave her the heebie-jeebies—but because he looked so freaking hot doing this. It wasn't the June sun beating down—and it was very much beating down—but because he was so into this. He loved making the kids' eyes go wide, he loved showing people around his beloved bayou, he loved being out here on the water, in the sunshine and fresh air.

She was being turned on by watching Owen talk about alligators.

She was in *so* much trouble.

"I see another mound over there," Owen said pointing at a spot a few yards in the other direction. "I'm gonna go check it out and see if maybe Betty has some eggs, too."

He gave everyone a grin and promptly stripped off his shirt.

Maddie blamed that for the fact that it took several seconds to process what he'd just said. It sunk in about the time that Owen turned and jumped into the water.

She was up and out of her seat immediately. As was everyone else. Every person on both boats got on their feet, watching Owen wade toward the shore. The water hit him just above the waistband of his shorts, then slowly dropped as he got closer to the land.

Holy shit. What the hell was he doing?

There were fucking alligators in that water. Not just that, but one female who definitely had a nest to protect and possibly a second.

Female alligators with nests were nasty. All alligators were nasty in Maddie's opinion, but females with babies were especially so.

She realized she was holding her breath while the rest of the people on the boat were filming and gasping and talking about how cool this was and questioning if he was crazy.

Yes, yes he was.

That was a fact. Owen took risks. Period. He liked to go hard, he loved the adrenaline rush. And he was cocky. These guys all thought they knew everything about the bayou.

Well, her brother had grown up on these waters. And he'd died here.

Suddenly Maddie felt a cold wave wash through her body. She gripped the arm of her chair, watching Owen pull himself through the water. She scanned the area. Where was Fred? Generally alligators were like other wild animals in that they preferred to avoid humans when possible. The Landry boys had been swimming and boating in these waters all their lives and they knew what to look out for. She kept repeating that to herself. But her brain wouldn't stop staying, "So did Tommy."

Then someone shouted, "Oh my God, she's in the water!" and Maddie swung around to see Wilma ease herself into the water.

And turn toward Owen.

Maddie suddenly felt like she was going to puke.

She couldn't lose him. She wouldn't survive that. There was so much she needed to say and do. Why the *fuck* was he out here risking his life like this when she was here now and they'd barely gotten started again?

Owen pulled himself up onto the bank and bent some of the tall reeds and grass to one side. He turned to the boat and gave them all a big thumbs-up. He'd found another nest?

Who the hell cared? So the stupid alligators were laying eggs. That just meant *more* stupid alligators. She watched, her body frozen, her mind whirling as Wilma headed for where Owen was. She saw him, Maddie was sure of it. That alligator was on her way over there *because* Owen was there.

She looked around. There were no trees for Owen to climb. That was a great go-to move. The ground he was on was marshland. Running away from Wilma/Betty/whoever-the-fuck-she-was—the second-best option to get away from a gator—wasn't going to work.

Shit, shit, shit.

Maddie glanced down at her shoes. She'd read about a woman who had scared an alligator off by slapping her flip-flops together. Would Converse work the same way?

"Oh my God, the alligator is getting so close!" someone yelled.

Maddie felt like her heart had frozen and she tried to pull in a deep breath.

Wilma was enough of a threat. But if that was Betty and that was her nest...

"There's another one!" one of the kids shouted, pointing.

Maddie felt a buzzing in her ears as she spotted the head and snout of another alligator also swimming in Owen's direction.

Holy shit, was that Fred? Did it matter? Females were smaller than males, but they were also vicious predators that didn't really give a fuck if Owen was a wild hog or just a stupid guy strutting for his tourists.

That was it.

Maddie swung around and located the metal box under her seat. She knew what was in there, and she knew how to use it. Maybe she hadn't actually done it in a long time, but she was going to have to hope that it was like driving an airboat.

She unlocked the box and within two minutes, even with hands shaking badly, she swung around holding a loaded rifle. She hadn't held a gun in years and her stomach twisted as she looked down at it. She couldn't shoot this thing. But then she glanced over to where Owen stood and the alligator that was within ten feet of him, and she lifted the gun.

One of her passengers noticed and gasped. Her husband turned. "Hey, what the hell?"

Maddie shook her head. "It's fine. I know what I'm doing."

"You have a *gun*!"

That caused people in Owen's boat to swing around. One of the women screamed. One ducked, covering her head with her hands.

Maddie would have rolled her eyes, if she hadn't been trying to keep her hands steady and her focus on the alligators that were getting closer to Owen.

But Owen's attention was on Maddie. And the gun.

"What are you doing?" he asked. He seemed genuinely confused.

"Gators. Two of them," she said.

"Yeah, I know. They live here. I see them every day."

"They're coming *at* you."

Owen turned to face the boat fully, his hands lifted. "Maddie, you know how this goes. They know I've got food. That's why they're coming over. Put the gun down."

"Just...come back to the boat," she told him, not really hearing what he was saying. Her eyes were firmly on the alligator to his right. "Then I will."

"It's okay," he said. "Everything's okay."

Her arms were shaking now, too, and she knew it was fear and adrenaline, but she told herself it was because she hadn't held a heavy gun in a long time. Or any gun in a long time. Did she want to shoot the alligators? Of course not. For one thing, the best way to kill an alligator was to shoot it right in the head. Which meant getting way closer to the damned thing than she ever wanted to be. But could shooting in the water *near* one scare it off? Sure. Theoretically.

"Owen," she said, noting that her voice was as wobbly as her arms now. "Get back in the fucking boat. *Now*."

Her eyes were starting to sting, but she had to keep them clear to see what she was doing.

One of the alligators was now only two feet away from Owen. She knew that the danger zone for an alligator strike was about half its body length straight in front and ninety degrees to either side. This was the kind of stuff she and the boys had all been taught by their dads and grandpas growing up down here. She'd never been a big hunter but the boys had, and Leo had insisted she and Kennedy learn to shoot and all the basic hunting safety the boys had to learn.

She was very grateful to Leo right now.

She just really prayed that she didn't accidentally shoot his grandson.

Maddie lifted the gun, rested the butt against her shoulder, and lined it up with the ground to the left of the alligator that was closest.

Oh God, I can't do this.

"Ah! That alligator is right by him!" one of the little girls yelled, clearly caught up in the moment.

Maddie's mouth went dry as the alligator put its front feet up on the mud less than half its body length away from Owen.

Fuck, fuck, fuck.

Maddie took a deep breath, pressed the safety, and then pulled the trigger.

The gun jumped, kicking into her shoulder and taking her breath. The blast was loud, everyone screamed, there was a splash, but Maddie instantly zeroed in on Owen.

Who was striding toward her through the water, his face stormy.

"Oh my God, did I shoot you?" she asked as he climbed aboard her boat and moved toward her.

He grabbed the gun from her in one hand and wrapped his other around her wrist, holding her in place. She didn't care. She ran her eyes over him, followed by her free hand.

"Are you all right? I didn't hit you?" Her palm ran over his shoulders, his chest, down his ribs, to his hip.

"Jesus Christ, Mad," he nearly growled. "No you didn't fucking shoot me, but you could have."

Her eyes widened. "I was aiming for the dirt! I just wanted to scare it!"

"Well you—"

His words broke off as she ran her hand over his abs, still, maybe stupidly, looking for injuries. Gunshot wounds, but also alligator bite marks.

Owen swore under his breath. He quickly unloaded the gun and bent to store it, with her hands running over him the entire time. Then he grabbed both her wrists, pulling her hands away. "You gotta stop," he said, his voice lower, but gruff. "I'm okay."

"They were coming right for you." Her voice sounded like a whisper but she didn't have enough air to put behind them.

"They always come to me." He blew out a breath. "You know how this goes. We feed them so they'll come up to the boats for the tourists."

She shook her head. "I didn't know that!"

He frowned. "Well, you *should* have. We've been doing this forever. The gators get used to the boats and to us coming out here with food. They swim up, but they wouldn't attack. They know us."

She took a deep breath and let his words sink in. They fed the alligators. Every day. The animals were used to them by now.

One of the women in the boat asked, "They *know* you?"

Owen glanced over. "They do." He shrugged. "They know my voice. And my smell."

"Come on."

"Seriously. There's a big old gator down the way that knows my partner, Sawyer. He won't come out for me, but he always shows himself for Sawyer's boats."

"You're telling me that you've trained these alligators?" one of the men asked.

Maddie let them talk around her, breathing deep. The

adrenaline was dissipating a bit now that he was standing here right in front of her and was fine.

"Kind of. Not exactly, but like I said, they recognize me, they know I have food for them. We do it for you all," he said to the tourists. "We can get them up close for you this way."

Yeah, she should have known that. She *had* known that. She'd just forgotten because it was Owen, and seeing even a *hint* of danger near him obliterated any rational thought.

Maddie swallowed, letting all of that sink in. "I'm really sorry I overreacted."

Owen's attention was immediately back on her. "I should have gone over it with you ahead of the tour. I'm sorry I didn't."

Maddie dragged in a huge breath and, looking into his eyes, realized that she'd screwed up big time. She'd pulled a *gun* out. And *shot it*.

Holy crap.

Her eyes started to burn and she had to swallow hard. "You jerk. You scared the shit out of me."

He nodded, his expression a little pained. "I know. I really am sorry. I can't imagine how I'd feel if I thought you were in danger like that. I'd probably kill the thing with my bare hands."

The intensity in his tone and eyes along with his words made the rest of her fear disappear. She wanted to kiss him. She wanted to *feel* him. His big, strong, hot body that was completely healthy and whole and uninjured. Well, she'd already made an ass of herself.

She went up on tiptoe, gripped his shoulders, and kissed him. And it wasn't a quick brush of her lips. It was a full-on, I-want-to-consume-you-right-here-and-now kiss with lips and tongues. Yes, plural. Because Owen didn't act even mildly surprised. He gripped her hips, pressed her against him, and kissed her back.

It took almost a minute, but eventually the wave of desperation and fear faded and she was able to let him go.

He stared down at her as she settled back onto her flat feet, his hands still gripped the denim at her hips. Finally he gave her a little nod. "You okay now?"

"Better, anyway."

He took a deep breath and let her go, stepping back.

And revealing two airboats full of people gawking at them. Even the kids.

Maddie's cheeks got hot and she gave everyone a smile. "Sorry, folks. I might have freaked out there a little bit."

"A little bit?" the guy in her boat asked.

She nodded. "Yeah. Sorry. It's been a little while since I've been out here."

"Looks like it's been a while since she did other things, too," the woman next to him muttered.

Well, she wasn't wrong. But Maddie felt her cheeks turn redder thinking about how she'd just forgotten everything else and kissed Owen like she was crazy about him and was ready to strip his clothes off right here and now.

Again, the woman wasn't wrong.

"You don't even know what you're doing?" the guy asked.

"I know..." God, she really didn't know what she was doing. Not out here. Not with the fucking alligators. Not with Owen. "I'm sorry," she said again. "Truly."

The guy didn't look convinced.

"Hey, it's all good," Owen said, moving toward the front of the boat. "We'll get you guys back to the dock." He jumped from Maddie's boat to his. The resultant rocking made the kids squeal and laugh. "I'll tell you what," he said to them as he got up on his seat. "You had something happen on this trip that doesn't usually happen. You've got a unique story."

"You can say that again," Maddie's tourist muttered.

She sighed. She'd apologized. This was minor compared to

some of her freak-outs. She could tell him about the shed, but she wasn't sure that would really help the situation.

Everyone watched as Owen opened the big blue cooler he had on board and pulled out raw chicken quarters.

"They're not cute, cuddly pets," he said as Wilma and Betty started for the boat. "But like any animal, they become a little tamer around humans when they're fed and when we respect their territory."

The alligators got closer and he tossed them each a hunk of chicken.

Everyone oohed and awed as the alligators ate. Owen tossed them more and gave everyone a few more fun facts about gators in general.

When the chicken was gone, Owen turned back. "Okay, who's got questions?"

He answered a few—probably questions he got on every tour—and then he got them all back into their headsets.

When they got back to the dock, Kennedy and Josh were there with complimentary water, soda, and sports drinks for the passengers. There was also no sign of the alligator stickers they usually gave out to the kids after they took a ride.

Josh helped dock her boat and after everyone had disembarked, she asked, "Owen texted and said you all needed to do something to smooth the feathers of the people who thought I was about to shoot them?"

He grinned. "Something like that."

"And we're avoiding giving out the stickers so that later, when their dad goes to write a review of the tour on a travel site, he doesn't look across the table, see the alligator on the sticker, and get all riled up again?"

"Exactly."

She blew out a breath. "That was bad."

"Owen thought it was great."

She glanced over to where he was talking to the older couple after having helped the woman off the boat. "Yeah?"

"He's been wondering when you're going to do something really crazy for him."

Her heart thumped at that. "Crazier than inventing a typhoid fever outbreak?"

He laughed. "Yep."

It was a freaking miracle she hadn't done something stupider because of Owen before this and they all knew it. "I kind of thought the shed would carry me for a while."

Josh chuckled. "Guess today was the expiration date." He gave her a little side hug. "Go on and get out of here. We've got this."

"This?"

"The complaints."

She groaned.

But she did make her way to the office. She just wanted to shut the door between her and everyone else for a little while so she could breathe and figure out what the hell was going on.

No, she knew what was going on. She was losing her mind. As usual in Autre. But she'd pulled a *gun* today. That was next level.

Maddie made it around the far side of the building and into the office, before she really started shaking. She closed the door and leaned back against it.

The chances of her shooting anyone on the boats had been slim. She'd shot a rifle before. She knew basically what she was doing and the barrel had been pointed away from them.

But it had been pointed at Owen.

Not *at* Owen, but near him. And she hadn't shot a gun in over a decade. She easily could have missed her target—the dirt next to Wilma/ Betty/ whoever-the-fuck-that-was—and shot Owen.

She dragged in a deep breath as her chest tightened. What the *fuck* had she been thinking?

Someone turned the knob, and the door she was leaning against pushed inward. She stumbled forward, barely missing knocking a huge stack of papers to the floor, and turned as Owen came through the door. He didn't look surprised to find her, which meant he'd come looking for her. He wasn't smiling, but he didn't look mad, either.

He shut the door behind him firmly and locked it.

12

Maddie felt her heart start pounding without even knowing exactly why.

He took the two steps to where she stood, grabbed her elbow, and pulled her in.

She went into his arms gratefully. As his arms wrapped around her, she started shaking. Adrenaline coursed through her and she felt jumpy and like crying and like she needed to push him away even as she slipped her arms around him and squeezed.

His arms tightened around her and she felt him kiss the top of her head.

And the tears started.

He just held her as she cried. She let it all out. The fear, the embarrassment, the confusion, the happiness.

Because, yeah, there was happiness mixed in there, too. She wasn't proud of her reaction. She hadn't used her head and had gone on pure emotion. That was stupid. It was also something she hadn't done in over a decade. Everything she did now was controlled and planned and rational.

Not here. Not with this guy. The guy she was clinging to like he was a life preserver and she was in the middle of the ocean, at risk of drowning.

She just cried, her hands gripping the back of Owen's shirt, for a few minutes.

He rubbed his big hand up and down her back and talked to her in a low, soothing voice. "You're okay." "I've got you." "It's all okay." "I'm right here."

And slowly the fear and humiliation started to fade, and in its place was a warmth—she hadn't been hugged and comforted since, well, he'd done it on the dock the first night she was in town. Before that, it had been a very, very long time. He was solid and warm, his heartbeat strong, his hold on her tight and secure. He made her feel safe. He made her feel like someone had her back. They all did. She'd freaked out, screwed up in front of customers, and yet her partners had just met her on the dock and worked on diffusing the situation as best they could, giving her a chance to get it together.

Partners.

They were her partners. But in more than business. She had no trouble believing that any of them would go out of their comfort zone for her if needed.

Her tears stopped, but she didn't let go of Owen. In fact, she cuddled in closer. God, he was so...*real*. He smelled like sunshine and dirt. He was hot, not just body temperature but from being outside in the sun for the past hour, too. He was hard, the planes of his muscles firm against her, and she knew that he could pick her up and carry her out of here if he wanted to. If she asked him to.

She really wanted to ask him to.

Of course, if she said, "Will you carry me out of here?" she'd also add, "and up to your bedroom?"

He'd do it. She knew that, too. They were balancing on the edge of tipping over into hot, crazy, this-is-going-to-tear-up-my-heart-but-I-want-it-anyway.

Part of her attraction was to his huge heart. The one beating a little fast against her ear, but also the one that allowed him to love big and completely. His family could do anything and he'd still be there for them. If someone said, "Hey, can you help me bury a body?", he'd show up with a shovel. And she knew that extended to her as well.

The arousal that was always coursing through her just below the surface when Owen was around grew stronger as the fear, mortification, and the muddled feelings faded. With a deep breath, she pulled back and looked up at him.

He met her eyes.

They just looked at each other for a moment. Then his hands moved up to cup her face.

"I didn't think about Tommy," he said gruffly. "I'm so sorry. That was part of it, right?"

She nodded. "Yeah. But I overreacted."

"No." He blew out a breath. "Fuck. I'm so used to going out there and doing that, it didn't even occur to me that you might think of Tommy. Damn, that was really stupid of me."

Maddie reached up and squeezed his wrists. "It's okay. It really is. And yes, I did think of him, too, but that was really mostly about *you*."

He took a breath, then nodded. "Okay."

"Are *you* okay?" she asked.

He gave her a half smile. "Why wouldn't I be okay?"

"Not scared of me?"

He glanced around. "If you left that Remington on board the boat, then I'm not worried."

She gave a small laugh, then groaned. "Oh my God, Owen, I'm so sorry."

He focused on her. "For?"

Her eyebrows went up. "For almost shooting you!"

"Oh, that." He shrugged.

"Oh, that?" she repeated.

"Would have been an accident.'"

She took a breath. "Okay, I'm sorry for not thinking about the fact that you know what you're doing out there. And that you know a lot more than I do about everything. I just..."

"You just what?"

Maddie wet her lips. "I guess you still make me crazy."

Something flickered in his eyes. Then he gave her a slow grin. "Well, Mad, I hate to tell you but, it's not me. It's you."

———

OWEN LET her go as Maddie blinked, then frowned. "What do you mean?"

He wouldn't deny that his heart had been pounding hard out on the bayou. Not so much from looking at the wrong end of a rifle barrel, but because of the sheer panic he'd seen in Maddie. He should have let her in on everything from where they'd be pulling up to stop, to the fact that Wilma and Betty and even Fred were going to be around and were not a threat.

Sure, they were wild animals. Alligators. It wasn't like he was going to bring one home to curl up on the foot of his bed. But he knew as long as he treated them with care, and brought them chicken, he was okay.

But he should have told her that. Honestly, he had not been expecting her reaction. He'd thought she'd remember how this all went. And no, he hadn't thought about Tommy. What had happened to Tommy was an anomaly. An accident. He thought about Tommy every single day and missed him, but what had happened with the shark didn't keep Owen off the water or out of the bayou.

Maddie hated alligators, he knew. He also knew that she was a pretty damned good shot, but hated guns. She'd gone out hunting with them a few times as a young teen, but she hadn't really enjoyed it. It hadn't occurred to him for one second that she might pull a gun out to protect him. That was so not in character that he was still having a hard time believing she'd done it.

But damn, she'd looked hot standing there, her hair blowing in the wind, her feet braced in the boat, that gun at her shoulder. Bayou girl indeed. Not because she could handle a gun, but because she was willing to do whatever she needed to do. Did she like guns? No. Was she willing to put her discomfort aside to confront a problem? Absolutely.

That made her hot.

She fit in here. She might not think so. She didn't like being out in the heat and humidity and dealing with the critters. But she would do it if she had to. *That* made her one of them.

And yes, he wanted her to be crazy about him.

He did. He couldn't deny it. Being a reason that Maddie would get tough and defensive and take a risk gave him a thrill.

But over the past several days he was realizing that her "crazy" had matured.

He crossed to the file cabinet and pulled the bottle of moonshine out of the bottom drawer. He looked around, realized that the cups hadn't gotten returned after they'd been washed, and unscrewed the top.

"What I mean," he said, "is that it's not *me* making you crazy."

"Oh, I think you're wrong," she said.

He lifted the jar to his lips and took a swig. Then held it out to her. "Take the edge off."

"You don't think what happened out there was crazy?"

He wiggled the bottle, sloshing the moonshine around. "Sure. But it wasn't because of me."

She stepped forward and took the jar. "It was completely because of you."

He leaned back against the desk behind him and watched her take a little swig from the bottle.

"It's you. You're protective," he said. "Of the people you care about. *All* of the people you care about."

She frowned and shook her head. "But I'm not *crazy* with anyone but you."

"You lied to that girl to get her away from Josh." He grinned. "You got all worked up about Snickers bars for the business. You went out on that airboat in the first place because of Sawyer."

Maddie took another swing of moonshine, then handed it back. She took a breath and said, "Yes, I did all of that. And maybe my reaction was a little...much...in those cases. *But,*" she went on. "All of those things made sense. They were *actually* problems to solve."

Owen recapped the bottle and set it to the side. He braced his hands on either side of his hips. His heart was pounding and she hadn't even said the rest of what she was thinking.

"And?" he asked.

"The alligator wasn't an actual problem."

"You didn't know that, though."

She shook her head. "I would have. If I'd thought about it. If I'd actually taken a breath and truly thought it through. Like I did with everyone else. The business decisions and Sawyer's situation were based on facts. The girl with Josh..." She paused and grinned. "That was a little more spontaneous, but it was pretty minor overall. And I did weigh options and decided to do those things." She sobered and met his gaze directly. "With you —the typhoid, snapping at Ellie, all of that today was pure emotion. Adrenaline. My heart pumping. I reacted because I saw you there in potential danger and...I *couldn't* think. I just did it. All I could focus on was you."

Fuck yes. Owen curled his fingers into the edge of the desk.

That was what he'd wanted. They'd been out of control as teens and it had been fun and wild and a thrill. That's how they'd thought love was supposed to be.

And it was.

In a way, anyway. Guns were a lot. Burning down sheds was a lot. But the emotion behind it? That was spot-on. Did he want a girl who would shoot a gator for him? Damn right. Especially when it was way out of her comfort zone to do so.

"When you were sixteen, you concentrated all of that protectiveness and love on me," he said, his voice gruff. "And I loved it. Encouraged it. I liked being the center of your universe and the focus of all your emotions. But now..." He cleared his throat. "You've grown up. You have more self-control. But you still have all of that love and fierceness in you. You're just spreading it around now. To all the people that matter. And that's awesome."

It was also why she couldn't paint here, though.

He couldn't avoid that thought. That realization. That's what tore him up about it all. Seeing her willing to protect and defend the people she loved...the people they both loved...and seeing that bayou girl inside her coming out made him want her with an intensity he hadn't even felt as a hormonal teenager. But now he knew that having that outlet for her emotions was taking away her drive to paint. He hadn't even known she could draw, not to mention paint pieces that other people would buy and hang on their walls, and now he was faced with the truth that the things that made her happy were very different than they had been twelve years ago.

If she wasn't fully happy about being that girl—if she didn't like being tough and protective and would prefer to paint out all her feelings instead—he couldn't be fully happy, either.

And that was the moment when he knew he was falling in love with her again. Because Maddie being happy was more important than Maddie being happy in Autre.

Or maybe he was *still* in love with her, but he'd finally grown up enough to realize what that really meant. Her happiness, whatever that looked like, was more important than what he wanted.

She swallowed hard. "It's Autre. It's in the air or something. I'm not like this in California."

Yep, that's exactly what he'd been afraid of.

Owen pushed up off the desk. "No. It's *you*. It's who you are. All that amazing passion inside of you..." He stuffed his hands in his pockets. "You just don't let yourself get close enough to anyone in California to feel that way about them. Here...you can't help it. We're a part of you."

That was going to make her turn around and storm out or—

Maddie took a huge step forward, grabbed the front of his T-shirt, and pulled him close. And kissed him.

She tipped her head immediately so that their mouths matched up fully, and she was the one to open first and lick along his lower lip.

Owen groaned, gripping her hips and bringing her up against him fully, happily returning every stroke of her tongue. Her little moan made sparks of need trip along his nerve endings and he needed *more*.

He turned her and backed her up, then lifted her up to sit on the edge of the desk. Papers went fluttering to the floor, but neither of them paused for even an instant.

Her hands slipped under the bottom of his shirt and slid up over his abs to his chest, sucking his breath from his lungs. She'd run her hands over him like this on the boat, too. As if she needed to convince herself that he was real and fine.

Well, he was *very* fine right now. He slid his hands under the back of her shirt and glided up over her smooth, hot skin to her shoulder blades, pressing her close.

She was wearing a bra but he felt her nipples hard against his chest, and his cock ached feeling how much she wanted this.

Maddie's fingers curled into his sides as if holding on and she wiggled her hips, pressing her fly against his. The pressure was relief and torture at the same time. They couldn't do this. Not this time. Someone—or more than one someone—was going to come looking for them soon. At least one of whom was going to be *pissed*.

But he didn't want to let her go. Not just right now, but...ever.

She'd been hot and fun and sexy as a teenager. She'd been more than happy to drop her panties on the floor of his truck. She'd thought he was amazing and she'd liked the crazy passion and the adrenaline rush between them. That had all been more than tempting. He'd been in love with all of that.

Now he was in love with *her*. The woman she'd become. The things she'd been through. The way she could still smile and laugh and had a sense of humor. Her protectiveness of the people he loved. The way she just took care of things that needed taken care of. The way she didn't let Sawyer's surliness keep her from seeing what he needed and the way she accepted Ellie's gruff form of love and the way she saw how special Tori was without needing to know her well. The way she was trying to make the business better even knowing she was leaving it because it was good for all of *them*.

She'd grown up. They both had. All of the stuff he'd been attracted to twelve years ago—her smile, her quick wit, her spontaneity, the sense of mischief, and yeah, her legs and tits—were all still there. But it was all...more now.

Maddie was the only woman he'd ever wanted *all* of. Not just sex, not just a good time, not just a few nights of partying. He wanted to make her laugh and he definitely wanted to strip her bare and bury himself deep. But he also wanted her in his arms when she was scared or sad or angry. He wanted to protect her. He wanted to be the one talking her down when she was riled up. And yes, he wanted her to paint. If that was what she wanted and needed, that's what he wanted and needed for her. If she needed to put all of this emotion inside a frame and put it up on a wall, someone *else's* wall, where she didn't even have to see it again after she'd poured it out, then he'd have to be okay with that. Because he wanted to be with her. Where didn't matter. He wanted to be the one that *knew* her, better than anyone did, and yeah, he wanted her to protect him, too. Even when she didn't really need to.

That had never occurred with another woman. He'd never felt particularly protective of them, and he'd definitely never cared if they were willing to fight a battle for him.

With Maddie he did.

He pulled back. He needed to tell her all of this.

He stared at her. She looked so fucking gorgeous. She was riled up right now, too, but this was a whole different kind. And this was definitely because of him.

"Mad—"

They were interrupted by a sharp knock at the door. "Owen, Maddie...we need to talk. *Now*."

It was Sawyer.

Fuck.

Maddie ran a hand through her hair. Her cheeks were flushed and her mouth pink from his.

"Wow," she said.

He couldn't disagree. "We're not done."

She wet her lips and nodded.

"Maddie! Owen! Right *now*!"

Owen stalked to the door and pulled it open. "What?"

"Are you fucking kidding me?" His angry gaze flickered to Maddie. "A *gun*? You pulled a *gun* while out on a tour?"

"It was...complicated," Owen said.

"It was a *gun*," Sawyer said.

His expression was hard and he looked ready to strangle someone. He was nearly vibrating with what seemed like anger, but Owen knew that it was mostly fear. The idea that one of them could have been seriously hurt had him rattled.

Owen used a calm, firm voice. "Everything is fine. We're fine."

"I should have never let you take that tour," Sawyer said to Maddie. "That's my fault. If I had my shit together you wouldn't have had to." He shoved a hand through his hair.

Awesome. Now Sawyer was blaming himself for this, too.

"There's a reason we have guns on board the boats," Owen said. "It's for situations just like that. If someone's in danger, we have ways to protect them. That's all that was. Maddie was doing her job."

"You weren't in danger," Sawyer snapped.

"She didn't know that. And if we'd been out there and I'd been in danger in your eyes, you would have done the same thing she did."

Sawyer scowled at him.

Owen stepped forward and put a hand on his cousin's shoulder. Man, he would do anything to take some of this anxiety and anger out of Sawyer. "Everyone is fine," he said, his voice again firm and calm.

Sawyer sucked in a breath. "Yeah, well maybe not *fine*."

Owen frowned. "What's up?"

"George Williams is here."

Owen felt his eyebrows rise. "What the hell is the sherriff doing here?"

"Apparently one of our guests didn't take kindly to the whole gun thing, even with free soda."

Owen blew out a breath and turned back to Maddie.

She was off the desk and coming toward them. "Well, of course," she said.

"He needs to follow up on the complaint. I'm not sure anything's really gonna happen," Sawyer said. "And if it does, we'll handle it."

Owen felt a crazy sense of satisfaction at that. Not only was Maddie here, loving and protecting his family, but they were doing the same. He put his arm around her and squeezed. "We've got your back."

She nodded. "I know."

Yeah, he liked that, too.

The three of them headed for the front office together. George was sipping a root beer and chatting with Kennedy as if he was out here for a fishing trip instead of following up on a complaint.

But he was in uniform.

"Hey, George," Maddie greeted as she stepped into the building. "It's been a while."

George chuckled and straightened from where he'd been leaning on the countertop. "I heard you were back in town and was wondering if we were gonna run into each other."

"You mean you were wondering when I was going to do something that you'd have to cuff me for," Maddie said.

"I never cuffed you," George said with a smile.

No, but after she'd burned the shed down, he had put her in the back of his squad car.

"So I guess you heard about my alligator encounter," Maddie said.

"Alligator encounter." George nodded. "Yeah, he mentioned a gator. But since you didn't hit it, I'm not so worried about you hunting without a tag and more interested in the complaint against you."

"What was the specific complaint?" she asked.

"Reckless endangerment."

"Now hang on," Owen said, stepping forward. "There was no endangerment. She shot exactly where she'd intended to shoot. No one was at risk. She shot *at* a gator that she considered to be a threat, which would mean she was protecting everyone."

"Guy said—" George pulled his notebook out of his pocket and flipped the cover open. "She was clearly unprepared for the encounter. She brandished the gun over the heads of several passengers and her hands were shaking so bad he thought for sure someone was going to accidentally get shot."

"That guy is a dick," Owen said. "He was never in danger, of any kind."

"How about you?" George asked Owen. "Guy said the shot came really close to you."

"Because the gator was close to me and she was trying to keep me safe. We carry guns on the boats for a reason," he pointed out to George as he had Sawyer. All the boats had guns and all of the captains knew how to safely handle them. Including Maddie.

George looked up at Owen. "Was it Wilma or Fred?"

Fuck. George had been out on their tour and he'd fished with Owen in that part of the bayou. "Betty," Owen admitted.

George nodded. "Uh-huh." He flipped his notebook shut. "So the gator wasn't a threat at all."

"No," Owen admitted. "But Maddie didn't know that."

"Fair enough," George acknowledged. "But she pulled a gun out and people *perceived* they were in danger."

"Come on, George," Sawyer scoffed. "Someone *perceiving* that they're gonna get robbed isn't the same thing as getting robbed."

Owen was surprised by Sawyer's defense. He'd been concerned just a few minutes ago. Then again, his concern had been about Maddie and Owen's safety, not the fact that some tourists had been spooked.

George gave him a nod. "Also a fair point."

"I was just trying to scare it off," Maddie said. "I know that it's hard to kill a gator from twenty feet."

George shook his head. "You still discharged a weapon in public."

"How is that public?" Owen demanded. "There were less than twenty people and we were out on the water."

"Public waters," George said. "And those weren't family and friends. They paid you to be out there. That's public as far as this is concerned."

His tone was a little firmer now and Owen knew he wouldn't be able to push too much harder. Just because George was a family friend, didn't meant he wouldn't follow the law.

"So what's the guy want?" Maddie said with a sigh.

"He doesn't need anything," Owen said with a frown. "You apologized. He didn't get hurt. What the hell is the problem?"

"He wants his money back," George said.

"I already processed the refund for him and his family," Kennedy said. "Sawyer said to do it. Sorry."

Everyone knew how Maddie felt about refunds. They had to be *really* deserved.

Maddie shook her head. "No, it's fine. It's my fault. I'll reimburse the business."

Owen shook his head. "No way. You're not doing that. This is your business, too. And that guy's a dick."

"Still," Maddie said.

"And he wants this on your record," George added.

Maddie swung to face him. "He wants me *arrested*?"

"He does," George said.

Owen felt anger tightening his gut. This guy was a piece of work. Most exciting tour he'd ever be on and this is how he was reacting?

"Where is he?" Owen asked, starting for the door.

"No," George said. "Unless you want to sit in the cell next to her for assault."

"You're gonna have to give me a better reason than that not to hit this guy," Owen said, yanking the door open.

"Owen, stop," George told him firmly. "The guy is pressing charges. Whether or not they stick is up to—"

"That's bullshit," Leo announced as he came through the door.

"Hey, Leo," George greeted.

"George." Leo gave him a nod. "Saw you pull up and I've been sittin' in Ellie's wonderin' when you were gonna come inside. Decided to come lookin' for ya."

"Your girl here is causing trouble," George said with a smile.

"Tell me somethin' I don't know." Leo gave Maddie a wink. "Got an earful about it outside from the poor guy who almost shit his pants because Maddie pulled a gun."

"That 'poor guy' is going to—" Owen started.

"Calm down. I was bein' sarcastic," Leo told his grandson. "So why are you so ticked off?" he asked George. "Maddie's shenanigans pull you away from a thrilling game of Fortnite?" he asked George.

Owen snorted. Everyone knew their town cop was addicted to the video game.

George laughed. "I was doing well," he admitted. "But, she's definitely making my day a little more interesting."

"This is the first thing since I've been home," Maddie protested.

Owen smiled along with everyone else, but he didn't miss her use of the word *home*. God, he fucking loved that. But he needed to keep his grip on reality. Her finally acknowledging that this was home didn't mean she was staying.

"You're not arresting her for what went on out there," Owen said. "It's her word against that guy."

"And everyone else on the boats," George said.

"You talked to everyone else?" Owen asked, knowing he hadn't.

"Not yet. But I could."

"Sure, I'll get you some names and numbers," Owen said agreeably. "And I'll give a statement. I'm a witness, too."

"Let me guess," George said mildly. "Your statement is that

nothing even happened and you'll get me names and numbers of people who will say what a fabulous tour it was and that they had a great time, felt totally safe, and don't even remember a pretty blonde with a gun."

"Well if you already know what they're going to say, you don't need to talk to them, do you?" Owen asked.

"Lying to law enforcement is a misdemeanor," George told him.

"Huh," Owen replied noncommittally.

"That could put you in that cell next to her, too."

"Huh," Owen said again.

George sighed. "It really diminishes my authority that the threat of jail does nothing to you."

"You mean your *feelings* of authority," Leo said. "Let's be honest about how much power you really have with people who know you're addicted to jelly beans and who saw you shit-faced on your birthday. Three years in a row."

George rolled his eyes, but he didn't argue.

Owen felt a little better. Basically, the local cop had just acknowledged that Owen would go to jail for Maddie. That was good. He could say that these people had no idea what all he would do for Maddie, but he thought that they really just might.

"Listen," George finally said. "No one was hurt and I know Maddie won't do it again. But the guy was making a huge stink and he's outside waiting to see what happens."

Owen pivoted toward the door again, but Leo stepped in front of him and George grabbed his arm.

"Whoa," George told him. "No fuckin' way are you going out there to talk to him."

"I wasn't really intending to do much *talking*," Owen said.

Okay, so maybe he wasn't totally over the urge to take a swing once in a while. At least not when Maddie was involved.

"No," Leo said to Owen firmly. "You'll make it worse."

"Wouldn't be the first time," Owen told him.

Leo shook his head. "All he needs is to *think* that she's in trouble for it," Leo said. He turned back to George. "He's not from here. He'll never know what you really do about it. Take Maddie down to the station. Let the guy see her sitting in the back of your car. Then get her a cup of coffee, pull the Oreos out of your bottom drawer, and spend a little time catching up. I'll haul this guy back to N'Awlins and drop him at the Hilton and everyone will be happy."

Owen sighed. Fuck. He'd rather punch the guy in the face. What was his problem? But he glanced over at Maddie. "You okay with that?"

She shrugged. "Better than an arrest."

"Okay then." George let go of Owen and gestured toward the door. "Let's go."

Maddie started forward.

"You think she needs the cuffs?" George asked Leo. Clearly joking.

But Owen heard himself growl. "You cuff her for this and I'll—"

Maddie herself slapped her hand over his mouth. "How about we don't add threatening a police officer to the list here?"

Owen wrapped his hand around her wrist, pulling her hand back and pressing a kiss to the palm. He saw the little hitch in her breathing. "I hate this."

"It's really nothing."

"Still bugs me."

Her smile was soft. "It still turns me on that it bugs you."

Now his breath hitched a little.

"Okay, let's go," George repeated. "Good lord."

Owen gave her another quick kiss, this time on the lips, and then let her go.

George grasped her upper arm and they headed out the door.

Fuck, he hated this. Owen shoved a hand through his hair. He really should do something so he could sit in the cell with her. At least keep her company. This was on him, too. But she wasn't actually going to be sitting in a cell. He supposed he could go eat Oreos with her. But that wasn't even the point.

It was all so stupid. But it was equally stupid to be this bothered by it. It was nothing. She wasn't getting arrested. She was going to spend an hour chatting with George downtown. But he hated that the tourist thought he'd gotten her into trouble.

"Hey, Leo?" he said to his grandfather.

"Yeah?" Leo was watching George take Maddie to his car. Past the group of tourists waiting for the bus to take them back to New Orleans.

The guy who'd started all of this mess said something as they passed and George paused for a moment to address him.

"You better get that guy back to NOLA quick. I'm still in the mood to hit somebody."

Leo nodded. "Me, too, boy. Me, too."

Owen looked at his grandfather. "But...you wouldn't, right?"

"I'd say it's about fifty-fifty," Leo admitted.

"Well," Owen said, clapping his grandfather on the shoulder. "I'm good for bail money."

Leo chuckled. "I don't think it would take more than what we've got in the jar."

Yes, the Landry family had a jar that sat on the back of Ellie's bar where they all deposited spare change on a regular basis. The jar said *BAIL MONEY* on the side, and the tourists, and maybe a few locals, thought it was a joke.

It wasn't.

They dumped it out regularly into a bigger bucket in back and with all of them contributing, the spare change actually added up. They'd only used it once and that was a few years ago so yeah, there was probably a pretty good amount in there.

"Well, then, I'll be the one to haul the bucket to the bank and turn it into cash."

Leo nodded. "Just promise that you'll leave me there for one night before you bring it down."

"Yeah?"

"George keeps that station like an ice box and the AC in my trailer is shit. It'd be nice to have a good night's sleep."

"You got it, Grandpa."

13

Owen heard the knock on his back screen door. He'd just pulled some leftovers from the oven. He tossed the hot pad on the counter and headed to see who it was. Sawyer, Josh, Tori and Kennedy just let themselves in. As did his mom, grandma, grandpa, aunts and uncles. So who the hell was this?

The second he saw Maddie standing on his back step, his heart rate went into overdrive.

He hadn't seen her since George had taken her downtown. He'd had two more tours, and she hadn't come back to the office after her coffee date with the sheriff. He'd come home restless, determined to give her a little space and time. But equally determined to find her tonight.

In the meantime, he'd looked up her art. He'd gone to the gallery's website and sure enough, a couple of her paintings were on the first page. They were good. Damned good. And they were so familiar—the bayou, the town, the storm clouds—that his heart had twisted. Seeing his beloved bayou, that he knew like he knew the back of his hand, on a canvas in a gallery in San Francisco was surreal. It was also obvious Maddie loved the places she painted, even if she was emotionally conflicted about it.

Owen swallowed hard as he pushed the door open. "Hey."

"Hey."

She looked fucking gorgeous. She'd showered and her hair was down and smooth, in contrast to the curls she'd had earlier from the humidity and wind. She was wearing another little sundress, this one white, with spaghetti straps, and simple white flip-flops.

"You okay?" he asked when she didn't step across his threshold.

"I need something," she said.

"Anything."

"You."

The oxygen he'd just pulled in jammed in his lungs and he just stared at her for a long moment.

"And when I say 'you', I don't mean that I want a cup of coffee or a glass of wine. I don't want to go for a walk. I don't want to talk. I don't want, or need, a hug. I don't need you to ask me if I'm okay or if I'm sure. I just want to get naked and kiss you and lick you from head to toe and then I want *you* to lick *me* from head to—"

He reached out, grabbed her wrist, and pulled her inside. He backed her up against the wall of the porch right next to the door. He braced his hands on either side of her face.

"Fuck yes."

A little smile teased her lips. "Really?"

"I'm all yours." For anything and everything for as long as she wanted him. He didn't have to say the rest. She knew.

She cupped his face between her hands, rubbing her palms over his short beard. "I want to feel this...in lots of places."

She heard the little growl that came from the back of his throat.

"You're going to, girl. *Lots* of places. Over and over again."

A little shiver went through her and he dropped his gaze to see her nipples pressing against the front of her dress. "I'm gonna need this," he said, reaching up to slip one strap off her shoulder.

"My dress?"

He nodded.

She reached for the zipper that ran up the side of the dress. She dragged it down, her eyes locked on his. Just like that. Not another question, not a single hesitation, not even a blush. She just unzipped.

Maddie shrugged her shoulders and the other strap fell as the bodice gaped. She pushed on his chest and he stepped back. She dropped her hands and the dress fell to a pool at her feet.

She stood in front of him in only a tiny pair of white silk panties and her sandals.

Owen's mouth went dry as he ran his gaze over her. Where to start? He wanted every inch of her skin against his mouth right now.

He bent and snagged the hem of the dress. She stepped out of it and he moved to the door. He pushed it open and tucked the dress through the loop of metal that made up the handle, hanging the dress from his back door.

Maddie laughed. "What's that?"

"You know how people put socks on their doors to show everyone they've got a girl inside and don't want to be interrupted?" he asked.

"Yeah."

"Thought this might be even more obvious."

"Is that what you usually do?"

He shook his head and stepped right in front of her. "I never have women over here." He dated exclusively in New Orleans and always went back to the girl's place, be it an apartment or a hotel room for the weekend.

Maddie gave him a smile. "You could just lock the door."

"With our family?" he asked. "If they didn't know what was going on in here, they'd either just beat on it until we can't stand it or one of them would pick the lock."

She didn't even correct him about the *our family* thing. They were her family as much as they were his and they both knew it.

"Someone can pick locks?" she asked.

"Three someones, actually." He gave her a look. "Are you really surprised?"

She thought about it for about one second and then said, "Not even a little."

He bent and lifted her into his arms. "And now, that's enough talking."

———

"Good afternoon, ladies."

The deep voice brought Maddie's head up from the spreadsheet she was reviewing. And she nearly slipped off her stool. She pulled her glasses from her face and stood quickly. "Oh my God. Hi. What are you doing here?"

The tall man pulled his sunglasses from his face in a much smoother motion, tucking them into the inner pocket of his suit jacket. "I wanted to come down after hearing about the typhoid outbreak, but staying away from that seemed wiser. But the near-death experience of a paying customer did catch my attention and I thought maybe it was time for an in-person visit."

Shit. That asshole who'd wanted to have her arrested had also *posted* about it? "You Travel?" she asked dryly.

"And Travel Time," he confirmed. Then he gave her a slow smile. "I've been trying to picture this but I just can't. I'm guessing you don't have need to be armed in the art gallery?" His eyes scanned her from head to toe. "Then again, seeing you dressed like this, makes it a little easier to imagine. I assume this isn't Armani?"

She was wearing cutoff denim shorts and a Boys of the Bayou T-shirt today, actually. She'd taken three shirts home the morning after she and Owen had first slept together. Slowly her style here was changing. The heat and humidity had driven her out of her regular work clothes within two days, but she'd stuck to sundresses after that, feeling those were close to her style, while still keeping her from heat stroke. But she felt very comfortable in denim and a shirt with a cartoon alligator on the front. It was something else she was choosing not to over-think. She was sure it was something about feeling a part of things and like she belonged. It could also be about wanting souvenirs once her time was up. But yeah, she wasn't analyzing it.

"Easier to wash bayou out of these," she said.

"Yeah, gator blood might be tough to get out of silk."

"Very true."

Maddie heard Kennedy clear her throat next to her. She glanced over. Kennedy was sitting up straighter, eyeing the man with interest.

Right. They hadn't met. Or at least, Kennedy didn't know they had.

"Sorry. Kennedy Landry, this is Bennett Baxter. Bennett, Kennedy."

Kennedy spit out her mouthful of sweet tea. All over Bennett's silk tie. That probably *was* Armani.

Bennett did nothing more than look down at his tie and then brush a hand over the spray of iced tea. "Hello, Kennedy."

Kennedy was staring at him. "Shit," she muttered. Then she shook her head. "Fuck."

Maddie smirked at the very Kennedy-like greeting. Which was probably *not* how Bennett Baxter was used to being greeted. Especially by women.

He was very handsome. He had that classic chiseled jawline, dark eyes and hair, broad shoulders, and, even more than how he filled out his suit, he had a confident, I'm-in-charge air that made people pay attention. It was clear he was used to commanding whatever room he was in.

Which was exactly why Maddie got such a kick out of his little-boy-excitement about the bayou and the airboats.

Kennedy reached under the counter and pulled out a roll of paper towels. She started to tear one off but fumbled the roll and dropped it. The towels unwound and Kennedy just watched them go, her lips pressed together.

Maddie, trying to hold back her smile, bent and grabbed them, tearing one off and handing it to Bennett.

He dabbed at his tie with the towel but his eyes were on Kennedy.

Kennedy's cheeks were red as she stared at his tie as if trying *not* to look at his face.

And Maddie didn't know what the hell to think. But she couldn't wait to tell...well, *everyone* about this.

So this is how they all felt when they couldn't wait to share something and when they couldn't wait to have all the juicy details. And how it felt to guess at those details until things could be confirmed. Yeah, this was fun.

"We should probably talk," Bennett finally said to Maddie.

She nodded, her smile and enjoyment dropping away. "Yeah, we probably should." Even without him reading about the guy she'd pissed off yesterday, her time was winding down here and they needed to figure out where they were all going from here.

She had an idea. But she hadn't run it past anyone. Including this man who was, very likely, ready to write a large check to the Boys of the Bayou.

"Kennedy, you okay if I duck out?"

Kennedy was attempting to return the paper towels to some semblance of a roll shape and totally seemed unaware that Maddie had spoken to her.

"Ken?" Maddie nudged her leg.

Kennedy looked up. "Yeah?"

"Bennett and I are going to meet up at Cora's. You okay here on your own?"

Kennedy narrowed her eyes as she looked at Bennett. "I'm fine. We're *all* fine. *Everything* is fine here."

Maddie glanced at Bennett and found him with a half smile on his face, clear interest in his eyes. Interest in Kennedy.

Maddie couldn't wait to tell Ellie.

"Glad to hear it. Would hate to inherit a bunch of problems," Bennett said as he turned toward the door, pulling his sunglasses out.

"Pompous ass," Kennedy muttered.

Maddie was eighty percent sure Bennett heard.

He paused with the door open, giving her a full-blown smile as he slid his sunglasses on. "See you around, Kennedy."

Oh yeah, he'd heard her.

The second he stepped out the door, Kennedy swung toward Maddie. "*That* is Bennett Baxter?"

Maddie nodded. "Yep."

"Ugh." Kennedy groaned, throwing her head back.

"What?"

"He's hot."

Maddie laughed. "Yeah, he is."

"I thought he was like fifty or something. I envisioned him balding and trying to make up for his small dick size with some stupid sports car and being into *golf* or something." She said "golf" the way people most people would say "garbage".

Maddie grinned and grabbed her purse from under the counter. "Well, he's thirty-two, has excellent taste in art, he really might golf, actually, but I think it's safe to assume dick size isn't an issue."

Kennedy wrinkled her nose. "I hate guys like that."

Maddie started for the door, laughing. "Uh-huh." She'd sobered by the time she'd pulled the door behind her, though.

"Ready?" Bennett asked, pushing off the railing across from the office door.

She took a breath. "As ready as I'm going to get."

He fell in step next to her and she headed for Cora's. At least there they'd have some privacy.

Her pit stop in Autre, Louisiana was about to be over.

––––––

"Hey, what's up?" Owen asked Kennedy as he came into the office to grab his next tour list.

"Bennett Baxter is a dick."

Owen looked at her. Okay, not the subject matter he'd been expecting. "He called again?"

"He's here. And he...wears these sunglasses. And he's in a stupid suit and tie. I mean, who does he think he is? Who wears a fucking *tie* to the bayou? What a dumbass. And he has these eyes and this smile. And I—"

"Ken?" Owen interjected Kennedy's rant. He had no idea why his sister was so riled. Kennedy didn't rant. She didn't go on and on and make no sense.

"What?" She scowled at him.

"Bennett is *here*?"

"Yeah, he's up at Cora's with Maddie. They're talking about the deal."

Owen felt a cold trickle down his spine. The deal. Her month was almost up. She'd also just spooked herself badly with the gun-and-gator thing yesterday. And Bennett Baxter, the complete stranger that was planning to come in and be a majority partner overnight, was now in Autre. Ready to sign on the dotted line. Fuck.

Owen shoved a hand through his hair.

It was time to make a decision.

"She's really leaving?"

Kennedy's question pulled Owen's attention back to her. He sucked in a deep breath. And nodded. "Yeah."

"You going to let her do that?"

He lifted a shoulder. "No choice. That's what's going to make her happiest. That's all I need to know."

"So you're going with her this time?"

His heart clenched. Kennedy had figured out what he'd just realized last night, when he'd been holding Maddie in his arms after she'd almost killed a gator and gone to jail for him.

He wasn't letting her go again. He wasn't letting her get away. If she was going back to California, then he was going with her.

He finally nodded at Kennedy. "Yeah."

She didn't look surprised. "I think that's good."

"You do?"

"Of course. If she goes back alone, she's going to end up all bottled up and by herself, thinking that she's nuts and she has to stay away from us to be okay. If you're there, you can make sure she's...well, happily nuts. Like the rest of us. You are the only person who can *really* make her like that. And make her okay with it. Also, if she's with you, she'll come visit and stuff."

Owen smiled at his cousin. "Happily nuts?"

"Well, if loving life and the people around you and saying what you think and being whatever and whoever you want to be is nuts, then yeah." She grinned. "But the important part is the happily part."

Owen leaned over and wrapped an arm around Kennedy's neck, pulling her into a short hug. "You're not all bad, Ken."

She let him hug her for a moment, then shoved him away. "Yeah, I know."

He looked down at the tour sheet in his hand. He really wanted to go find Maddie and Bennett. Actually, Bennett most of all. He needed to talk to the guy before he told Maddie his plan.

A second later, Kennedy plucked the page from his fingers. "I've got this covered. Go."

"Go?"

"Cora's house. They've been up there for about forty-five minutes."

"You sure?" he asked, already moving toward the door.

"I'm not going to offer again. If that door isn't shutting behind you in five seconds, you're taking this retirement party out to look at gators."

The door shut behind him three seconds later.

Owen made his way toward Cora's. His heart was pounding, but it wasn't with nerves. He was sure of this. But he needed Bennett Baxter to be on board.

He stopped short at the end of the path leading to Cora's porch. A tall man in a suit and tie was just putting sunglasses on as he came out of the front door.

Bennett Baxter. Had to be. No one wore a tie to the bayou, Kennedy was right.

The man spotted him and stopped at the top of the steps. "If you're looking for Maddie, she just headed over to the bank. I stayed here to make a couple of calls, but I'm meeting her up there in a little bit."

"Looking for you, actually," Owen said.

The man came down the steps and Owen met him at the bottom. He stuck out his hand. "Owen Landry."

"Bennett Baxter."

"So you want to be a swamp boat tour company owner."

Bennett's face stretched into a grin. "I do."

"How would you like to own another fifteen percent of Boys of the Bayou?" Owen felt his chest tighten even as he said it. He'd planned to say it. This was why he'd come to find Bennett. But he was giving up the business, the thing that had brought him joy since he was a little kid. Maddie was worth it. Being with her was worth it. But it still felt weird.

Bennett's eyebrows rose over the top of his glasses. "I'm listening."

"I'm heading to California and I'm looking for a buyer for my share," Owen said. "My fifteen will put you at fifty percent ownership."

That made his chest tighten even further. With Maddie and Owen's shares together, Bennett would own more of the business than Sawyer did. It didn't seem right to put a stranger in that much control, but Owen didn't know what else to do.

Bennett didn't react right away. But he took his glasses off, meeting Owen's gaze directly. "Have you spoken with Maddie about this?"

"Not yet. Getting my ducks in a row first."

Bennett nodded. "Okay. Then my answer to your question is yes, I'd be interested in buying your share as well."

"I'm going to insist on some commitments from you," Owen said.

"Such as?"

"You can't sell for at least five years. You have to invest fifty percent of your share of the profits back into the business. You can't get rid of Sawyer or Josh. That kind of stuff."

Bennett didn't seem offended or frustrated by Owen putting

contingencies on the sale and Owen was reminded that this man was a businessman. He was used to negotiations and deals. Owen felt pretty good about seeming firm on those stipulations, too. The truth was, if Bennett didn't agree to those things, Owen was in a bind. He was set on selling. He didn't really have another option. He couldn't own a portion of the business but never be here to help run it. That wasn't fair to Sawyer and Josh at all.

"Is there a reason you think I might want to get rid of Sawyer or Josh?" Bennett asked.

"Not unless you get full of yourself and think you can do a better job than they do or something," Owen told him.

"I don't see that happening," Bennett admitted. "This isn't about taking something over. This is just about being a part of it. You guys and the way you run the place are part of its marketability."

Huh. Was that right? Owen hadn't thought about that.

"In fact, the idea of losing one-third of the guys who make this place what it is, on top of the recent loss of Tommy, makes me wonder if Boys of the Bayou will really be all it can be going forward."

Owen frowned. That was nice and all, but he wasn't part of the deal. If that changed how Bennett was looking at this whole thing, they might all be in trouble. "You might not be interested if I'm not here?" he asked.

"I'll have to think about it," Bennett told him. "This company isn't just about floating down the bayou or spotting an alligator or egret here and there. It's about you guys. Your love for it all, your knowledge of the area because this is your back-yard, your protection of it. The bayou and the area down here all benefit from having you guys running the tours and fishing trips as much as the tourists benefit from it. Maybe more. If people from the outside come in"—Bennett paused, clearly meaning him—"who don't understand it all and are just here to make money, then the bayou and the natural balance out here suffer."

Owen frowned. "You're an outsider who sounds like he knows what he's talking about."

"There are oil companies, logging companies, tourism companies, any number of people who don't care if they're destroying the marshlands. People like you need to stay here, claiming the territory and helping protect it."

Owen squinted at him. "Aren't you…"

"A rich guy who only looks at how to get richer?" Bennett asked.

Owen shrugged. "Something like that."

"Yes and no. I'm a rich guy. But I have a law degree, along with a master's in biodiversity and conservation."

"You're a scientist?" Owen couldn't hide his surprise.

"I am. But I decided that I could be even more effective using my knowledge and passion combined with my money and network than I could trudging through the swamp. So I invest in green technology and conservation programs and I lobby politicians and other investors on behalf of those efforts."

"You don't want to get richer?"

Bennett grinned. "Green technology has tons of potential."

"Ah." Owen couldn't fault the guy for using what he knew and had to get more. He was giving back, at least. "You're going to run for office eventually?" Owen guessed.

Bennett nodded. "Eventually."

"But now you're investing in a swamp boat tour company so you can also trudge through the swamp once in a while."

Bennett grinned. "Yep."

"So you'll keep the company and the business as is? And invest in it?"

"I really like what you guys do. Not just for all the reasons I gave you but because you also show people a hell of a good time." Bennett shrugged. "I don't have a lot of friends who can take apart an airboat and put it back together or who can kill, clean, and grill up an alligator."

"And you're into that?" He had to admit the guy standing in front of him looked nothing like the guys who gathered around the bonfires and twisted the heads off of crawfish.

"I'm a stereotypical nerd who wants to be one of the cool kids."

Owen laughed. "You might have low standards for cool kids, but you're in the right place if you want to get dirty and drunk and dumb once in a while."

Bennett laughed. "Boys of the Bayou will be safe with me," he said. "But I am concerned about you not being a part of it."

"I don't have a choice, man. I'm going with Maddie."

Bennett seemed to ponder that. Finally he nodded. "Okay."

They stood for a long moment, neither saying anything.

Finally, Owen asked, "So now what?"

"Write up an offer. Let me know how much you want, when I could take ownership, all of that."

Owen nodded. But he had no idea how to really do that. He wasn't a businessman. Not really. He could balance a checkbook and knew his log-in information to get into the online banking. And that was about it. "Is there a standard form for stuff like that or something?" he asked. He would have expected to feel a little intimidated by Bennett Baxter to be honest, but he didn't. Bennett seemed like a straight-forward guy.

"How about for now, we can just write something up that lists all the stuff we both want and agree to," Bennett said. "I've made business deals on reams of expensive linen stationary and I've made deals on the backs of bar receipts."

Owen relaxed a little. "I'm definitely more of a bar-receipt guy."

Bennett smiled. "Think Cora has a notebook or something?"

"Absolutely." Owen led the way back up into Cora's kitchen and twenty minutes later, he and Bennett both scrawled their signatures across the bottom of a piece of paper that read GROCERIES AND SH*T at the top and had a bear carrying a basket of food in the corner.

Owen felt good as they made their way over to Ellie's for lunch. Their agreement, written like that, felt like the partnership agreement Leo and Kenny had written up out at the fishing cabin all those years ago. Was it completely legal? Well, maybe. But more importantly, it spoke to the commitment of the two men who'd signed it. Owen was going with Maddie. He'd officially put it down on paper.

And now she *had* to let him tag along to California. In another week, he wasn't going to have a job in Autre anymore.

———

"So, everyone knows that Bennett Baxter is in town," Maddie said later that evening as everyone—sans Bennett—gathered around the big table at the back of Ellie's. It was another "partner meeting" which meant that Cora, Ellie, Leo, Kennedy, Mitch and several other random friends were also there and that there was food. "He wants to meet you all, but he didn't want to crash our dinner. He's staying at Leo's tonight and is over there working now."

"He's crashing at *Leo's*?" Josh asked. "The trailer?"

Leo had been living in a trailer behind the bar since he and Ellie had split up. It was nothing fancy. It didn't even come close to fancy. And that was where the big millionaire investor was going to stay?

Owen actually chuckled at the thought. Bennett seemed enamored with all things bayou and "downhome"—anything different from his rich upbringing. He'd probably love the trailer.

"Where's Leo going to sleep?" Mitch asked. "Don't tell me you're putting Baxter on that couch. He'll never walk straight again. And that couch will snap Leo in half."

"Really, he could just go back to New Orleans to stay," Kennedy said. "He can have people kiss his ass at some swanky hotel instead of expecting us to all do it. At least they'd be getting paid for it."

"He doesn't expect anyone here to kiss his ass," Maddie protested.

"So when he asks me for something tomorrow, I can tell him to fuck off?" Kennedy asked.

Maddie sighed and everyone else laughed.

"Guess that depends what he asks you for," Owen said with a wink. He hadn't missed that Kennedy was particularly annoyed by Bennett, and he hadn't missed that her irritation probably meant something was up between the two of them.

"No, you cannot tell him to fuck off," Sawyer said. "He's going to be your boss."

Kennedy scowled at him. "Well...not really."

Sawyer nodded. "Yes, really. He'll own part of the business. You work for the business."

"Yeah, but Josh and Owen own part of the business, too. I don't listen to them."

Sawyer gave his little sister a look. "That's because Josh and Owen let you get away with that. I don't think Bennett Baxter will."

Kennedy did not look happy about that.

"*Anyway,* Bennett is staying in town for the next couple of days," Maddie said, clearly trying to steer the conversation toward her big announcement.

"He can sleep at my place," Mitch said. "I can crash at Owen's. His couch is great."

"Well, why not just put Bennett on the couch?" Kennedy asked. "His rich ass can't sleep on a couch?"

"Kennedy," Sawyer said, sounding tired. "Enough."

"I'm just sayin'."

"You mad that we're not putting him up at your place?" Mitch asked.

"Fuck off, Mitch," Kennedy muttered.

"That's not a no."

"There are a ton of beds and couches available between us all," Sawyer said. "Leo, you can come to my place."

"I'm good," Leo said, waving that off.

"Where are you staying?"

"Don't you all worry about where Leo's sleeping," Ellie piped up. "He'll be fine."

Everyone turned to look at her—and Leo—as one.

"Oh, he will, will he?" Josh asked his grandmother.

"I see how it is," Kennedy agreed, nodding.

"Oh, you all shut up," Ellie told them. "Go on, Maddie."

It was funny to see their grandmother blushing. And she most definitely was.

So Trevor was staying in New Orleans and they weren't supposed to worry about where Leo was sleeping. This dinner was interesting.

And it was typical.

Damn, he was going to miss the hell out of all these people.

"*Anyway*," Maddie said again. "Bennett is here for the next couple of days and we're finalizing the deal." She looked around the table. "He is going to be a part of Boys of the Bayou."

No one said anything, but the smiles fell away and a few people shifted uncomfortably on their chairs.

Maddie sighed. Owen knew she'd been expecting their reactions but it was hard to disappoint people you cared about.

"I know that you're worried about bringing in someone new. But I promise you that he has the business's best interests at heart. He's excited about this. We talked at length about plans." She took a deep breath and looked around.

Owen wanted to reach out and take her hand but she was too far away. He wanted to face his family and tell them that change was sometimes inevitable and didn't have to be bad. He wanted to believe that, too. Life in California was definitely going to be a big change.

"We need his money," Maddie said, her voice softer. "We need help if we want the business to keep going. That's just a fact."

"We've always found a way to get through things," Ellie said. "Together. We figure things out."

Maddie blew out a breath. "I know. I get that. This is me helping to figure things out."

"Without the rest of us," Cora pointed out.

Owen bit his tongue. Literally. He loved Ellie and Cora. But they were each a force to be reckoned with and together they were...impossible. And they were almost always together on things. Owen couldn't remember the last time they'd disagreed about something. It was either that, or they disagreed behind closed doors. A lot like parents not wanting to fight in front of the kids. In front of the kids, they presented a united front.

Apparently one or the other of them had decided that they were upset about Maddie selling and they decided to be upset together.

He got it. Cora's granddaughter was home and clearly happy here. They didn't know about her issues with her painting. And honestly, in Cora and Ellie's minds, nothing was more important than family and Autre. Having Maddie back had only fueled their belief that this was where she belonged.

"There are other details I want to share with you," Maddie said. "But it's really important that you all accept Bennett and understand that this is a good choice."

She said it firmly, but it was clear that Cora's comment had hurt. Owen felt his hand tighten into a fist. Maddie didn't need his help here, and he didn't want to yell at Cora. But dammit.

"Everybody just fucking listen," he said.

Okay, so he hadn't yelled, but he was clearly talking through clenched teeth. Cora and Ellie both looked at him and he met their gazes with eyebrows up. He knew his look said *knock it off*.

"Really? You don't want her to stay?" Ellie asked.

Owen looked at Maddie. "No. I don't want her to stay."

14

"What?" Cora demanded. "What are you talking about?"
"This isn't where Maddie wants to be." Owen looked at Sawyer and Josh. "We need to bring Bennett in. He's the answer to...all of it."

"All of it?" Sawyer cocked a brow. "What's all of it?"

"What's going to happen when Maddie and I go to California."

Everyone was completely silent for several long seconds.

The first person to speak was Maddie.

"What the hell are you talking about?"

He nodded. "I'm coming with you this time. I'm not letting you get away again."

She sprung to her feet, her chair scraping across the floor. "Are you crazy? You can't leave Autre. The business."

"I can," he said firmly. "And I'm going to. You need to be in California. That means I need to be in California."

"No," she said. "No, Owen."

Owen got to his feet, too, facing her across the table, feet braced, hand on his hips. He *would* convince her of this. Or not.

He'd still show up in San Francisco. He'd show her, eventually, that he meant what he said.

"Bennett is buying me out, too," he said.

Maddie's mouth dropped open and she started shaking her head.

Not the reaction he'd been expecting.

"We talked about it." Owen gave her a firm nod. "It's official."

Maddie's eyes widened. "What do you mean 'it's official?'"

"We wrote up an agreement. We both signed it—"

He hadn't even finished the sentence when Maddie stomped around the end of the table and headed for the door. What the hell?

"Mad!" he called after her.

She didn't slow down or look back.

"Maddie!" he shouted. He started after her.

"I'm going to talk to Bennett!" she shouted back.

"Madison Evangeline! Stop!"

She swung around to face him. "I'm going to undo this! This isn't final."

He stopped nearly on her toes. "Why? Why are you going to undo it?"

"Because you can't give this up, Owen!" She pushed a hand through her hair. "I've been watching you for almost a month. *This* is where you belong. Not California."

"I can belong in California."

"No." She shook her head. "No, you can't."

"Hey."

"I know you, Owen. I know California. And you would be miserable there. I'm not doing that to you."

"You need to be somewhere else to paint," he said. "If you're somewhere else, I am, too."

She looked confused. "You *just* found out that I paint but now you're willing to *move* your *life* to California so I can do it?"

"Yes."

"Well, that's ridiculous."

No, that was a grand gesture. It was fucking romantic, dammit. It was the kind of thing the Landrys specialized in and it was something Owen had never done before. Because it was clear to him now that Maddie was the only person he would do it for. And this was a pretty great gesture, if he did say so himself.

"I'm coming to California, Maddie," he said firmly.

"That is *not* happening."

"You don't want me there?"

"No! *Definitely* not."

Well, that was not what he'd been expecting. Where was the squealing? The throwing herself into his arms? The kissing and happy crying and I-love-you-so-much-Owen he'd been ready for?

"Maddie—"

"I *have* to talk to Bennett." She looked very angry. "Just stay here."

"Here at Ellie's right now or here in Autre forever?" he asked dryly, his growing anger seeping into his tone.

She frowned. "Both."

"Great," he said tightly. "Got it."

He didn't get it. Not at all. What the hell was happening?

Maddie looked like she wanted to say something more but she snapped her mouth shut, turned and left, presumably to find Bennett and rip up his agreement with Owen.

Fuck.

The door shut behind her and Owen took a deep breath.

Well, that had definitely not gone the way he'd planned.

"You're not going after her?"

This came from Ellie.

Owen turned back to face his grandmother. "Of course I'm going after her."

Ellie crossed her arms. "When?"

"As soon as I pack for California."

"That's not happening until we talk." This came from Sawyer. He stood, his face stony. "What the fuck, Owen?"

"I'm in love with her, man. This can't be a total shock."

"You leaving and selling your percent to Bennett Baxter?" Sawyer said with a scowl. "Yeah, it's a shock."

"I'm sorry but—"

"We have a partnership agreement," Sawyer broke in. "You have to give us thirty days."

Owen braced his feet and put his hands on his hips. "You're kidding, right?"

"Not even a little."

"I have to wait thirty days to go to California with Maddie? What's going to change in thirty days, Sawyer?"

"Well, a total stranger won't own fifty percent of our fucking business!" Sawyer snapped. "That's one thing."

Owen sucked in a breath and let it out slowly. "I think Baxter is a good guy."

"I don't fucking care what you think," Sawyer told him. "You're giving me thirty days to figure out what to do about your fifteen percent. You're not selling it to him!"

"Maddie's over there telling Baxter the same thing," Josh said, his voice calm. Though the frown he sent Owen said he was almost as pissed as Sawyer was. "If anyone can get Owen out of this, it's her."

That was a little emasculating, but it wasn't totally untrue. Owen still frowned back. "I don't *want* out of it."

"It's bullshit," Sawyer said. "It's complete bullshit. We should have the chance to buy you out."

"You can't afford it!" Owen reminded him.

"Not Tommy's thirty-five, but maybe fifteen." Sawyer shoved a hand through his hair. "But we'll still be a man down and I doubt very much that Baxter knows how to...do any damned thing that might be helpful at all."

Owen hated seeing Sawyer and Josh wound up and worried. And pissed. "What am I supposed to do, Sawyer?" Owen finally asked. "She's leaving. I can't just let her go."

"She doesn't want you to go with her," Sawyer pointed out.

"Yeah, well, that's too bad." But something nagged at the back of his mind. She said she couldn't paint here. That was what bothered him the most. Her painting was important to her. But it wasn't working here. She said it was because all of the emotions she normally put into her art were coming out other ways.

If he was in California with her, would that do the same thing? Would she not be able to paint if he was there? That seemed crazy. It seemed like a terrible reason to not be together. But, he had to admit, it seemed pretty damned selfish of him to assume that she'd choose being with him over her painting. Maybe that was why she didn't want him to come?

Or maybe she just wasn't feeling what he was feeling. And had he ever *said*, "Hey I'm in love with you. Again. Still", or if he'd *asked* her what she wanted, maybe he wouldn't be standing in the middle of his grandmother's bar, facing his entire family, and feeling like the world's biggest ass.

"Seems like maybe you need a drink," Ellie said, moving toward the bar.

Well, it wasn't milk and cookies and a big hug, but he had to admit, at his age and in this situation, his grandmother had exactly the right offering.

———

MADDIE STALKED down the path in front of Ellie's.

What in the *hell* was Bennett doing? He'd made an arrangement with Owen? Who did he think he was? He was going to buy another fifteen percent of the company? Just like that? That was *not* the agreement.

And Owen couldn't sell his portion. He needed it. The Boys of the Bayou needed him. There was no way Owen should be in California. He couldn't leave Louisiana. What the hell was *he* thinking?

She was just past the Boys of the Bayou office when she saw a flash of light out of the corner of her eye. It made her pause. What was that? She walked back a few yards and peered into the darkness.

There it was again.

It looked like a flashlight.

Frowning she immediately started in that direction. Who the fuck was skulking around the office at this time of night? All of the partners were up at Ellie's.

She rounded the corner of the building just as a tall shadow stepped into her path. Without thinking, she immediately swung, her fist connecting with his jaw and snapping his head back. She knew it was a him because of the deep "oomph" sound he made when she hit him.

He stumbled back and she took a step forward, thinking quickly. There was a broom just inside the door to her right. She wasn't sure how much damage she could actually do with that, but she was willing to try.

"Jesus, Maddie!" the man said, rubbing his jaw.

She froze with her hand in her purse, feeling for her keys. She frowned. Did she know that voice? Again, all of the men she knew were up at Ellie's. She latched onto her keys and pulled them out. She could do some damage with those if she couldn't get into the office.

She jabbed out with the longest key clutched between her second and third fingers. "What the fuck are you doing down here?"

"I was on my way to Ellie's and I heard one of the airboats take off. I came down to check on things."

Maddie squinted into the darkness. "Bennett?"

"Yes!" he shouted. "Who the hell did you think it was?"

"I thought it was someone trying to break in!" she shouted back. She had a ton of adrenaline pumping, first from Owen's big announcement and her anger at Bennett, and then from coming down here to confront a possible intruder.

Her anger at Bennett. Hey, yeah, she was mad at this guy. She dropped her keys into her other hand, pulled her fist back, and punched him again.

"What the *fuck*?" he roared, his hand going to his face. "Are you crazy?"

"Yes! Maybe I am! But I don't care!" she told him, advancing on him and gratified to see him backing up. "What the *hell* were you doing buying Owen's share of the business? I told you what was going on! We had a deal!"

Bennett stopped with his back against the railing of the dock. If he leaned back any farther, or she hit him again—which she was seriously considering—he'd go over backward into the bayou.

She'd actually really like to see that. She took a step forward and Bennett held his hands up in surrender.

"I'm not actually buying him out," Bennett said.

"He said you signed an agreement."

"We did," Bennett agreed. "With no witnesses and on paper that's very...rippable."

She narrowed her eyes. "Rippable?"

"We can rip it up."

"Why did you sign in the first place?" Maddie was nearly on top of his toes now.

"Because if he was serious, then I was definitely interested. But I knew it wouldn't fly. Not once he heard that you were staying."

"Wait, you didn't *tell* him that?" she asked.

"I thought *you* should tell him that."

Maddie took another deep breath and opened her mouth. But then shut it.

She hadn't told Owen she was staying.

Shit.

In her anger and worry about Bennett signing an agreement with Owen for his portion, all she'd been able to think of was getting to Bennett and ripping that up. She hadn't actually *told* Owen that she'd changed *her* deal with the millionaire.

"How do I know you'll actually rip it up?" she asked, taking a step back.

"Seriously?" Bennett asked, straightening and smoothing a hand down the front of his shirt. "I'm not here to stage a takeover. I need these guys as much as they need me. I want this to be good for everyone. Owen was determined. And honestly, going over his demands in our agreement showed me even more what this place means to him and to all of them. Leaving this, selling to me, would have been one of the hardest things that guy ever did."

Maddie crossed her arms.

"Why are you freaking out?" he asked. "You don't trust me?"

She thought about that. "I guess...I do trust you," she finally decided.

"Then what was *this* all about?" Bennett rubbed his jaw.

"Going to find you was about protecting Owen," she admitted. "He doesn't *really* want to leave. And then I saw someone down here and that was about protecting the business."

"You didn't think maybe you should get help protecting the business?" Bennett asked.

Maddie sighed and shook her head. "Thinking things through isn't my strong suit. Not here, anyway."

"And the protecting Owen? You just swing first and ask questions later?"

She narrowed her eyes and nodded. "Yeah. I do. And if you're going to be one of our partners, you should remember that."

"I *am* going to be one of your partners," Bennett said. "With seventeen and a half percent."

She gave him a nod, but she was still frowning.

"Does Owen need your protection?" Bennett asked, suddenly seeming amused.

"Doesn't matter," she said with a shrug. "It's me, not him. Not them. I feel first and think later."

"Good to know."

"So let's go," she said turning on her heel.

"Where?"

"To rip up your agreement with Owen."

"Okay, but..."

"Yes?" she asked, glancing back.

"Did you hear the part about the airboat being stolen?"

Maddie turned fully, facing him. "What?"

"Someone took one of the airboats out. Unless it was one of the guys?"

Maddie frowned. "No, everyone is up at Ellie's. Even Mitch and Leo." She looked behind Bennett. Sure enough, one of the boats was gone. What the hell?

"I found a couple of beer cans and this cap on the dock," Bennett said, holding it out.

She looked at it closely. It seemed familiar. It was gray with dark blue Greek letters. She pulled her phone out of her back pocket and dialed Owen.

"Maddie." He sounded relieved.

"Hey, we have a problem. I need you."

"On my way."

Her heart stuttered at that. He didn't ask what she needed. It didn't matter that they'd just had a fight or that she'd basically told him she didn't want him in California with her and had walked out without any further explanation. It didn't matter that he thought she was still leaving. He would be there for her anyway.

"I'm at the dock," she told him.

"Oh."

"Yeah." She took a breath. "Bring everyone."

Two minutes later, Owen, Josh, Sawyer and, yes, everyone else, was there.

"Someone stole an airboat." Maddie held the cap out. "And I think I know who. The drunk guys Sawyer kicked off the tour the other day were wearing these caps."

"Shit," Sawyer muttered, taking the cap. "What the hell?"

"Revenge?" Maddie suggested. "We wouldn't give them a ride so they decided to take one on their own?"

"Dumbasses," Owen said. "There's no way they know how to drive an airboat, is there?"

"And in the dark on the bayou?" Josh asked. "No way."

"So we have to go after them," Owen said.

"Guess so," Josh agreed, looking just as irritated.

Maddie's hand shot out, grabbing Owen's arm. "Wait, what? You can't go out there."

"Why not?"

"You don't know who they are for sure. And maybe they have guns."

"Why would they have guns?"

"Maybe they're...hunting. Or think they are." Maddie thought back to the guys who crowded into the office, pissed off. "They're a bunch of stupid college guys who think they know more and are way cooler than they actually are."

"So chances are that they're joyriding with an airboat and are more a danger to themselves than to us," Owen said. "They'll probably end up stuck in the grass and will be whimpering, sure the gators are going to eat them by the time we get there to rescue them."

She was suddenly scared. "We don't know for sure who took the boat, or what their intention is, or what they have with them, and what they might do if they get spooked or were angry...or both."

He nodded, his expression serious. "I know. But we have to go after them. They could hurt themselves. Or someone else. If they get stuck, they're not getting out unless we go after them."

There weren't many people who lived out on the deeper bayou but there were a few along with a series of rental cabins on one branch. People could rent them for hunting and fishing, or just getting away. They all had docks and sat close enough to the water that an airboat could absolutely go crashing into one of them and hurt someone.

"I'm coming with you."

Owen scowled. "No."

"Yes."

"*No.*"

"It's my airboat, too."

Owen paused at that. "For a few more days anyway, right?"

She frowned. "No, I—"

"Let's go!" Josh shouted. "We can do all of this later. Let's get *our* boat back here."

Owen looked down at her. He seemed to make a decision. He leaned in and pressed his lips to hers. "We're not done with this."

She nodded. "We're definitely not done."

Emotion flared in his eyes briefly, but then he turned toward the boats. Josh and Sawyer were in one and Owen headed for the other with Maddie on his heels.

Their boat was actually in front so they'd be the first out. She jumped on board and grabbed a headset as Owen untied the boat and then climbed into the driver's seat. He started the engine as Sawyer fired the second boat up.

They were only a few yards from the dock when they saw a

boat come around the trees at the bend. It was getting dark, but the sunset wasn't completely gone. It was enough to light the area. Kind of. For a little longer.

Maddie turned to look back at Owen. He'd already seen the other boat. He was scowling ahead. He glanced back at Sawyer and made some hand gesture. Sawyer gave him a thumbs-up and Owen headed for the boat coming at them.

It had to be their stolen airboat.

Maddie gripped the bench seat she was on as Owen sped up. She didn't know what Owen's plan was here. Maybe to more or less sheep-dog the boat, making sure it was headed back to dock.

The guys on the other boat were waving their arms and she thought she could see them shouting, "Help!"

Shit. They were in trouble and they knew it.

Maddie jumped when she felt Owen's foot nudge her shoulder. She looked back. He pointed at her, then at his seat. Then he pointed at his chest and then at the other boat.

She frowned and shook her head, not understanding.

He pointed at her again and then at his seat.

He wanted her to drive?

Then his pointing to the other boat made sense. He was going to get on *that* boat? How the fuck was he going to do that? He was going to jump from this boat to that one?

"You're crazy!" she shouted, assuming he could at least read her lips.

He nodded and shrugged.

And it hit her. She loved this man. She'd already known that, but in that moment, it hit her directly in the face. He would do anything he needed to do to make things right. He would put himself at risk to *jump from one moving airboat to another* to save the jackasses that had stolen the damned thing.

Oh, she was going to chew some drunk-frat-boy asses when

this was over. But for now, yeah, she could help Owen do what he needed to do.

She stood and climbed over the seat to stand next to the driver's seat. Owen let up on the accelerator as the other boat went speeding past.

"Hang on!" Owen shouted.

She couldn't hear him, but she clearly saw what he said. Maddie grabbed the back of the seat in front of her as Owen turned the boat to follow the other. She almost lost her footing, but she braced herself and hung on, even offering up a little prayer.

When they were behind the other boat, Owen climbed down, holding the rudders straight until Maddie was in place. She blew out a breath and wrapped her hand around the controller. It was still warm from Owen's hand and she had a moment of, "This is a terrible idea."

But she gripped it hard and focused.

I really should have told him I was in love with him before this.

That thought hit her hard. Fuck. She was *not* letting more time go before saying it.

Owen started to move to the side of the boat, but she reached quickly, grabbing his sleeve and tugging. He looked back.

"I love you!"

She knew he wouldn't hear her, but those words were easy to read on lips.

He gave her a grin. "I know!"

She laughed, relief going through her as she let go of him. He moved further up the boat, holding on as he got to the side. He motioned for her to catch up with the other boat. Maddie accelerated, her heart pounding. She could do this. She *had* to do this. Owen was going to jump either way and the closer she got him and the steadier she held it, the safer he'd be.

Calm settled over her and she focused carefully on the other boat. She moved up next to it. The guys on the boat were watching with wide eyes. The guy in the driver's seat looked petrified.

Maddie glanced up toward the Boys of the Bayou dock. Damn, they were getting close. Airboats didn't have brakes. They needed room to coast to a stop. Or thick grass or low water to slow them down. There was no grass or low water here. Even with Owen in the driver's seat, they needed space more than anything when it came to stopping.

Owen got right to the edge of the boat, balancing, waiting for her to pull up close enough. Maddie held her breath as she got within about two feet.

Owen glanced back to her and mouthed, "I love you, too!"

She grinned. And then he jumped.

Maddie gasped, then blew out the breath when he landed. She let up on the accelerator so *she* would have room to stop. But she felt her heart pounding as she watched Owen on the other boat. She frowned. He wasn't taking the driver's seat. What was he doing?

The next thing she saw was Owen throwing three frat boys into the bayou and then jumping in after them.

Holy shit. Her eyes widened as she realized what was going on. There wasn't room for the boat to stop at the speed they were at. It was going to crash. Right into the Boys of the Bayou's second dock. She turned her boat slightly, coasting to a stop as she watched with a horrible feeling of helplessness and shock washing over her as the airboat plunged into the dock, collapsing the pilings, throwing wooden slats every direction. She sucked in a breath, holding it as the boat headed toward the main building. But it jammed into the thick mud, coming to an abrupt stop before hitting the main building, and Maddie breathed again.

Three men climbing aboard her floating boat pulled her attention away from the crumpled metal and shattered wood.

Owen turned and offered a hand to the last guy to come out of the bayou.

The driver. The guy who'd bitched at her in the office about Sawyer cutting their tour short. The jackass.

Maddie slid off the high seat and beelined for the guy. He'd barely straightened by the time she'd pulled her fist back, and his eyes widened slightly just before her fist connected with his jaw.

His head jerked back and he splashed into the bayou.

Owen shook his head, bent and kissed her, then leaned over the side of the boat and offered his hand again. He pulled the guy onto the boat. The kid gave Maddie a look that was shocked and scared.

Good. Scared was good.

She returned to the driver's seat and started the engine again, heading for the dock. One of the two that was left.

She really wanted to hit the guy again. Yeah, that was her go to tonight. It probably beat a can of lighter fluid and a match, though.

Once they were again at the dock, she jumped off the boat right behind the kids.

Apparently Owen anticipated the move.

"Mad!"

He tried to grab her, but she was prepared, too, and she dodged his hand. "Better get that tied up," she called, gesturing to the boat. "Hey!" she yelled to the kids. "Stop!"

The three guys stopped and turned. She marched right up to the them.

"What the *fuck* did you think you were doing? Who do you think you are?"

"We're just having some fun," one said. He was the one who had been drunk last time.

"Bullshit," she said. "You committed a crime. More than one. You broke in, stole a boat, and then smashed our dock!"

"Take it easy," one of the guys said, holding up a hand.

Maddie's blood pressure shot into the red zone immediately and she stepped up to the guy. She had to tip her head back slightly to look him in the eye, but she did it. "And you put the love of my life in danger!" Then she pulled her hand back and swung.

A big hand caught her wrist before she could connect with the guy's face, though.

"Whoa." Owen's deep voice sounded in her ear. He wrapped his other arm around her waist and picked her up, turning her away from the guy.

She kicked and squirmed. "Hey, I wasn't done with him."

"I don't want George to have to take you downtown for smacking that guy," Owen said. "I've got plans for you tonight."

"George wouldn't."

Owen inclined his head to where the sheriff and a state trooper were coming down the dock. "Let's not risk it," Owen said. "That guy isn't worth missing out on our celebration."

Her anger drained away and she stared up at the man she was madly in love with. And who had, again, almost ended up in the hospital tonight.

She launched herself at him, wrapping her arms around his neck and her legs around his waist.

He caught her under her ass with a little chuckle. "What's this for?"

"I love you so much. And I'm not leaving. I want to be *here*. I should have told you that before I left Ellie's tonight."

Emotion flared in his eyes. "What about your painting?"

"I think I'll paint again," she said. "And if not—" She glanced at the Boys of the Bayou sign, then at the people gathered at the end of the dock. "Painting was how I let my feelings out. And it was just a substitution for everything I can have here." She looked into Owen's eyes again. "I can laugh and yell and fight and love here. Out loud, in person, up close. I don't need paintbrushes here. This is all *real* and it's...what I want. What I really need."

She felt Owen's hands on her ass squeeze. "God, I love you so fucking much. And I'm going to give you a *ton* of ways to let your feelings out."

Maddie kissed him deeply before pulling back and frowning at him. "But you have to quit doing stuff that could put you in the hospital," she told him.

He squeezed her ass again. "Not if it gets me *this*."

"I'm serious, Owen. You almost gave me a heart attack."

He looked at her for a moment. Then he shook his head. "If I hadn't done it, you would have."

"Jumped onto the other boat to take over and keep those guys from crashing into the dock?"

He nodded.

Her eyes went to the jackasses being led to George's car. The ones that would have been seriously injured. Or killed. Even though it would have been their own stupid fault. She sighed. "Yeah, *maybe*. Or something."

"It's the 'or something' that is part of why I love you so much," he said. "And it's part of why you love me."

"You think so? You don't think it's your magic tongue?"

He squeezed her ass. "Oh, it's also my magic tongue. But you think I'm sexy when I'm taking care of other people."

She gave in. "It is. And God knows there are a lot of them to take care of down here."

"There are. And I could really use some help."

"Taking care of *you* might be a full-time job."

He grinned. "I think you're up for it."

She hugged him tight. "I am. I'm all in." She let him go and slid down his body. "So now what?"

"To my house. To celebrate."

"Celebrate what?" she teased.

"Everything."

Her heart melted a little at that. But she asked, "By burning your agreement with Bennett, right?"

"You and burning stuff," he said, shaking his head. "Can we just tear it up?"

"Burning seems more final. And dramatic."

He rolled his eyes. "It will also take longer. Which means longer until I get you naked. And longer to tell you I love you a few million times."

She started to reply, but George interrupted.

"Maddie, Owen, we're going to need a statement."

Maddie sighed. Owen grabbed her hand and lifted it to his lips for a kiss. "Think of how boring life was without police paperwork."

She laughed and they followed George up the wooden slats.

"Of course we're pressing charges," she overheard Bennett saying to the state trooper.

"And you are?" the trooper asked.

"Bennett Baxter. Co-owner."

He said it with absolute confidence and it gave Maddie a strange sense of security. Bennett was used to dealing with high-powered people in high-powered positions. They could use a little of his experience and poise. Poise was definitely something lacking around here.

"Baxter's kind of impressive," Owen commented.

Suddenly she stopped, jerking Owen to a stop with her. "Oh my God, I still didn't tell you."

"Tell me what?" he asked with a concerned look.

"I only sold Bennett *part* of my portion," she said.

Owen stopped and stared down at her. "What?"

"I'm staying but we need his money. And—" She glanced in Bennett's direction. "I think maybe we need him, too."

Owen gave a single nod. "Maybe. So, he's got how much?"

"Seventeen and a half percent. Half of mine."

Owen seemed to be thinking about that.

"And that means that Sawyer, with his thirty-five percent, is the only majority owner. He'll be the main decision maker. The big boss."

Slowly Owen smiled. "I like that."

She nodded. "Me, too."

"Things are going to be so good."

"Yeah." Maddie again looked up at the sign over the front of the building, then out over the group of people who were here, involved, driving her nuts, *making* her crazy, but loving her no matter what.

Owen kissed the top of her head. "I love you."

She looked up at him and smiled, her heart full. "I love you, too. This is definitely where I belong."

He gave a little groan.

"What?" she asked.

"I've never wanted to throw you over my shoulder and take you straight to bed as much as I do, hearing you say that."

She stepped in and snaked her arms around his waist. "I'm not too crazy for you?"

"Just crazy enough."

He bent to kiss her, George stopped him.

"Oh, no you don't. Statements. Now."

Owen stared down at her. "Come on, George. I've been waiting twelve years to have this woman back."

"So, another hour or two won't hurt you," George said.

"Another *hour or two*?" Owen asked.

"Quit doing stuff that you have to give statements for and we won't have to keep doing this," George said.

Owen looked down as Maddie looked up at him.

"Yeah, that's probably not going to happen," Owen said.

Maddie laughed.

George nodded. "That's what I figured." He gave Maddie a wink. "Welcome back."

Her eyes stung with tears. Happy tears. She hugged Owen. "It's really good to be home."

EPILOGUE

F*our days later*

"DAMN, GIRL, THAT LOOKS *GOOD*," Owen said.

"It really does. Wow," Josh agreed.

Maddie took a deep breath. Her latest painting, the one that had poured out of her after the huge fiasco at the dock, the one that was full of bright, vibrant colors and people—the first time she'd ever painted people—was displayed in the front window of one of the art galleries on Royal Street in New Orleans.

The gallery was, appropriately, named *Crazy Creatives*.

Owen had talked her into loading her newest painting into the truck and taking it to New Orleans. "What's the worst that can happen?" he'd asked. And hey, they were coming to town today anyway. So she'd done it. They'd driven past the gallery and she'd seen the name and immediately ordered Josh to stop. The gallery owner had flipped for the painting and had put it right up front.

The painting was of Ellie's and all the characters that filled the place with laughter and life every day. Maddie almost didn't want to let it go. She'd envisioned it hanging on the wall in Ellie's, straight across from the bar.

But Owen was trying to be supportive, and she knew it would reassure him that there was now nothing she was missing about California. She'd been so amazed when she'd awakened the morning after telling him she was staying and that she was in love with him and had headed to Cora's and started painting immediately.

It seemed that she could channel happy feelings, too. Perhaps she just hadn't enough of them over the past few years. Or the ones she'd had hadn't been so overwhelming that they poured out through her brush.

That wasn't going to be a problem anymore. She now felt happiness and love and hope and an incredible sense of belonging that was too much to keep inside.

"Okay, we'll leave it here," she said, taking a breath.

"It looks amazing." Owen squeezed her hand.

It did. But she still kind of wanted to keep it.

Josh's phone dinged with a text message. He looked down. "Bennett's there," he said. "We should head over."

"What did the guy say again?" Owen asked as they approached the attorney's office.

"Just said that they wanted to make a deal. They thought they had an idea about how to make this all work out for all of us without having to go to court," Josh said. "The other kids are all still waiting to see a judge, but this one wanted to talk."

"I'm still having a hard time believing that kid is going to medical school," Maddie said. "Not sure that makes me feel real secure about the medical system in a few years."

"He's from Virginia," Josh said. "Probably don't need to worry about him working on you."

Maddie rolled her eyes. "That guy is a dumbass."

Owen couldn't argue. He reached out and pulled the door open for her. Then he swatted her ass as she passed. "Try not to call him that in front of the lawyer."

She grinned at him. "Guessing the lawyer already knows."

They crossed the lobby to the elevators. Josh looked around and whistled. "This is nice. Kid can afford high level lawyers."

"He's from Virginia?" Maddie asked as they stepped onto the elevator.

"Alexandria," Owen confirmed.

"Great." She sighed. "His daddy's probably a Senator or something."

Josh nodded. "Possible."

"Little shit thinks he's going to get off," Owen said.

Chase Dawson, aka the little shit, had hired an attorney immediately who had reached out within twenty-four hours of his arrest. Maddie had been willing to listen. Chase was headed to medical school in two weeks. Obviously a jail sentence for stealing their airboat and destroying it and their dock was going to get in the way of him showing up for day one of gross anatomy.

"Well, we already lied to Sawyer about this meeting," Maddie said.

The elevator arrived on the sixth floor and they stepped off.

"We can't let this kid off. Sawyer is so pissed already. If this kid doesn't get *something* for what he did, Sawyer might have an aneurysm."

"Oh, he'll have to do something. Pay for everything at least, right?" Josh asked.

They stopped outside of the suite and looked at one another.

"So the kid has a rich dad who's going to try to pay us off," Maddie said. "Are we going to go for that?"

"What's our alternative?" Owen asked. "Make him sit in jail? That doesn't get the dock rebuilt and..." He shrugged. "We've all made some pretty bad decisions and done some stupid stuff, right?"

Josh and Maddie had nothing to say to that. Because yeah, of course they had.

"Okay, so let's hear what they have to say," Maddie said.

Josh pulled the door open and they went inside.

Bennett was already in the conference room with another man in a suit. They both looked completely comfortable in the leather chairs around the mahogany table in front of floor to ceiling windows that overlooked the French Quarter.

"Nate, this is Madison Allain, Owen Landry, and Josh Landry. My partners," Bennett said, coming to his feet and buttoning the top button on his suit jacket. It seemed like a habit and Maddie smiled. The guy was as comfortable in Armani as Owen was in blue jeans. It was so interesting to see the guys next to each other.

Owen and Josh were both in khakis and button-down shirts today, though. That was as dressed up as they'd likely get, but they cleaned up good.

Nate shook each of their hands and indicated that they should sit. "Chase and Juliet should be here soon."

"Chase and Juliet?" Owen asked, holding a chair out for Maddie and then taking the one next to her.

"Chase paid his bail but his sister, Juliet, came down and made sure he stayed. She intends to have him make up for what happened."

Bennett lifted a brow. "Chase's sister is going to make *him* make up for what happened?" he repeated. "What does that mean?"

Nate nodded. "Juliet is an attorney in Virginia."

Maddie remembered him threatening to call her when

Maddie had refused his refund. So his lawyer sister was coming to bail him out after all.

"Oh great," Owen said. "The kid has a lawyer for a sister."

"So she has an offer to pay for everything or what?" Josh asked.

"I should wait for them to get here," Nate said. "But..." He trailed off and eyed them each. "I maybe shouldn't tell you this, but Juliet and Chase are the daughter and son of Wilson Dawson."

Bennett frowned. "Wilson Dawson?"

Nate nodded.

Bennett shook his head. "Wow."

"Who's Wilson Dawson?" Josh asked.

"Billionaire investor," Bennett said.

"We were right," Owen commented. "Thought maybe the kid had a rich dad."

"He does," Nate said. "But he has an older sister who's determined that he, in her words, not turn into an asshole."

Maddie felt her eyebrows rise.

Nate nodded at their surprised looks. ""Juliet's older brothers both work for their dad. Juliet, on the other hand, is a lawyer who does a lot of work as a patient advocate and a lobbyist for healthcare. Chase is her little brother and she's determined to make sure he becomes a good guy."

"It's important to her that he shows up for medical school on day one then," Maddie said.

"It is," Nate agreed. "But she also wants Chase to be held responsible for what happened in Autre. So she wants to talk."

Just then the door to the conference room swung open and a woman tumbled in. She was juggling an armful including a big leather bag, an accordion file folder, and a coffee cup.

All of which fell to the floor in front of her as she turned her ankle and pitched forward.

Josh, the closest to her, shot up and caught her before she face planted into the table.

"Whoa there," he said, setting her back on her feet.

Maddie looked around the table. All of the other men were also out of their seats and reaching for her, as if by instinct. Maddie turned her attention back to the woman.

She was...gorgeous. Like, stunningly gorgeous. The type of woman even other women said, "wow" about.

In spite of the fact that the bun on top of her head was falling down, her pale blue suit jacket was hanging off of one shoulder, her black-framed glasses were sliding down her nose, and her cream-colored skirt was now splashed with coffee. But it also looked like maybe it had been spotted with something else—barbecue sauce maybe—even prior to dropping her coffee cup on Nate's office carpet.

The woman looked up at Josh, then at the others in the room as she pushed her glasses up, straightened her jacket, and patted her hair.

"Um...hi."

She must have felt that her hair was coming down because she pulled the elastic band from it and shook it out. The dark strands were streaked with blond and red highlights and fell to the upper curve of her ass.

It was a great curve, too. Even Maddie had to admit. It went perfectly with the very...generous...curves behind the cream-colored silk tank she wore under her jacket. In contrast with her curves, she had a tiny waist and had to be only about five-three. She was little and curvy and beautiful. And possibly a bit of a klutz. Then again, maybe she was just having a bad day.

"I'm Juliet Dawson," she said, giving them all a big smile. She glanced at the organizer—which was still nicely put together because of the tight elastic band around it—and coffee cup—which was *not* nicely put together—on the floor behind her. She grimaced. "Sorry about that."

"It's not a problem at all," Nate assured her.

"Are you okay?" Josh asked.

"Can I get you another coffee?" Bennett asked.

"Oh no," Juliet told him with a smile. "Not without my spill-proof cup. Because... well, you see why. But thank you."

"Of course," he told her with an unnecessary level of sincerity in his tone.

Maddie smirked at that. No way did Bennett Baxter get people coffee.

"Um." That was all Owen managed.

Maddie looked up at the man she was crazy about. He was staring at Juliet like a dumbass. But she forgave him. Juliet was just...really hard not to stare at.

Maddie elbowed Owen and he quickly glanced at her. He immediately realized why she'd poked him.

"Sorry."

Maddie laughed. "I'd be more worried if you didn't look."

He ran a hand through his hair. "Quite an...entrance."

Maddie nodded. "Yeah. That's what I was thinking." Right. The truth was, Juliet looked like a lingerie model dressing up as a lawyer for Halloween.

The fact that she was an attorney made Maddie like her a lot. Clearly the woman had brains, too. But there was no way that she walked into a courtroom without every single person thinking, "Wow." That had to give some kind of advantage in trials.

"Have a seat, Juliet," Nate said, pulling out a chair between him and Bennett.

Juliet bent to retrieve her bag and the folder and Maddie thought Nate was going to tip over leaning to watch.

She straightened and smiled again. That smile made her seem very sweet.

Maddie hoped underneath it, Juliet was a barracuda.

Then she frowned. No she didn't. She wanted Juliet to feel bad about what her brother had done and make it right.

Juliet stepped around the table and took the chair Nate had been holding for her. "Thank you." She set her bag under her chair and then opened the folder on the tabletop, looking confident and poised, even though she'd just, literally, fallen into the room. "Chase should be here soon. We—"

"I'm here."

They all pivoted to look at the doorway. Yep, Chase was the guy that she'd refused to give a refund. The guy who had been driving the airboat Owen had jumped onto.

Something must have shown in her face because she felt Owen's hand clamp down on her thigh. "Easy there," he said softly.

Or maybe Owen just knew her really well.

"Chase," Juliet said.

Something in her tone made Maddie look over. Juliet was looking at her little brother with a mix of annoyance, worry, and affection.

Maddie knew what it was like to feel all of those things at once for someone. Currently, she was feeling that combination for Sawyer.

"Sorry, I'm late. I couldn't find parking."

"I told you—" Juliet started. Then she pressed her lips together and shook her head. "I'm glad you made it," she said. "Have a seat. Let's get going on this."

Chase didn't make eye contact with anyone else in the room. He rounded the table and took a seat three chairs down from Maddie.

"First," Juliet said. "Chase would like to apologize." She looked at her brother. "Go on."

They all looked at Chase.

"I'm sorry," he said. He spoke clearly, but he still didn't look at any of them. "It was really stupid. I didn't intend to do any harm and I deeply regret the damage I caused to your boat and dock."

Maddie frowned. "How about the lives you endangered? The people on the dock, Owen, your *friends, yourself*?" she demanded. "Do you even realize what could have happened?"

Chase glanced at his sister. So did Maddie. Was Juliet going to defend him? Argue with Maddie? Tell her to back off?

Juliet was watching Chase. She lifted a brow at him and said nothing.

Chase blew out a breath. "Yes, I'm very sorry about all of that. It was, as I said, stupid."

Maddie scowled, but didn't say anything more. In part because of the squeeze Owen gave her leg. In part because, well, what else was the kid supposed to say, really?

"We have a proposal," Juliet said, drawing the attention back to herself. "The damage Chase caused must be rectified. However, he needs to report to school in two weeks."

"The estimated amount to do all repairs was in the report we sent," Bennett said.

Again, Maddie was grateful to have him. He'd handled a lot of the communication with their insurance company and had pulled strings—or maybe flashed a check—to get three bids on the repairs within twenty-four hours.

"Yes, I got that," Juliet told him. She started to write something down on the page in front of her but suddenly there was a small puddle of ink spreading over the page. "Dammit," she muttered, picking up the pen that had, somehow, exploded. She bent to dig in her purse and by the time she sat back up with a new pen and a tissue to blot the leaked ink, there was a streak of black on her tank top. She noticed, started to blot the spot with the tissue, forgot she was still holding the broken pen, and simply succeeded in making it ten times worse.

Maddie shot Owen a look. He was watching Juliet with a confused, but slightly amused expression.

"But we're not just going to pay the estimate," Juliet told Bennett without missing a beat. It was almost as if she was used to these things happening.

"You're not?" Bennett asked, seemingly distracted.

Maddie watched the other woman. Was this just a technique to keep the people around her off-kilter?

"No. Chase is going to work the amount off."

No one said anything for a moment. Then Josh asked simply, "What?"

Juliet turned slightly toward him in her chair. "Chase is going to work off what he owes you. He can help rebuild the dock for starters. He doesn't know anything about boat repair, but he can do other things that will add up to what the boat repairs come to."

"Oh." Josh blinked at her. Then he looked at Chase. Then back to Juliet. "Does he know how to...build things? Use tools and stuff?"

Juliet didn't seem offended by the question. Neither did Chase, as a matter of fact.

"Actually no. He'll need some training. And so will I."

"Or you could...just pay us for it," Owen said. "We could do the work."

"We *could* just pay you," Juliet said. "But you shouldn't have to do the work. And it's important to us"—she gave her brother a look—"that this not be that easy. Chase needs to get his hands dirty. He needs to see what goes into rebuilding what he broke. He needs to help make it right."

"But he doesn't know how to do the things we'd need him to do," Owen pointed out.

"No. But we're both quick learners and it would be a great chance for us to do something new."

Owen frowned but Maddie was the one that asked, "You? Both of you?"

Juliet nodded. "I'm coming, too. Having two of us will make the work go twice as fast."

Josh coughed and Maddie could read that it was a "yeah right" cough.

"But you'll both need training?" Maddie asked.

"Yes. Though I've already started researching."

"Researching?" Maddie asked.

"How to build docks. What kind of materials are needed, how they go together, that kind of thing."

Maddie elbowed Owen before he could reply. "Oh, okay, well, great," Maddie said.

Building a dock wasn't like building a house or something. It was essentially a bunch of wooden slats hooked together and stuck on posts. The girl would need to know how to use a saw and hammer, but neither took a college degree. Though for some reason the idea of Juliet swinging tools around and using sharp things seemed like a bad idea.

"Like I said, Chase needs to be ready to start classes in two weeks. So we'll both come and help work off what he owes you," Juliet said.

Finally Bennett leaned in. "You would have to make something like four hundred dollars an hour to pay off what you owe in two weeks."

Juliet looked at him, as if expecting him to go on.

"No offense, Ms. Dawson, but I don't know that I believe your carpentry skills are quite up to that level."

Juliet tucked her hair behind her ear and smiled at Bennett. "Of course not. I'm much better with depositions than drills. But we'd like a chance to work off what we can and then talk about paying the difference."

Okay, so she was realistic about her skills. And she was a pretty quick thinker. Maddie liked her.

"I think it's great," Maddie said.

"You do?" Owen asked.

She elbowed him again. "I do."

Bennett gave her a look. "I think we need to talk about it."

Juliet dug through her accordion file and pulled a page out. "Here we go," she said. "There was a case in Oregon where a couple of twenty-one-year-olds stole a car and drove it into a play structure in a public park. The judge ruled that they could do jail time or rebuild the structure." She looked up. "So there's some precedent."

"No judge is ruling in this case, though," Bennett said.

"We were hoping to avoid that," Nate said. "If we can settle this and Boys of the Bayou drops the charges, then there's no need to involve a judge. Saves us all time. And money."

"I think we need to—" Bennett started.

But Maddie interrupted. "Guys, can I talk to you in the hallway for a second?" Maddie stood and started for the door before they'd even answered.

"Wha—" Bennett started, but then he got up and followed when he saw that Josh and Owen were already out of their chairs.

They all stepped into the hallway and Josh pulled the door shut behind them.

"This is a...surprise," Owen said, pushing a hand through his hair.

Maddie nodded. "I know. We should totally do this."

Josh frowned. "Do this? You mean let them come down and work off the damages?"

Maddie nodded. "As much as they can in two weeks anyway."

"Why?" Bennett asked. "Why would you want that?"

"There's no way they're going to be any help at all," Josh said.

"Oh, I don't know about that," Maddie said. "I think she's perfect."

"She's *perfect*?" Owen asked. "What the hell for?"

"Sawyer."

They all just stared at her for a second.

Then Josh asked, "*What?*"

Maddie nodded, completely sure of her plan now. "Look, Sawyer is going to insist on overseeing, hell, *helping* with the rebuilding, no matter who does it."

Since the accident at the dock, Sawyer been even worse about trying to keep an eye on everything and everyone in line. Maddie hadn't thought that was possible.

"He's talked to Skip and Tanner about it already," she went on. "But they're charging us extra because they know he's going to be a pain in the ass and we all know they'll end up quitting on day one when he starts bitching at them. But Juliet and Chase will *need* his help. They know that. They'll listen and let him be bossy and they can start right away." Skip and Tanner couldn't start the project for at least two more weeks.

"But they don't know what they're doing," Josh pointed out.

Maddie shrugged. "Come on. It's not brain surgery. Sawyer can show them what to do. And," she added. "Juliet seems really serious about wanting Chase to make up for his mistake. We all know how it feels to mess something up and *not* be able to make it right. Let's let them do this."

They all stood, clearly thinking it through.

"You know," Josh finally said. "That's not crazy."

"It *is* crazy," Bennett said, shaking his head.

Owen blew out a breath. "I don't know. You're not there every day, Baxter. Having Sawyer paying attention to someone else for a while sounds nice."

Bennett sighed. "He's gonna be pissed. He doesn't even know we're meeting with them."

Maddie nodded. "Yeah. But I'm worried about him. He needs a break from...everything. We all know he won't take two weeks off and get away, but this could be a nice...distraction."

"Oh, I think he'll find Juliet Dawson very distracting," Josh agreed.

Maddie grinned.

Bringing Juliet Dawson to Autre might be a disaster.

But they'd survived disasters before. And they'd come out stronger on the other side. She was sure this would be no different.

Besides, in her opinion and experience, there was a fine line between disaster and destiny.

———

Thank you so much for reading Maddie and Owen's story! I hope you loved **Sweet Home Louisiana!**

And we're not done in Autre, Louisiana yet! Up next is Sawyer and Juliet in **Beauty and the Bayou!**

Grab it now!

Sawyer Landry knows he's been beastly to be around for the past few months. But the beauty who just showed up on his boat dock doesn't seem a bit intimidated by his growling.

The big, gruff boat captain is the first person in a long time to want to watch out for her and Juliet finds that hotter than his grandma's jambalaya.

But Sawyer doesn't need any more people to worry about long-term and the things that make him feel protective of Juliet aren't going to go away. So this two-week adventure can't be anything more than a fling. With Juliet around, there's an even bigger risk than snake bites and hurricanes. There's the very good chance of someone of ending up with a broken heart.

You can grab it now!

**Learn more at www.ErinNicholas.com
under the BOOKS menu!**

And if you loved the Boys of the Bayou, you'll also love the **Boys of the Big Easy**! Sexy New Orleans guys who are also single dads!

MORE FROM ERIN NICHOLAS

If you loved Sweet Home Louisiana, don't miss the rest of
The Boys of the Bayou

My Best Friend's Mardi Gras Wedding

Sweet Home Louisiana

Beauty and the Bayou

Crazy Rich Cajuns

———

And there's more Louisiana fun in the
The Boys of the Big Easy

Easy Going (prequel novella)

Going Down Easy

Taking It Easy

Nice and Easy

Eggnog Makes Her Easy (Christmas novella)

———

If you're looking for more sexy, small town rom com fun, check
out the
Billionaires in Blue Jeans series!

Diamonds and Dirt Roads

High Heels and Haystacks

Cashmere and Camo

ABOUT THE AUTHOR

Erin Nicholas is the New York Times and USA Today bestselling author of over thirty sexy contemporary romances. Her stories have been described as toe-curling, enchanting, steamy and fun. She loves to write about reluctant heroes, imperfect heroines and happily ever afters. She lives in the Midwest with her husband who only wants to read the sex scenes in her books, her kids who will never read the sex scenes in her books, and family and friends who say they're shocked by the sex scenes in her books (yeah, right!).

Find her and all her books at
www.ErinNicholas.com

And find her on Facebook, BookBub, and Instagram!

CPSIA information can be obtained
at www.ICGtesting.com
Printed in the USA
BVHW071658220221
600776BV00005B/249